PIONEERS WANTED

the heading proclaimed. Though he knew it was sheer promotional jazz, Scot felt a certain thrill, and his hands shook a little.

It described in general terms an uninhabited planet, "Conquest," circling the star Gienah in the constellation Cygnus. It was 63 light-years distant. Four small moons revolved around it, but apart from that it was quite Earthlike. Gravity was 1.03, slightly greater than that of Earth but hardly objectionable. There was more land area, less water, making the overall climate more vigorous—but so much of the land was near the equator that many more people could settle in the mild subtropics. In short, Conquest was highly habitable.

PIERS ANTHONY

BUT WHAT OF EARTH?

A novel rendered
into a bad example

TOR

A TOM DOHERTY ASSOCIATES BOOK
NEW YORK

TABLE OF CONTENTS

Introduction

This is not exactly a novel. It is the *story* of a novel—a book that was lured into an unfortunate liaison, then brutally violated and cast out upon the cynical market to expire in shame. It was not the fairest of books to begin with, though it had its secret aspirations; after its degradation it was sad indeed. In this volume I shall describe in graphic detail exactly what happened.

But for those who simply want entertainment without didactic complications, that too is available. Skip the rest of this introduction, go to the novel proper, and read it through without paying attention to the numerous superscripts (elevated numbers) that call out the footnotes massed in the rear. *But What of Earth?* may not be the best novel written, but neither is it the worst; it is merely the least significant of the novels I have done. It is, ironically, intimately associated with my most significant novel, *Tarot*—but irony permeates this whole situation.

Those who prefer to assimilate the complete sordid story at the outset should read the rest of this introduction, then go through the novel, looking up the footnotes along the way. A traveling bookmark or two should help—one to keep place in the main text, another to do it for the footnotes. Why haven't I put the notes at the feet of the pages where they are called out? Because some of the notes are pages long! This novel was the offspring of my fancy, and my anger at its treatment cannot be contained in token notes. For perhaps the first time in this genre, the Writer is talking back to the Copy-Editor—in public, on the pages of the manuscript. The whole story is capped by the Conclusion, which describes what I did about the affront at the time. I trust that the reader who goes the whole route— Introduction, Text, Notes, and Conclusion—will feel rewarded for his effort; certainly he should understand more about writing and publishing than he did before.

Some may prefer to compromise: read the novel, then go through the Notes in a mass, trusting memory to make their contexts clear. These are not research paper–type notes; they are in a number of cases separate little essays that can be grasped apart from the particular passages to which they relate. Some readers may sample Notes randomly, or look up only those that promise to be interesting. Whatever—it's optional. Now let's get on with the story about the genesis of the novel.

I keep records of just about everything. My Daily Work Record notes how I have spent every day of my life since retiring to full-time professional writing in 1966, and that record is available now. It indicates that I wrote to the person I shall simply call "Editor" on January 4, 1974, sending him some material for consideration for publication. I didn't do this blindly; I remember that he had phoned me to request a submission, so I had obliged. Thus I believe I first heard from him in December 1973, and waited for the holidays to clear before trusting my material to the mail. Like some folk who depend on the mails for delivery of both product and payment, I tend to be moderately paranoid about it, and try not to provide any pretext for the loss of anything therein. Glutted December is dangerous; cold January is relatively safe.

Editor did not accept the material; it wasn't quite what he was looking for. This is standard Editorialese; these folk normally keep what they *are* looking for a secret from writers. After all, who would respect an easy editor? And in due course he sent me a letter suggesting that I try something really ambitious, in the mode of Isaac Asimov's *Foundation* trilogy. (Since then, Dr. Asimov has profited from a system I believe I pioneered, and added a fourth novel to that trilogy. Trilogies stretch farther if they run to four, five, or six novels.) The notion intrigued me; why not show that I could create on just as grand a scale as the Good Doctor A? So I settled down and worked it out, formulating the *Cluster* trilogy. I sent a sixty-page presentation to Editor—and he rejected it. I was in the process of learning the hard way: if there is one thing an editor is sure to bounce, it is exactly what he says he is looking for. Later my agent showed *Cluster* to Avon, who hadn't asked for anything like it, and therefore bought and published it. That series, incidentally, has done better

commercially than anything Editor published,
which illustrates another rule that writers understand: what an editor rejects is often superior to
what he accepts.

Somewhere along the way, he suggested that I try
what he termed an "Anti-Homosexual" novel; he
could virtually guarantee a sale on that, he said. So
I worked up a notion and routed it to him through
my agent. More is possible in science fiction than in
the mundane world, so I had consequences of
homosexual involvement such as men bearing babies. I happen to be emphatically heterosexual
myself, but my fiction does not necessarily indicate
my preference on anything; it indicates my ability
as a writer. Evidently this treatment wasn't what
Editor wanted, for he never responded, not even to
reject it, to the annoyance of my agent, who was left
with an unsettled file. In retrospect I find this
interesting—this direct invitation to write on the
subject, and then this complete tuning-out. Could
this suggest that I was dealing with a closet member
of this persuasion? I have no idea. I regard each
person's sexual preference as his own business, and
that of his partner—except when it impinges on my
writing-time. I really don't like having my time
wasted.

My record indicates that I made my first notes on
the project that was to become *But What of Earth?*
on February 6, 1975. Editor had informed me that
the new line of science fiction books he would be
publishing was intended to appeal to a mundane
readership, so as to draw in readers who normally
did not enter the SF-genre section of the store. He
wanted none of the hard-core space opera that
ordinary folk would not comprehend. He explained
that by appealing to this broader market, he hoped

to sell a quarter-million copies of each novel in the line. Impressed, I agreed to try that sort of writing. Today I have sales in that range for my series-fantasies, but then it was more like 50,000 copies per novel. What writer could resist a shot at such a moon?

So I worked up a summary for a notion I had: that the level of civilization in the world may be governed by population. Just as an elephant is more complicated than an amoeba because it is larger, not larger because it is more complicated, so also may civilization have come to mankind because of increasing numbers, not vice versa. Such notions intrigue me, and I like to work them out— especially if I can earn my living while doing so. But how could I test this, fictively? Well, suppose I reversed it? Arranged to have the population decline, and see whether civilization declined with it? Yes—an excellent thought-experiment!

But what would account for a non-catastrophic decline in population? Remember, this was for a mundane audience that wouldn't understand alien invasion by slimy Snail-men or some loathsome telepathically-transmitted disease, attractive as those notions may be to hardened genre addicts. Well, I did have this framework in which people were being matter-transmitted to colony planets, in *Cluster*. Could I adapt an aspect of this? Peaceful emigration that steadily depopulates Earth? Yes— that should do nicely. Thus I developed *But What of Earth*?

On March 8 Editor phoned me to accept my summary. In fact he expressed interest in a sequel. Always ready to oblige such a request, I quickly worked up a summary for *And What of Conquest?* that ran into immediate difficulty: my agent re-

jected it. That is, the man who represented the
commercial side of my literary interests, and who
marketed my fiction for me, getting me decent
terms and better treatment than I had had when I
was on my own, refused to market *Conquest*. He
found it unconvincing, and it was not his policy to
inflict such material on editors. Now don't get
outraged about this; there will be occasion enough
for outrage later in this narrative. Agents, increasingly, serve the useful function of winnowing out
the chaff in the literary marketplace; that's one
reason they can get better terms for an author.
Editors claim to be deluged with appallingly bad
material "over the transom" from unagented writers; they hate to wade through that slush pile. But
when they receive a submission from an agent, they
know that this is far more likely to be good material, and they approach it with a more positive
attitude. Thus an agent can get faster attention for a
writer, and sometimes can sell material that the
author would not have, because of its getting lost in
the slush from the transom. My agent was doing his
job. BUT—this was a *solicited* submission. That
put it in a different category, and he should not
have rejected it. Even the best of agents can make
mistakes. So I sent it directly to Editor—who liked
the notion, but rejected it because he felt it was too
juvenile in treatment. This was not an insult; the
Juvenile market is perfectly respectable. He just
wasn't publishing Juveniles. Actually, I had not
pitched *Conquest* as a Juvenile; it had adult theme
and treatment. But it is an editor's privilege to
purchase what he wishes, and to reject what he
wishes, for whatever irrelevant reason he chooses.
At least I had the sale on *Earth?* to keep my creative
juices flowing, as Editor liked to phrase it.

The new line of books was shaping up to be pretty classy. Several novels were to be published each month and put on sale in separate racks set apart from the common SF herd. There would be a distinctive series-format, and one of the top genre artists was to paint every cover. Editor really was going for that quarter-million sales figure.

The contract on *Earth?* arrived—and I discovered to my dismay that it gave me only two months to deliver the novel. I had told Editor I needed at least three months, because I do three drafts, and even a short novel takes time to do properly. But the contract was dated April 16, 1975, and had a delivery deadline of June 15, 1975. I had started to work on it, in anticipation of the contract, so I had a couple weeks head start; even so, this was going to be close. For one thing, there were mundane distractions: we were in the process of buying land in the forest. I was raised in the forest and retain a liking for it; we had managed to save up some money, because my wife had a regular job (writers seldom are able to save money on what they make writing: this is a matter of economics, not lack of discipline), and we were investing it in land. We had made two trips to the country eighty miles to our north to look at acreage, and had gotten mired in sugar-sand for an hour and a half, but had found some we really liked. It was in fact the land we now live on. Buying land and building a homestead on it can be a time-consuming process. We really had to be sure it was *right*. But writing novels is how I earn the money to survive, so I buckled down to the novel. Two months? I would do it somehow!

Then I discovered another problem: the contract also specified a length of 55,000 words. Now that's short; I was then moving into the 100,000 word

territory, which category I have been comfortable
with ever since; it seems to be my natural length.
My typical novels now run 120,000 words. This one
for Editor had to be half that length, and it is *not*
easier to write short than long. I need room to
express myself; 55,000 words was like squeezing
through a narrow drainpipe, instead of walking
freely along the surface. But I feared that if I ran
overlength, Editor would simply lop off some to
make it fit his format. I *had* to keep it short! So I
eliminated chapterization so there would be no
space-consuming chapter-ends, and struggled valiantly, and finally managed to come in at exactly
55,000 words. Whew! It was not the best work I
could do, because of the double-bind of time and
wordage, but I felt I had risen to the occasion and
done a decent job despite the handicaps.

I shipped it off, and Editor accepted it as it stood,
sending my agent written notice to that effect, and
in due course I received payment for it. All well and
good. This should ordinarily have been the end of
the matter. (Do you hear that faint but sinister
music in the background?) Had I But Known . . . !

Meanwhile, other things were developing. Not
long after signing the *Earth?* contract I discovered
that my research for the novel was expanding
voluminously, and of course I just didn't have time
for that. But a juxtaposition of events led to the
sudden revelation of what was to become the major
project of my career, *Tarot.* Some of the research
was religious, for Brother Paul, who is a character in
this novel. I had met a disciple of a semi-religious
group in the course of my classes in judo; he and I
were helping to haul out the heavy mats that form
the *tatami* or cushion to protect students when
taking falls. He arranged to send me some of their

literature. It arrived on the same day as a recording
of a lecture by John White on an aspect of a
seemingly supernatural phenomenon. So I played
the recording while going through the voluminous
literature—and *Tarot* was born, extending the
framework I had used for *Cluster* and *Earth?* The
sale of the *Cluster* trilogy to Avon occurred at about
that time, so it was easy to integrate the three
projects. *Tarot* was to have a more complex history
than either of the other two projects, and the three
wound up spread across three and a half publishers
(Jove was the half), but it all started here in *Earth?* I
never showed *Tarot* to Editor, having realized that
if *Cluster* was too strong for him, *Tarot* would give
him a stroke. As it was, it almost gave the editors at
Avon, Del Rey, and Berkley strokes, before Jove
bought it—and was in turn bought by the conglom-
erate that owned Berkley. *Tarot*, like *Cluster*, has
been more successful in print than most of the
novels published by the publishers that bounced it.
I mention this in an offhand manner, but with
enormous private satisfaction.

Editor called me: there were some spot changes
he would like to have me make in *Earth?* A prologue, an epilogue, that sort of thing. His suggestions seemed reasonable, and I immediately wrote
up the material, which included a technical clarifi-
cation in the body of the novel, and sent it to him. I
really hadn't had to do this, as the novel had
already been accepted as it stood, but I always try to
give an editor what he wants. (Do you hear that
background music getting louder?)

Then he called again: he wanted additional edito-
rial revisions. He said that he had hired a new and
excellent copy-editor, who had gone over my manuscript and come up with some points: minor items,

scattered throughout the text. There were so many that it would be better to retype the manuscript for the printer. (The music is now deafening, but like the folk in movies, I simply did not hear it.) He assured me that I need not concern myself with this; he would simply have another writer do the job of retyping and incorporation. Now, I really did not believe that my novel needed this attention, but certainly I didn't want to retype it just to include scattered minor changes. My commitments had multiplied while I worked on *Earth?*; I had sold four novels in a single month (the *Cluster* trilogy and a non-genre collaborative martial-arts novel) and my time was really hard-pressed. So I went along with this, since Editor planned to pay the other writer a fee for the retyping, and the other writer happened to be a friend of mine. Why torpedo an easy buck for a friend? Editor was sure I would like the result, and of course the other writer would send me a letter to clarify exactly what was being done. (Absolute chaos in the orchestral score!)

Time passed. I received no letter from Writer, and no further word by mail or phone from Editor. Maybe they hadn't bothered with the changes after all. I wasn't worried.

But when I received no galley-proofs to correct, I queried. When two queries brought no tangible result, I had my agent speak for me more firmly. A writer does after all have to put his foot down somewhere.

Editor responded with a copy of the printed brochure covering the forthcoming novels 34 through 48, which listed *Earth?* as number 44. My jaw dropped—for it was listed *as a collaboration* with the other writer. Now this was crazy; the contract specified that it was a solo novel, and it specifically prohibited any oral changes in the agreement. Until they had my written agreement, nothing could be done to my novel, and I had signed no such agreement. Naturally I challenged this immediately. (The music had finally penetrated!) Editor phoned. It turned out that he was sure I had not only approved the collaboration, but had agreed to give future profits from the novel to the other writer, who had only been paid $500 for his services initially. The Editor may have convinced himself that I had consented. I had not. Where was the necessary revision of the contract? (He had, on the phone, described the retyping as being "like a collaboration"—that may be where he got the notion that I had no objection. But his description was a simile; had he said, "it *is* a collaboration," I would have said, "No way.") Technically there was no question: the publisher was in violation of the contract. But Editor assured me that I would be pleased with the book, and that if I were not, the other writer's name would be stricken from future editions and no share of the profit would be paid to him. (I wonder what he told the other writer?) He gave examples of the flaws I had had in the novel that had needed correction. I told him they were spurious; there were no such flaws. It was now evident to me that something was seriously amiss; what had they done to my novel, and why?

Concerned, I bought a copy of the other writer's solo novel for that line, which was already in print. I had gotten to know him through fandom, and long-time fans tend to think they can write better than the professionals can. Copy-editors seem to have the same notion. That is seldom the case.

Certainly it was not the case here. The novel was a conventional post-holocaust effort, such as I had done for *Battle Circle*, basically pedestrian in treatment, limited in perspective, and without literary pretension. He was adequate, but hardly a writer of ambition. The cover artist, who professed to pay meticulous attention to every detail, had portrayed the protagonist *reversed*. Since the chief attribute of the protagonist was having half his face horrendously scarred, this did make a difference. It was reported to me via the fannish grapevine that the artist had described *Earth?* as unreadable until the other writer had remedied its flaws. Well, a larger jury will now have opportunity to judge. I had always admired the work of that artist, and still do, and find it hard to believe he said such a thing; the report may have been a misrepresentation of his attitude.

When *Earth?* was published, I bought a copy and read it nervously. Alas, my worst fears were realized: the thing had been entirely reworked. Major scenes had been deleted, and grammatical errors had been introduced such as the run-on sentence, misuse of the preposition "like" and abuse of the subjunctive mood. It had been expurgated in the areas of sex, race and religion. Characterization had been fudged, and the rationale of the protagonist's major mission had been deleted, rendering the novel pointless. I was ashamed to have my name associated with this atrocity. Delete the other writer's name? Better to delete *mine*!

Editor had assured me that all was well when he had in fact been ravishing my innocent novel in the back room. Not only was this unethical and indeed a breach of contract, it was foolish on two grounds.

First, a poor novel had in effect been substituted for a decent one, so that the readers would be turned off and the line would suffer. Second, he had done this to Piers Anthony, who had a well-deserved reputation as one of the most ornery authors of the genre. I don't look for quarrels, but I generally do finish them, and only an idiot would quarrel with me twice.

I intended to have Editor's head.

But before we get to the manner in which I sought my objective, let's present the novel, so that everyone can see what I'm talking about. Perhaps my reader is assuming that I am overstating the case, reacting with undue sensitivity to minor and necessary modifications. Oh, yeah?

I recovered the copy-edited manuscript from the other writer, who of course had also been misled, being assured that I had approved the rewrite. His initial letter to me had been sent to the wrong address (his error; he had my correct one but evidently had forgotten that I had moved six years before, so used the defunct one) and so had never reached me. But he was basically a decent person; I'm sure he thought he was improving my novel. Very few living writers can do what I do better than I do, which is one reason I am now well up in the top one percent of all writers in commercial success, but he honestly thought he could. The more subtle aspects of my writing simply were not apparent to him. I am sincerely sorry that he was brought into this mess; as I said, he had been a friend of mine.

Read the novel now, with or without looking up the notes. Then read my Conclusion, wherein I detail what happened *after* publication of the novel.

As I explained, handicaps of time and length caused this to be the least of my novels, but it does have its points and it does fill in some background in the *Cluster* and *Tarot* framework.

—Piers Anthony

But What of Earth?[1]

"Here comes the love scene," Scot said. "Care to keep pace, Fanny?"

"Stop it, Scot," the girl snapped as his arm encircled her shoulders a bit too intimately. "I want to *see* the movie, not wrestle it."

He relaxed his grip on her, concealing his irritation. If she was this stuffy at a drive-in, how would she be elsewhere? He had spent his whole week's entertainment allowance setting up for this, paying the exorbitant prices for gasoline, restaurant food and theater admission: the best he could afford on his student budget.[2]

At first he had respected her hands-off attitude, but it was becoming increasingly awkward. She was, after all, his fiancée; would the barrier really drop when she was his wife?

She turned, alerted by his silence. "Why don't

you wait and find out?" she asked him, brushing
back the loose strand of red hair from her face and
smiling. Fanny was an exceptionally pretty girl,
especially when she smiled. She had a sense of
humor, she was intelligent, she finished whatever
she started, and she had other strong recom-
mendations—which was why she *was* his fiancée.
His irritation faded.

Actually, it wasn't much of a love scene, and not
much of a movie, despite its expense. Either he was
getting jaded, or the quality of such entertainment
was deteriorating as its price went up. He would
have been better off taking her for a walk in the
park—except that the park was hardly safe at night.

Scot looked out the window, across the massed
cars to the city skyline beyond the edge of the roof.
The atmosphere glowed with the diffused light of
myriad streets and buildings, the pinpoint sources
fuzzed into a dull ambience by the smog. Once
there had been strict environmental regulation, but
that had passed with the series of intensifying fuel
crises. Now only the rich could afford to breathe
really clean air; they had it piped into their sealed
houses and cars at phenomenal expense.

No stars were visible; the city atmosphere took
care of that too. Scot looked up, experiencing a
frustrated nostalgia. He coughed, suddenly aware
of the acrid aftertaste of the air. He felt suffocated,
but knew it was largely in his mind. The really toxic
wastes were still controlled, theoretically; breathing
might not be sweet, but it was government-
certifiably safe.

The screen darkened and the speaker went silent.
"Oh no—not another power failure!" Scot
groaned, though he had not really been paying
attention to the show.

Fanny shrugged. "It'll come on again in a moment."

"That's not the point! This is the third failure this week. For the rates they charge for electricity the least they could do is keep it coming. This business of—"

"Don't shout," she said. "You know they can't help it. Their facilities are overextended."

That was the difference between them. He railed at interruptions, price increases, inferior merchandise, poor service, false representations; she accepted them as part of the price of a burgeoning population. Her way undoubtedly gave her greater equilibrium, but did nothing to correct the situation. Actually, neither did his own way. So they were even—but it was a fundamental difference that manifested in times of stress.

"There are too many people on this Earth," he muttered.

She shrugged again. That seemed to be much of her philosophy of life: a shrug. "How are you going to do anything about that? You can't just murder them."

"It's got to start with birth control," he said. "An absolute moratorium on procreation for two or five years, to stop the population surge. Then very limited—"

"I thought you wanted a family," she said. "You have always seemed eager to start work on it."

Ouch! "That's not the same. I want—"

"Oh?"

Oh-oh. She didn't believe in birth control—not the artificial kind, anyway. She would be glad to wait five years to start a family, if that meant no sex. That wasn't his idea at all, as she well knew. Scot didn't want to resume that argument with her. So he punched on the car radio. The battery could take that amount of drain for a while, and it was better than sitting in unromantic silence.

Raucous music blared out of the speaker, making Fanny wince. "Turn it down. Find some news," she said.

Good suggestion. Her suggestions were always practical, in the minor compass. She had a mind in her head. Too bad she seldom applied it to major problems.

He cut across stations until he picked up news-in-progress. It, like the rest of his world, was routine but crowded: stock exchange down four points, hit and run killing, provocative remark on national policy by an ambitious senator, unemployment rate up again, weather cloudy and cooling.

"They don't deign to mention the power failure," Scot muttered. "It's broad enough to be newsworthy." He looked out across the city again. The stoplights were dead, the skyscrapers dark. This one covered square miles!

"It happens all the time," Fanny said.

"That doesn't justify it!" he snapped back. "They should refund—"

"Sh," she interrupted him. "Something interesting."

"I don't care what—"

Then, abruptly, his attention became riveted to the news. ". . . matter transmission," the announcer was saying. "Breakthrough in a years-long effort. The procedure is said to be instantaneous, effective across thousands of light-years. It is claimed that it represents a window to the stars."

That was all. Obviously the item had been inserted as a fillip to spice the news, like a rumor of a duck-footed man or interview with a drunken ghost. Everyone knew that instantaneous matter transport was impossible!

"But if it were true . . ." Scot breathed.

"What difference would it make?" Fanny asked, taking advantage of the hiatus to do some knitting. Many girls knitted today, as a necessary hedge against the cost of clothing.[3] "The space exploration program doesn't improve *our* lives."

There was the narrow compass again. "What difference!" he cried. "The light-speed limitation on velocity in space has stopped us from doing much more than explore the nearest planets of our own system. We know there are other planets out there, circling other stars, *but we can't get to them.* If we had instant travel, we could colonize . . ." He drifted silent, overwhelmed by the sheer vision of it: walking on some exotic far-distant world, two suns in the sky, one red and one blue, humming vegetation, rainbow-hued streams, the fragrance of new-mown hay everywhere . . .

"Who would want to leave Earth?" she asked complacently.

"*I* would!" he said—and realized with a start that an inner truth had sprung forth. Even if it were some barren rock-planet, it was his notion of heaven. The very thought filled him with an enthusiasm akin to love. "I'm sick of Earth! Everything here is sour; it just gets worse and with no remedy. I'd leave it all in a moment!"

"*I* wouldn't," Fanny said.[4]

He saw that another fundamental difference had opened between them, but that only made him more vehement. "I'd like nothing better than to say good-bye to Earth forever, to go somewhere where I could breathe fresh air and see the stars at night, have room to—"

"Remember Philip Nolan," Fanny told him.

"Who?"

"Philip Nolan. The man without a country. He said he never wanted to hear the name of his country again, so the judge gave him his wish."

"Oh. A story. Well, I didn't mean it exactly that way. I don't mind if I hear about Earth—but I *would* leave it for a pioneer planet."[5]

She turned her chin away in a small, elegant gesture of negation.

"What's so good about Earth?" he persisted unwisely. "Do *you* like perpetual power failures?"

"*Intermittent* power failures. I don't like them— but it's better than no power at all, which is what you'd have on a new world. We're really pretty comfortable here, all things considered."

"Comfortable? We're stagnating!"

"If we *were*, we wouldn't be inventing matter transmission, would we?"

"What good is matter transmission, if the lights don't work?" he demanded.

"Exactly," she said, and he realized that he'd somehow lost an argument. He'd gotten reversed; *she* was the one who cared about the creature comforts instead of theoretical explorations of space.

As if on cue, the power returned. The movie picked up where it had left off. Fanny turned off the radio and returned to the film as though there had been no interruption.

But the notion, so suddenly introduced, would not let go of Scot's imagination. Matter transmission—could they mean it? They had said it was instantaneous, and that was suspicious. The news service so often got things muddled! Not light speed, which one would reasonably expect, but *instant*. At light speed it would take four years to reach the nearest star, and a hundred thousand to cross the entire galaxy. That was no good. But instant travel—[6]

No. It had to be a mistake. Relativity said it was impossible.

But if it *could* be true, invoking some principle that Relativity didn't apply to. Not travel, but duplication at the receiving station, from the human blueprint—[7]

"Will you stop muttering?" Fanny said. "I can't hear the dialogue."

"The universe opened to man, and all you care about is third-rate dialogue!"

"Well, if you're going to be difficult about it—"

"Damn, I don't see why—"

"Why what?" she asked, turning to him.

Why we can't forget that damn movie and just neck, he thought vehemently. *See how far we could go in a car*. But he couldn't say that. She would hit the roof.

"Why *what*?" Fanny repeated. She was challenging him to back down, to apologize, as he had so many times before. Yet there was a limit.

"Why we can't skip the movie and—"

"Let's go home," she said coldly.

He had been wrong. She hadn't hit the roof. She had frozen up. But he was mad now. "What *is* it with you?" he demanded. "You don't care about the horizons of science, you don't care to neck." In his mind he used a stronger term. "Where does your mind orient, anyway?"

"There is a middle ground."

"The vast mediocrity of the radical center!"

"You ought to know. You asked to marry it."

"I'm having second thoughts," he said.

"Oh?" She put her hand to her engagement ring.

What was he doing! She had called his bluff, and he had to back off now. "I didn't mean it that way! Of course I love you. But why must we quarrel?"

"Why?" she asked, turning his question back at him in the way she had.

Why, indeed? *She* had started nothing; *he* was the dissatisfied one, beating his head against walls foolishly. By his own definitions, he was stubborn and unreasonable. Perhaps he saw in Fanny a stabilizing complement to his headlong personality. Her normalcy balancing his abnormality. It would be folly to throw that away.

"Because I'm an ornery ass," he said, defeated. It was evident that she could function better without him than he could function without her.

"You are a dedicated person," she said, softening. She was always a gracious winner.

"Same thing." And he had his second revelation of the evening; they *were* the same thing. To be dedicated was to be ornery. Her way was to yield gracefully to the necessities of existence, like a flexible willow. His was to stand firm like a gnarly oak—and therefore risk being uprooted by the storm. Could the two of them really make it together, or would that fundamental difference in nature inevitably tear them apart?

He started the motor, put the car in gear, and eased out, using his parking lights. He made his way to the exit ramp and started down, circling the building several times in descending spirals until reaching ground level. Down here not even the skyline was visible; it was like the bottom of a foggy pit. Perhaps that was the real attraction of the rooftop cinemas: for a few hours they lifted a person up out of the depths, nearer to seeming freedom. Though the theaters would soon close if many more people committed suicide by ramming their vehicles over the ramparts to fall into the chasm of the street . . .

He drove Fanny home and kissed her chastely at the door. Her attitude was just right—yet he knew she was upset. They had fought, however deviously, and there were hidden wounds.[8]

. . .

Scot circled the block for twelve minutes, watching his gas gauge nudge down, before snatching a place to park. Ordinarily he avoided downtown, having little patience with the perpetual congestion. But the space colonization recruitment office was there. Maybe he should have taken the bus—but the fares were so high now it would have been no saving, and it would have taken three times as long.

He paused for a moment, staring at the neon MT emblem. Already they were accepting applicants for emigration! People were crowding in.

In fact there was too much of a crowd. There was no chance for any interview. His time on the parking meter would run out before he got through this line. Scot saw a pile of pamphlets on the counter: promotional literature. He took one and squeezed on out.

A man was in his car, hands reaching under the dash. Or a boy, by the stature. "Hey!" Scot cried, breaking into a run. He had removed the ignition key, of course, but today's car-thieves were smarter than the manufacturers. He had never thought someone would want his old clunker, but evidently even thieves were getting desperate.

Sure enough, the engine roared into life as Scot came up. No doubt the thief had seen him enter the MT station and thought he would be in longer.

Scot dived at the driver's window of the car, grabbing at the boy inside. He knew the thief could not move his hands effectively while driving the car, even if he had the ignition-shorting cables clamped already. The reach through the window was awkward, but he got hold of the front of the shirt and yanked. The material ripped away. Scot grabbed again, desperately, trying to bring the thief up against the car door so he could not drive. His fingers closed on flesh—and froze.

It was a woman.

But she didn't fight with her hands. Not directly. She used the car. She backed it out rapidly, and Scot was dragged along by his arm in the window, his fingers clenched around the material of shirt and bra.[9] Then his arm dragged free and he was thrown clear. He took a hard fall on the pavement, cracking his head.

. . .

The cool pressure of a hand on his forehead woke him. Scot opened his eyes, fighting off the brief pain of too-bright light. "Hello, Mom," he said.

Mrs. Krebs smiled. She was 45, but looked older. "I'm so glad you're feeling better, dear," she said. Her hair was tinted dark to conceal the early gray hairs, but it didn't help. The cheap quality of the tint had not kept the color true.[10]

Actually, Scot felt awful, but he smiled back. "I know this sounds silly—but I don't remember coming here. What happened?"

She paused, trying to smile and not quite succeeding. She had more wrinkles than she used to, perhaps because of the weight she had lost. Once she had been short and plump; now she was lean, but somehow seemed shorter yet. Was she developing a permanent stoop? "I'll bring your father," she said.

Then he knew it was bad; his mother did not like to discuss unpleasant matters openly. In that way she resembled Fanny. Probably no coincidence, Scot thought wryly; no matter how they cast about, men generally would end up marrying women like their mothers. Or so it was said.

Arthur Krebs came in immediately. He was taller than his wife, and unashamedly graying. He was three years older, but pride kept him young. He too had lost weight, though he remained hearty. "How're you feeling, son?" He started to reach out as if to embrace Scot, then shifted to a proffered handshake, but paused as the two truncated fingers of his right hand came into view, and went back to the embrace. Either gesture was awkward, since Scot was lying down. They settled for a brief mutual elbow-grip, and Scot tried valiantly to hide the sudden pain the pressure brought to his bruises there. His right arm had been lacerated, by the feel, though obviously it wasn't that bad. "I don't mind telling you, you gave us a start."

"Dad, I really don't know what happened. One moment I was on the street, and now—" Scot shook his head—and felt a headache he hadn't been conscious of before. And now he did remember pieces of it:[11] ambulance siren, the quick sting of shots or blood tests, bandages. "Was I mugged?"

"Look at you," Mr. Krebs said. "Lanky, brown-haired, intelligent face—"

"Dad—"

Mr. Krebs looked at him penetratingly. "And as stubborn as ever. You really don't remember?"

"Dad, you act as if you're playing games with me. What *is* it?"

"You were clutching a—an item of feminine apparel."

Scot wrinkled his brow. "A what?"

"And you seemed to have been hit by a car. Mostly bruises and scrapes, but your shoulder's bashed pretty bad, and you had a concussion. Must have been some tiff."[12]

"My car!" Scot cried, remembering. "She was stealing my car!"

His father's expression cleared. "The woman was not an acquaintance of yours? We were afraid—"

"Of course not. The bitch was shorting out my ignition, and I grabbed her shirt—" He smiled. "That was some grab!"

"Evidently. The car was insured?"

"Yes." Scot sighed. "For the balance due. So I get nothing. The payments were too high anyway." He looked up at his father. "So you thought I was a rapist or something—"

"Nothing like that, son. But you might have been taken in by one of those hookers—"

"But you took me in anyway." That sounded wrong.

"They said you should stay in the hospital for observation, but there was no room. As it is, the doctor's bills—"

"I've got medical insurance too."

"That was the first thing they verified. They said it wasn't enough."

"That figures. You can't *get* enough insurance to cover today's medical bills. They just keep on going up, and the policies all have limits based on last year's obsolete averages."

"Don't we know!" Mr. Krebs agreed with feeling. He spread his hands. "So what else could we do?"

"I appreciate it," Scot said warmly. "But you don't have room for me here, and—"

His father pushed him back down, gently. "You can't go back to your apartment. The bills—"

"Oh, no! You mean my trust income's been attached?" A moderately wealthy uncle had made arrangements for the most promising children of the family to obtain college degrees despite the expense. It had been a godsend for Scot.

"Afraid so, son. The medics won't even treat you these days unless someone signs the liability waiver. We had to do it. We—"

They had had no choice; Scot knew that. He could not blame them. "I can camp out at the college for a while. My tuition's paid through the month." But after that, what? The trust had been a mainstay, and now it was gone, swallowed in one gulp by one of the serpents of the caduceus.

Mr. Krebs shook his head. "You can't leave town until the court settlement."

"Court settle— Oh, you mean that business about the bra."[13]

"We had to keep you here. I know this business can be cleared up, now that we know what happened. Maybe they can use the clothing to identify the girl; she's probably got a police record. But that will take time."

"So meanwhile I'm broke." Scot shook his head, carefully. "No car, no home, no money."

"You have a home, son. We'll take care of you. That's what families are for."

"What's your current income?" Scot asked, giving his father a direct stare. He knew Mr. Krebs had worked many years at the machine shop, going from blue collar to white collar to forced early retirement. That meant a financial situation that was unfondly termed The Squeeze. All too apt!

"We'll get by."

"You can't afford to feed yourselves, let alone me! Look at the weight you've lost already! If I had known how bad it was with you, I'd have shunted some of my trust income to you, somehow. And you've hocked most of your furniture——"

There was no denying the bareness of the premises. "Fixed income, and this damned inflation," Mr. Krebs muttered. "How do they expect a family to live? But we've got to take care of our own."

"I'll get a job. Repay you . . ." But they both knew there was little chance of that. With three years of college, Scot had not been able to find steady work before. He had tried, between semesters. There were too many unemployed with better credits. With a degree, he'd have a better chance. But that was out, now. One condition of his trust income had been that he stay out of debt——and thanks to his accident, he was in debt now. And even if he weren't, the trust was gone.

If only he had had the sense to let the thief take the car! That would have been expensive and inconvenient, but he could have gotten by. But the sudden medical bills had ruined him. He had known something like this could happen any time, but had never really believed it could happen to *him*. There were more bankruptcies owing to medical expense than any other category.[14]

There was an awkward silence. "You had stuff in your hand," Mr. Krebs said.

"A bra. I know. She must have had fun driving that car in her bare—"

"No, the other hand. Pamphlet—"

Scot looked at it. "MT! That's the start of all this!"

"Empty?" Mr. Krebs right eyebrow screwed up. He had never quite mastered the elegant lift, but he still tried it.

"Letter M, letter T—Matter Transmission. I went down to their office, picked up this bit of paper—and now I'm here." Now, for the first time, he had a chance to read it.

PIONEERS WANTED, the heading proclaimed. Though he knew it was sheer promotional jazz, Scot felt a certain thrill, and his hands shook a little.

It described in general terms an uninhabited planet, "Conquest," circling the star Gienah in the constellation Cygnus. It was 63 light-years distant. Four small moons revolved around it, but apart from that it was quite Earthlike. Gravity was 1.03, slightly greater than that of Earth but hardly objectionable. There was more land area, less water, making the overall climate more vigorous—but so much of the land was near the equator that many more people could settle in the mild subtropics. Plants and animals differed from the familiar; there were no true trees, but many treelike species. The animals had vague resemblances to a number of Earthlike species, being four-footed, furry and warm-bodied. In short, Conquest was highly habitable.[15]

Scot's eyes drifted past the paper. He visualized settling with Fanny in a mockwood log cabin,

hunting mock buffalo for food and hides, fetching
fresh spring water in buckets formed from the huge
closed seashells there. No cars, no machines, no
pollution, just clean wilderness. Maybe every few
months a barn-raising, celebrating with mock
pumpkin pie and homemade ice cream.
"Conquest . . ."

To be a genuine pioneer! To plow virgin spring
turf behind mock horses—and it would take only a
few weeks to come to think of them as real horses,
and what difference did it make, since there were
hardly any genuine horses available on Earth itself
for such mundane chores, anymore? Skid logs in
the winter's snow. To be free of the rat race! By the
sweat of one's own brow, to earn one's own living
from the soil.

"It's a pipe dream, son," Mr. Krebs warned. "I
looked at that pamphlet. How can you judge a new
world, where nobody's settled before? The original
Western Hemisphere pioneers didn't have it easy; a
lot of them died."

"Maybe so . . ." But the vision was upon him. He
could accept a lot of uncertainty and hazard on a
distant world, if only to be free of the certainty of
this Earthly grind.

"And think of the cost," his father persisted.
"Several million dollars per person. None of us can
afford even a hundredth of that."

The vision began to dissipate, like mist beneath
the morning sun. What good was an unspoiled
world, when there was no way to get to it? Sixty-
three light-years . . .

"The way we have it figured," Mr. Krebs said,
"we'll keep you a week. Then you can stay with your
brother Tully a week. Maybe by then—"

"Spread the burden," Scot agreed. How sad a commentary on the times, that two weeks was all they could afford to plan ahead! "So we won't *all* go bankrupt. God, I wish I could get *off* this planet!"[16]

"Don't we all!" An expression of futile longing crossed Mr. Krebs' face, surprising Scot. He had supposed the dream belonged to him alone, or at least to his generation. "Now you rest and recover. We'll get by somehow. You can listen to the radio, sleep—just don't aggravate anything."

Scot didn't ask why he couldn't watch the TV. He could guess: it had been repossessed when they tried to assume responsibility for his medical indigence. A medical shock was a financial shock, and any financial shock was too much. Better to spare them the embarrassment of telling him; what was done was done.[17]

"I'll rest—for a while," he promised. "I'll find some way to make it up to you."

"Of course, son." His father stood up, smiling but not quite concealing the tension he felt, and left the room. The prodigal son had returned, bringing inadvertent ruin . . .

Scot shook his head. There was no question his folks wanted to help him—but the mathematics of financial solvency indicated that they could not support him without being drawn under themselves. The years-long depression, somehow never reflected in official statistics but now considered normal economy, left no leeway for frills. Every person had to pull his own weight—even when there was no rope to pull on, no place to stand.

No wonder crime was rampant! The woman who had stolen Scot's car had done it in order to make her own living. Probably she had children at home, hungry. All Earth was becoming a ghetto of poverty and crime. However bad it was in this neighborhood, it was worse elsewhere.

And that very poverty, his greatest inducement to leave Earth, prevented him from doing so.

In a bleak mood, he turned on the little radio. It crackled as it warmed up, showing signs of age and fatigue, but at least it was cheap and it worked. For fifteen minutes he listened to popular songs mixed with ads and patter. Perhaps by no coincidence, these things mirrored his own concerns. The craving for release, the desire to be free, productive, secure; the need to establish new horizons, broader and better than the old.

Oh, the old standby love songs were there too, but their love seemed to be less for attractive young women and more for attractive new lifestyles. It was possible to learn a lot about a culture simply by listening to its songs, its humor, and its advertising. When the focus was on pretty girls, Texas spending and larger cars, times were good; now it was on marketable skills, unemployment jokes, and super gas mileage.

Then the news. "The Matter Transmission Agency has announced a new bonus recruiting program. Any volunteer found suitable for planetary colonization and willing to revoke all his Earthly holdings will have his transport to a new planet provided by the government."

Scot stiffened as though electrified. *Transport was free!* Well, not exactly free—but for poor people like him it amounted to much the same thing. He could afford to go![18]

For the rest of the week, while his body slowly recovered, Scot moved in suppressed jubilation. He tried to eat very little, but his folks forced more food on him, going hungry themselves. It was spring, but still too early for the little garden patch in the back yard to bear, so money was their only source of food. The excitement of the new MT program was his best medicine.

"It's one-way, son," Mr. Krebs warned. "If it doesn't work out, you can't come back. You don't even get your choice of planets; you're at the mercy of the bureaucratic process. The decision is irrevocable, for better or worse. There's a lot they aren't telling us."

"I've got to check it out, though," Scot said.

"Not until you've recovered!" his father said firmly. "Remember what happened the last time you were downtown!"

Scot smiled ruefully. "You win, Dad!" And he felt a warm surge of appreciation for what his folks were doing for him.

Fanny came to see him, dutifully, having borrowed her folks' old car. She was very solicitous, and Scot had the nagging impression that she was overcompensating, that she liked him better this way than in full health. He showed her the literature and told her about the bonus program.

She shook her head dubiously. "Why can't you be satisfied here? It's probably just a gimmick to get rid of poor people. Better than conscription, or sending out press gangs. A one-way trip—how do we *know* they're doing well? Or that the émigrés are even alive?"

Scot paused, shaken. His father had implied as much, but from Fanny, who had to go with him, the objection was more compelling. "No—our government isn't a mass murderer. And the other big nations are setting up similar programs. It's *got* to be legitimate."

"All the same, I'd prefer to meet someone who's been to one of these fine colony-planets—and returned."

They took a slow walk around the block. It was another chill, windy day, with snow in the air belying the season; it seemed that the very world was becoming colder as the new ice age dawned. Lack of adequate clothing intensified the effect. Fanny wouldn't even kiss him in the open, so the emotional climate seemed as thin as the physical. But at least she had taken the trouble to visit him. His excitement over the MT program was wearing down, and he was at a low ebb, and he really appreciated her brief presence, however restricted.

• • •

The following week Scot went to his brother's suburb-farm. Tully Krebs was five years older than Scot, shorter but more powerfully built, with a sturdy wife and two children. They were health nuts, eager to proselytize. Scot would not have gone there, had he any real choice. But he had to stay *some*where while his body healed.

Tully didn't have a car. He came on a tandem bike. Scot mounted the rear seat and pedaled[19] until his leg-muscles went numb and his breath rasped, while his brother seemed unaffected.

"Take it easy," Tully said. "I know you aren't used to this, and you've been ill. Just let your feet go round, and I'll do the pushing."

"Thanks." As much for the excuse as for the physical relief. He would not have done much better had he been in normal health. The distance to go was ten miles—nothing in a car, but a real chore this way. At least it wasn't snowing!

What was there to do but put a positive face on it,

as Fanny would do? "You know I wouldn't be here if I could avoid it," Scot said. "But maybe I won't be with you long." He showed Tully the MT pamphlet as they waited at a busy intersection. He expected the same objections his father and Fanny had raised.

Tully only glanced at it. "We're familiar with the program, and we approve of it. You might say we've been preparing for it for years."

"For years! They only announced it ten days ago!"

"By learning how to do for ourselves. We use bicycles instead of a car; we raise most of our own food here on the farm; we burn wood instead of using oil heat; and we have a solar water heater. I'm going to put up a windmill when I can scrounge the materials; then we'll be almost entirely free of commercial power."

"All those things are to save money," Scot objected. "Lots of people do them."

"True—but they'll work just as well on a wilderness world. Probably better. We plan to emigrate ourselves, as soon as we can wrap up our affairs here. Maybe next year."

Scot stared at Tully's neck. "You really mean it? I thought you were the down-to-Earth one in the family."

"Why not? Think we want to raise our children on super-refined foods, in a polluted environment?"

There was the health fanaticism again. Scot turned that subject aside. "But their schooling—"

Tully laughed shortly. "Fifty kids in a classroom built for thirty? You call that education? Even their up-to-date texts are way outdated in attitude. Do you know they still distribute General Mills propa-

ganda directly through the classrooms?" His voice
went into a high mimicry: "Sugar-cereal is *good* for
children, and especially for their dentists!" He
hawked and spat, literally. "Better to get 'em out in
the wide open wilderness, learn about nature. Better for all of us."

"Except for General Mills and the dentists."[20]

This time Tully's laugh was wholehearted. "Let
'em eat sugar! No, we're going!"

Scot could have asked for no better recommendation—yet now he hung back. "How do you
know it's legitimate? That there really *are* good
planets out there? That volunteers aren't just being
duped, maybe dumped in radioactive mines or sold
into slavery?"

"We *don't*. The first parties will have to go on
trust. But they'll win the best territory on the best
worlds, if they win their gamble. They'll send
messages back; that won't cost much, comparatively. In fact, I'll bet the government provides free
postage, as a publicity mechanism. Nothing like a
satisfied customer."

"What's to stop the government from faking the
messages? Making Hellhole IV sound like Paradise
III?"

Tully sobered. "There *is* that. We both know our
government is corrupt enough to do that. *Any*
government is." He pondered a moment. "Tell you
what: if you're uncertain—and I don't blame you
one bit—I'll send you word. Some key only you
and I know. Maybe a nonsense word from our
childhood code: FREB if it's good, DOLP if it's bad, no
matter what the rest of the message says. The
message may be censored on the way—but if it
doesn't contain one of those words, you'll know it's
fake. How's that?"

"That's great!" Scot agreed. His older brother had always had a ready way with problems.

They were cruising through a factory area. The smog was worse here, and unkempt men loitered. Three young punks moved out across the road in front of the bike as though to cut it off. Scot quailed—but he saw Tully's shoulders hunch, the muscle bunching, and knew his brother was staring the pedestrians down.

And—the three gave way. Scot could never have bluffed them down like that—but Tully was no bluffer. His fists, on the few occasions he used them, were like sledgehammers.

Suppose I had been alone? Scot thought. And dared not answer himself.

The trip only took an hour, thanks to Tully's indefatigable pedaling. Maybe there was something to be said for the healthy life; if anybody was ready for the wilderness, it was Tully!

"You go on in; Jan's expecting you," Tully said. "I've got to go fetch the mail."[21]

Not even tired! Scot got off, and watched his brother pedal on down to his bike shed. Yet now Tully looked nervous. Why? Scot turned and approached the house.

Janice met him at the door, her seven-year-old son Tyler peeking from behind her skirt. "Come in, Scot; I know you're tired."

She was not even aware of her condescension. This was part of the problem about being a freeloader. Scot changed the subject as he entered: "I hear you're going to emigrate."

She made a noncommittal sound as she closed the door. The house was unheated; they were economizing on their fuel, of course, even though it was only free wood.[22] Tully was right: they were already halfway into the pioneer mode, right here on Earth.

"Let me heat some soup for you," Janice said.

"Don't waste power for that," Scot said, half-facetiously.

She brushed back her dark hair with a callused hand. Scot was momentarily repelled: muscle and callus on a woman?[23] And then he thought: *Is this what Fanny would look like, as a pioneer?* "No waste," she said. "We make bouillon with our hot water."

And the hot water was free, from their solar system. They really had it down to a science. "Thanks anyway; I'm not really hungry." He sat down on a homemade bench. This place looked more like a workshop than a home! "But I really am impressed that you plan to emigrate—"

She shook her head. "Tully wants to, but I'm afraid I'm not ready to make the irrevocable commitment. I'm just not much of a gambler. I want to know more. I admit it's very tempting, but—"[24]

The door opened and a little girl, only four or five years old, came in. In one hand she clutched a ragged graham cracker; in the other she held a paper cup tied to a length of string. She was crying.

"What is it, dear?" Janice inquired, kneeling down to take the child in her arms. The pair of them together were an inspiring sight: the mother a well-fleshed woman, seemingly constructed precisely for enfolding and comforting children; the daughter almost comically cute in her misery, bearing a strong family resemblance that suggested what the mother had looked like ten years ago. What the daughter *would* look like, in ten or twelve years.[25]

But the child, supported, only cried harder, her

words tumbling over each other so rapidly that nothing could be distinguished.

Then the phone rang. Scot was surprised to discover they had one—but of course they did, for they had arranged to pick him up by phone.[26]

Janice tried to disengage herself, but the little girl clutched her tightly. "I'll get it," Scot said quickly.

It was Tully. "Now don't make an exclamation," Tully said. "I don't want the children to hear."

"Right," Scot said, wondering what was up. Why should his brother phone from in sight of the house?

"Actually, I'm glad you answered," Tully continued. "Look—I've been laid off my job at the plant. I've been afraid of this; been checking the mail personally, to intercept the letter."[27] So that was why he had seemed nervous! "I want to break the news to Jan gently, without the kids. Are they with you now?"

Scot looked at Jan and the child. The boy was watching him, too. "Yes." He could not say much more, lest he give it away. Whatever it was that remained to be given away; obviously they knew something was up, already.

"I—" Tully paused. "Damn! She's going to take this hard, and I can't hold you on the phone while I make up my mind. I shouldn't have called like this, but it came as a shock even though I— I mean, to have your livelihood knocked out from under—"

"I understand completely," Scot said.

"Yes, yes of course you do. Sorry. Well, I've got to tell her—something. Can you—I mean— No, of course I'll have to tell her myself. No way out. Put her on."

"Yes." His brother was really shaken, for ordinar-

ily he was a decisive man. Scot had never seen this
weakness in Tully before, and was embarrassed. But
he certainly did understand. The loss of a job was
no longer a mere inconvenience; it meant a complete change of lifestyles, and for the worse. Far, far
easier to fall into the black hole of unemployment
and deprivation, than to climb out of it! *There were
not enough jobs!*[28]

Scot steeled himself, then called out to Janice.
"It's Tully. Something's come up."

"Oh, no!" she exclaimed. "He's been—" She
glanced from one child to the other, her lips thinning. Little lines appeared around her mouth. She
was taking it hard, all right! "Tyler, go upstairs and
do your homework. Jody, why don't you go outside
with Uncle Scot and tell him all about it. I know he
can fix it." She looked up pleadingly at Scot.

"Oh, sure," Scot said awkwardly. "Come on,
Jody—I'll give you a piggy back ride." He put out
his hands, and to his surprise she came into them,
still sniffling.

"Piggy bank ride," she said.

"Piggy *bank* ride?" He started to lift her, then felt
his healing bruises and had to renege. "I forgot—I
was banged by a car last week, and I can't pick you
up."

"That's all right," she said obligingly.[29]

They went outside. "Now what happened?"

"Mona hit me," Jody said clearly.

So it was something tangible. Already Scot felt
more competent. "Who is Mona?"

"Little girl, like me. I took her this cracker, and
she hit me."

Scot knew there was a missing element. "Why
don't we go and get her side of it?"

"All right." He was surprised again by the child's

ready agreement. She certainly didn't seem to be difficult to get along with. Why *would* a playmate strike her?

Meanwhile, this was giving Janice and Tully time to talk, to work it out without the children listening. The new poverty . . .

Jody led him around the house, across the back yard, past assorted stacks of cut wood and compost piles, and to a neighbor's house. No other child was in evidence. "Are you sure—" Scot asked gently.

"I was going to play telephone with her," Jody said positively, showing her cup and string. Now Scot recognized it; he had made similar devices as a child. A length of string was stretched tight between two cups, so that it really did function as a crude voice-transmission system. A great novelty for children.

"Maybe she didn't want to play the game," he suggested.

"*She* did—Anna didn't," Jody said firmly.

"There were two children?" Already the ramifications were developing. "Anna was the one who—?"

"Mona threw sand at me and hit me."

"Mona wanted to play with you—but *Mona* hit you?" He knew something was amiss.

"Yes." Jody looked at her bedraggled cracker and began to cry again.

"I'll talk with Mona's folks," Scot said quickly. "You're sure this is her house?"

The child nodded. He rang the bell.

A young woman answered. "I'm Scot Krebs, this little girl's uncle," he said. "It seems your daughter hit her, and I'm not sure I have the whole story."

"We prefer to let children handle their own problems," the woman said coolly.

Scot suppressed a flash of ire. He could see part of the problem already. Parents who didn't even want to know what their children were doing . . . "I prefer to get the facts before taking action," he said.

The woman came out. "Mona—get over here!"

Mona turned out to be playing with another little girl of similar size. Reluctantly, she came.

"Why did you hit Jody?"

"She wasn't playing nice," Mona said.

Just like that, a confession. Scot had anticipated some evasion, but evidently the children were not that sophisticated.

"Did she hit you?" the woman demanded.

"No . . ."

"Then why did you hit her?"

"Anna said to . . ."

"Well, you get right on into the house," the woman said severely.

"I suppose Anna felt three was a crowd," Scot suggested. But the woman was already going back to her house, obviously not pleased at having been brought into this. Probably he had interrupted a favorite TV program.

"Let's go home," he said to Jody. Had he done the right thing? He had gotten a little girl punished, but that was unlikely to improve neighborhood relations.[30]

Janice was off the phone and composed when they got back. "What's the story?" she inquired, evidently not eager to talk about the layoff yet. There was a continuing tightness about her mouth that made her unpretty, but her voice was controlled.

"It seems Jody went out to play with Mona," Scot said, feeling like a detective at the denouement of a successful case. "But Anna didn't want to share her playmate, so instigated hostilities. She talked Mona into hitting Jody." A small case, but a good one; he had solved the problem.

"The hypocrites!" Janice said vehemently.

"Anna didn't actually do—"

"I *know* what Anna did. We've had trouble with her family for a long time. We caught their boy committing vandalism on our property, so we took him home and told them we wanted it stopped. We always go to the concerned party first, instead of going roundabout or making anonymous complaints. After that, the vandalism got worse, and the boy started threatening and then attacking our children. Last time it happened we called the police, and Tully had a confrontation with the other father that almost came to violence. So now they don't do anything directly; they just instigate."

So there was more to it than had met his eye! "Nice neighbors," Scot commented. Setting one little girl on another, to "get even" for a prior complaint—the complaint being that direct action was taken to halt that family's unsocial behavior. Just the way a gangster would try to get even with the police who jailed him, as though no law could apply to him.[31]

Janice waved one hand. "All too typical. Sometimes I think the whole world's like that. We try to raise our children to be gentle—maybe we should be teaching them how to handle guns."

She was vehement because of her distress about the layoff. Scot could hardly condemn that. Now his brother was in the same fix he was—but his brother had a family to support. Everything seemed to be crumbling at an accelerating rate, cutting down even those who tried to help themselves. If Tully could be brought low by the imponderable flux of society's economy, who on Earth could survive?[32]

"This is the last straw," Janice said. "We'll emigrate."

The neighbors could be just as bad on a colony planet, Scot thought. And there would not be very effective police to call. But he could hardly blame her—and anyway, it was not really the neighbors who were driving them out. It was Earth—its entire, decaying structure. When the ship was sinking . . .

"I—I'd like to go with you," Scot said, feeling a bit like a rat deserting the sinking ship he had just visualized. "If I can talk Fanny into it."

"Call her," Janice said. "I'm going to pack."[33]

So suddenly was the decision made! But without work, without prospects, what real chance was there? Better to go down fighting a legitimate wilderness, than to be chipped away by the wilderness of Earth's deterioration.[34]

. . .

Fanny came, though it was evident that she had serious misgivings. Tully picked her up on his tandem bike, because the gasoline shortage prevented the use of her family's car. This in itself was a bad omen: she would not arrive in a good mood.[35]

They swung into the drive, and Scot saw that Fanny was pedaling too. There was something elegant about the synchronous movement of their legs and the gliding motion of the bicycle; like a canoe, it coasted smoothly to the door. *We are bilaterally symmetrical*, Scot thought. *Two arms, two eyes, two legs—things in pairs please us estheti-*

cally. Hence the beauty of dancing—and of the bicycle built for two. Odd he had never appreciated it before.[36]

"Here she is!" Tully said cheerfully.

Fanny dismounted with neat efficiency and nodded to Scot. She wore a nicely tailored riding habit complete with cap, and was so pretty he wanted to take her in his arms right there. But of course she would have none of that.

Tully parked the bike and busied himself with preparations for departure, sorting out things to store and things to dispose of. He had an orderly mind, and would leave the farm in good order even though he knew he would never see it again.

Scot took Fanny in to meet Janice. The two women shook hands diffidently, then Janice returned to her own work. Apparently Janice didn't quite approve of Scot's taste in fiancées.

He showed Fanny the literature. "Planet Conquest is the first one—a giant step for mankind," he told her. "It's just about Earth's size, but it's mostly land, so it has much more area to settle. They're going to transport a million people there in the course of the next month or so. It costs something like a million dollars to ship each one, but we can get it free—if we act in time. Maybe they'll find another planet just as good, and maybe they'll pay the pioneers' way there too—but why gamble on that? Soon the money'll run out, and the colonization program will stop, and our chance will be gone. I think it's now or never—and I want to go along with Tully. So we can stay together. If only you'll come too! Will you?"

"Yes," she said.

"It's really a nice world, with deep forests and

such pretty dragonflies—look at the photographs! The soil is rich, it's never been depleted, and there are hundreds of species of fruit trees and hardly any dangerous animals." He paused, something incredible sinking in. "What did you say?"

"Yes."

"Yes, it's a good world, or—?"

"Yes, I'll emigrate with you."

Scot had been so sickly certain she would refuse, at least on the first several importunings, that he didn't quite know what to make of this. "You'll come with us to Conquest?"

"This becomes repetitive," she said, frowning prettily. "Do you want me to change my mind?"[37]

"Oh, no, no, no, of course not! I just thought— This is great!" He drew her over for a kiss. She yielded with a graceful lack of enthusiasm. She never did like to have her makeup disturbed; it was too expensive and time-consuming to apply. Why she chose to use such attractants when she obviously didn't care to have them work as intended was one of the annoying little mysteries about her. Were all women like that? But at the moment Scot could not work up much ire.

"I'll tell Tully!" he exclaimed. "We'll have to get married before we go. Hey, I'm so glad you— Come *on*!" He drew her along after him, like a tug towing a yacht.[38]

Tully met them outside with a smile. "I can see the news radiating from your face," he said. "Congratulations."

"How does one proceed?" Fanny asked him.

"We'll have to make application as two families," Tully said. "The Tullus Krebs and the Scot Krebs families. Then we all go for the physical—"

"Physical?" She frowned.

"To make sure we're healthy. They don't want any contagious diseases carried to Conquest. That's one of the blessings of emigration: we leave sickness behind us. But they also need to make sure none of us have any degenerative illnesses that might interfere with our ability to live and work on a pioneer planet. No failing hearts, kidneys, lungs or brains; no cancer or leprosy. And we have to be generally fit—able to walk several miles without collapsing. So they will give us the most complete physical examinations and necessary spot treatment we can imagine. All part of the grubstake."[39]

"You make it wonderfully clear," she said, smiling as only she could smile.

"You sure do," Scot agreed. "I'd forgotten about that disease bit. That's halfway to paradise already! No more common colds, no more fevers— What's another annoying contagious disease?"

"Syphilis," Janice said, emerging from the house. "Tully, can you help me with some boxes? I've loaded them too full for me to move."

"Sure, dear," he said. "Scot, do you want to bike her back home? You know the way."

Scot thought of the toughs they had encountered before. How could he protect Fanny from those? A bicycle was so *exposed*, with hands and feet occupied. No way to run, no way to fight—as if he *could* fight. Yet how could he decline to see his fiancée home?

"How is your injury?" Fanny inquired.

Actually, Scot was feeling better, physically. But it was a legitimate out. "I'm not sure about my endurance," he said.[40]

Tully paused at the back door. "Oops—I had

forgotten about that. With that physical coming up,
you can't afford to overextend yourself. I'd better
do it."

"I guess so," Scot agreed gratefully. But at the
same time he resented the situation. Having to
draft his brother to take his girl home! Tully had
better things to do, and for Scot it was a wasted
opportunity. If only he weren't such a coward about
physical things . . .

Well, things would be different on Conquest! He
would have his full health back, and there would be
no idle toughs. Just a beautiful virgin planet, an
almost literal heaven in the sky, where hard endeav-
or would bring success and satisfaction like none
available on degraded Earth.

It seemed almost too good to be true.

. . .

The physical was every bit as thorough as Tully
had predicted, and it included psychological questioning of an uncomfortably penetrating nature.
Scot didn't mind; he knew that this sort of selection
would eliminate the punks that he worried about on
the bicycle. No bullies on Conquest! He was not in
top condition, but they knew he had been injured
and would recover; that was not the same as a
degenerative illness.

MT was efficient. Three days later they received
the results by mail. No actual data; they had been
advised that if they wanted the specifics they would
have to reimburse the government for them: a
matter of about $500. "Worth it," Tully had
opined. "We have to give up everything to go,
anyway. But I'd as soon take their word I'm healthy;
I wouldn't understand the technical data." And

Scot had agreed. Now he heard the excited talking and entered the living room where Tully held the notice.

"Oh—mail's in?" Scot inquired as if he hadn't known.

"Our acceptance for emigration to Conquest," Janice told him. "There's a letter for you too." She held it out to him. "I would have called you, but got distracted—"

"Who wouldn't?" Scot agreed. He tore it open, forcing himself to concentrate on the print of the form letter that seemed to want to dance out of focus.

Greetings SCOT KREBS:

> *Owing to negative findings in your* PERSONALITY PROFILE *your application for emigration to the colony planet* CONQUEST *is hereby denied without prejudice. You are permitted to make reapplication for authorization to emigrate not sooner than* SIX (6) *months from this date, ameliorated to within* MT *tolerance by that date.*
> *Regrets.*
> [illegible scrawl]
> *Director, Matter Transport*
> *Procurement*

"Oh-oh," Tully said, reading Scot's expression. "Bad news?"

"They rejected me," Scot said dully. He knew he was making it sound worse than it was, perversely; they hadn't actually rejected him, merely postponed him. But it was probably the same thing. They'd cancel the bonus plan before the time was out, and then he'd never be able to go.

"But we were all going together!" Janice protested with feminine illogic.

Scot dropped the accursed notice on the table and walked out. He didn't mean to be impolite; he was simply numbed. He had never anticipated this!

He sat on the back step, the developing heat of his reaction seeming to drive out the chill of the morning. He knew what was responsible: that accident report with its implied morals charge. If only it had been a *male* car thief! That inadvertent handful of feminine apparel—the bitch hadn't even *looked* female, or he would not have grabbed her there![41]

If he ever encountered her again— But what could he do to a *woman*? She had cost him his future, and he didn't even know who she was. She had worn a cap or something, concealing her hair, or maybe it had been cut short, and her shirt had seemed straight, like a man's, not full. He couldn't even remember her face; it had been entirely plain, no makeup. He could pass her on the street and not recognize her. Which meant any revenge he might have in mind was completely thwarted. No redress at all; he couldn't even make her testify at his trial, to exonerate him—assuming she would if asked. Why should a thief care?[42]

He looked at the sky. There, behind a solitary cloud, he fancied he could see Planet Conquest, floating serenely. Deep forests, huge harmless dragonflies, no pollution, illness or crowding—garden of Eden, contemporary style!

All gone, for him.

Little Jody came out, squeezing out the door sidewise so as not to bump him with the screen. "Aren't you coming, Uncle Scot?" she asked, her eyes big and blue.

"Honey, they won't let me," he said. Oddly, he

could talk to this child, when he would have been taciturn with an adult.

"But that's very sad," she said, her face puckering into the sweetest, cutest possible expression of misery.

He put his arm around her. A child, unversed in duplicity: what she said was from the heart, and the way she looked was artlessly sincere. "Yes it is," he agreed.

He knew she would quickly and painlessly forget him, on Conquest. But for the moment, her grief was the comfort he needed.

And Fanny—at least he still had Fanny. The dream of a far planet would be sterile, without her along, and Earth remained worthwhile, with her. He could not go to Conquest with his brother, but he and Fanny could go to some other colony planet. His future had only been delayed, not eliminated.

Provided the bonus plan lasted for at least six months.

It *had* to!

. . .

In only two hectic, glad, miserable days, Tully, Janice, Tyler and Jody were gone, never to be seen on Earth again, and Scot had inherited the farm. They had taken the special train to the transport unit in another state.

The house was silent. It was hard to believe that he would never see his brother or little Jody again. Yet the separation was utterly final, and could not be disbelieved. Scot could not reconcile the two feelings, and was depressed. *Is this the way schizophrenia begins?* he asked himself. *Two mutually exclusive beliefs that split the personality . . .*

No! He could not let the stress of separation

affect his sanity! It was only a dream he had been denied, and not even a certain one; until he heard from Tully with a confirmation, an on-the-spot progress report. And only one dream of two. He still had the other, still had Fanny.

He turned on the radio. The news was of the MT program, so promisingly launched with the first transmissions to Conquest. Scot changed the station, and intercepted the top new song hit: *Emigrate With Me!* He felt a pang like heartbreak and turned it off.

He picked up the phone to call Fanny, but changed his mind before dialing. He didn't want to tie up the phone right now. If there were any last-minute hitch, the line had to be open.

Maybe there'll be a mechanical failure at MT, and they'll have to delay the Conquest program six months, he thought. Then chided himself for his selfishness.

When his watch said 1400 he knew they had made it. Something let go in him; nothing he could do now would change what had happened. The MT transports were supposed to occur exactly on time, to the microsecond, because everything had to be coordinated. The capsule on the colony planet was exchanged with the one on Earth, so neither crashed into a spot where air or other substance existed; a misalignment of as much as a second could wreck the mechanism, as he understood it. So every fifteen minutes meant another 256 people, day and night. Until they had the one million or so total for the initial colonization of Conquest. The figures were on all the news media, in every conversation. Man's giant step to the stars!

And not for him. Almost, he would have left

Fanny, to indulge in that pioneer dream. Almost. He was, he realized, a man of two loves, one romantic, the other idealistic. Their seeming combination when Fanny had agreed to go had been irresistible; now the half-dream that remained to him was less than satisfying.[43]

That female who had stolen his car, stolen Conquest . . .

Yet he hoped Tully would remember to send the message. FREB for good, DOLP for bad, no matter what else the letter said. The insidious truth, lurking in one recess of his hurting mind, was that he was a little relieved at not going. Of course he had *wanted* to go, more than anything else, but he had also been afraid it wasn't real. That people would actually emigrate to some hideous fate . . .[44]

He shook his head. No—he couldn't wish that on his brother, selfishly preserving himself! Pray that Conquest was as bright and wonderful a challenge as the literature implied. Even half as good, was good enough—still so much better than what lay behind on dismal Earth.

1415. Now they were there, and he found he could not imagine what they were experiencing, sixty-three light-years away.

Suddenly crowded, noisy, polluted planet Earth seemed unbearably still and lonely. He picked up the phone and called Fanny. He hadn't seen her since Tully biked her home; they had been too busy preparing for the departure.

Her mother answered, somewhat tightly. "Fanny isn't here. Who's calling?"

"Scot. Scot Krebs, her fiancé."

There was a pause. Then: "Is this a joke?"

"I don't understand."

Now her voice was angry. "Scot and Fanny emigrated hardly fifteen minutes ago. I don't find your call funny."

"Emigrated!" he exclaimed, feeling a shock as of a blow on a mental funnybone: a strange, half-ecstatic kind of pain. "That's not so! I failed the physical and couldn't go. Didn't she tell you?"

She sounded doubtful. "If you're Scot Krebs—I admit you sound like him—tell me something no one else would know."

What sort of game was this? "Last time I was at your house, you had a headache. Fanny was dressing, and I just had to wait. You were wearing a red—no, it was a plaid bathrobe, and you said the coffee tasted bad. And I said *all* coffee tasted bad at the prices we had to pay for it. And you said—"[45]

"All right." He knew she was shaking her head. "Scot, I don't know what to make of this, but our daughter emigrated at 1400. We took her to the train ourselves, and only got back a few minutes ago. We—we stopped for a drink. We just couldn't— This whole thing was so sudden, our only child. We assumed you were already in the train—"

"Fanny—MT'd?" He felt dizzy.

"Yes. She's gone. And you—"

"I think I've just been jilted," Scot said heavily. "She left without me—deliberately. She knew I couldn't go."

"Scot, believe me—we didn't know! She never said—"

"I understand. I— Good-bye." He had to hang up.[46]

Fanny had sneaked off to Conquest, thereby breaking their engagement irrevocably. The break hurt—but the manner of it hurt worse. Why hadn't she *told* him?

Scot was not a drinking man, mainly because the price of anything alcoholic was prohibitive. But now he wanted to get drunk, much as Fanny's folks had felt a similar need. Some things could not be borne by the naked mind—not in the first awful siege.

He searched through the house, but found nothing, for his brother was a teetotaler. Then he discovered a jug of cider, evidently forgotten in the bike shed. It was well-turned. In fact, that might be the reason it had been set out here: because it had become alcoholic. In time it would turn all the way to vinegar—no doubt why it hadn't been thrown out, for Tully hated waste and Janice could use vinegar. But right now it was excellent.

. . .

The cider didn't last long, and it didn't really make him feel any better, and life continued unremittingly. Scot had to eat, so he foraged in the cellar for the stored potatoes. He knew he would have to eat next year too, so he tended the garden Tully had established, blistering his hands the first day on the hoe, getting splattered with mud as he set out the water sprinkler. If he missed any area, the plants wilted, and that made him feel sad in much the way the little girl Jody had been sad: a poignant emotion that was soon remedied by proper attention to the problem.[47]

He kept forgetting to start the circulating pump on the solar water heater, and as a result had cold water until he got himself trained. The heater had a series of copper pipes or tubes laid out in a glassed-in panel on the roof, the metal painted black; the rays of the sun passed through the glass and struck the metal, and the heat passed into the water circulating through those pipes, enhanced by the oven effect of the enclosure. But the natural tendency of the hot water was to rise, and so it would stay up on the roof unless forced down into the hundred-and-twenty-gallon tank on the ground. A simple system, but effective—when properly taken care of. Like the garden.[48]

Scot worked hard, learning through his mistakes. He tried to sublimate his sorrow in the heat of the effort, setting himself daily goals. There was a lot of work to be done around a farm!

But the chores were dull. He was depressed and lonely.

MT was in the news everywhere. At first he turned off the radio whenever the subject came up, but he needed the radio's company. The headlines in the daily newspaper delivered to his yard forced more MT information on him. So many thousands of people rushing away from Earth every day—while he had to stay behind!

Tully had saved some money, and left it with Scot. But he discovered that inflation was becoming logarithmic rather than linear. MT, supposedly the solution to the ills of overpopulation, seemed to have the opposite effect, at least temporarily. Prices of merchandise in the local stores rose almost 40% in the first month after MT started, with no letup in sight. At this rate, money itself would soon be worthless.

His near neighbors were caught up in the throes of it. In a week one family was gone; in a month, two more. Vandals broke into the newly-deserted houses, looting, wantonly destroying. Some attacked Scot's property, but he banged on the wall with a pan, making a big noise, and they scattered. They were only children, hardly ten years old. Not even worth notifying the police, who were so busy with serious calls that they no longer responded to minor ones like burglary or assault.

Then the lights went out. Too many people had moved out; it was no longer economical to maintain the lines in the face of the vandalism and attacks on linesmen. This was the fringe of suburbia; a few blocks farther in, power was being maintained. Just a necessary, minor, temporary adjustment, the company's polite note explained. Until the economy stabilized, and it became economically feasible to expand services again.

Minor? No lights and no hot water, for now the electric pump was defunct. No refrigerator. No radio. It was a major change in the local lifestyle! Scot's remaining immediate neighbors moved out hastily, finding lodging with relatives or merely taking over the homes of émigrés within the power zone. This was not legal, but in practice squatters' rights prevailed. The police ignored it, so long as things were quiet. Within a week, Scot was alone on his block.[49]

Fortunately Tully had laid in kerosene lamps and many gallons of kerosene. One lamp was a beautiful circular-wicked affair with a mantle: a little net that glowed in the flame and magnified it into a pure white light. Scot liked it; this really was as good as an electric bulb![50]

The hot water was more difficult. Scot made a labor-exchange deal with a neighbor in the next block, and the man helped him get the solar collector unit down off the roof. On the ground it was lower than the water storage tank, so that when properly connected the heated water rose to collect in the tank. This was a more primitive, natural system, and completely automatic. Not as much direct sun reached the ground, however, so the water was not as hot. It didn't matter; when really cold, he lit a fire in the fireplace and stayed there admiring the brilliant embers, feeling a certain comfort. Man had always admired fire![51]

At first he read books by lamplight, but he soon decided to conserve fuel and shifted to daytime activity. At night he washed in the dark and brooded. What was all this coming to?

And he had an answer of sorts: it was coming to the same thing Earth was. Regression, loss of technology, of the standard of living. At least, out here in the sticks. A temporary effect, of course; every advance in technology brought concurrent layoffs and failures in outdated systems, and MT was probably the biggest advance in man's history. But for him, left out of it, it was inconvenient and annoying. He was like the candlemakers when electricity spread: a depressed industry.

But perhaps the candlemakers would have the last laugh . . .

His phone was disconnected: economic reasons, again. It hardly mattered; telephone rates had tripled since MT. It was as though the city were trying to make him move out. But he refused, obstinately.[52]

One evening there was a knock on the door. Scot felt for the hammer he kept in his pocket, just in case; one could never tell, these days. He opened the door.

A black-haired beauty stood without. "My car broke down, and I don't care to spend the night outside," she said. "I'd like some food, a bath, and a place to sleep. I'll wash dishes or whatever." She spoke rapidly, as though it were a memorized spiel.[53]

"You're alone?" Scot asked, taken aback by her abrupt approach.

"I am."

"So am I," he said. Then, to alleviate the awkwardness: "The rest in this house emigrated."

"So did my family." Her speech was more natural now. She stood there, awaiting his decision.

"Oh. Sure. Come in, if you—"

"It's all right?" she asked. Her attitude reminded him of the time Fanny had agreed to come to Planet Conquest; he had reacted much the same way.[54]

"Well, there are neighbors down the street with women in the house, I mean. I thought you'd rather . . ." He was not certain he was doing the right thing. A woman could be every bit as dangerous as a man, as his car theft episode showed. But the house was so eerily silent by itself! He had lived alone before, but now that it was by necessity instead of choice it was much less comfortable. Quite apart from the more primitive conditions. He'd have to take the risk.

"Thanks." She entered. "I'm Wanda."

"Scot." She hadn't given her last name, so he didn't either. Maybe that limited anonymity was best.

"I tried several other houses," Wanda said, explaining almost as an afterthought. "The women were worse than the men."

"Oh."

"I know what you're thinking," she said. "Why would a woman come into a lone man's house, unless she wasn't what she seemed? But I'm really not the advance scout for a raiding party. And you were just here, not out—looking. So the chances are you're safe. But it's no great risk for me—there isn't anything I have that you'd want. I'm broke." She took off her jacket, and he saw that it was dirty and worn. "Except maybe one thing—and I suppose I'd rather make a gift of that instead of having it taken—if that's the way it has to be. Just so I can sleep easy."[55]

Her gesture and her manner expressed her offer more clearly than her words: the way she thrust out her bosom momentarily and tilted her head. Yet obviously it was desperation that motivated her. Hunger, not sexuality. Even the curls of her hair seemed listless, fatigued. "That—that won't be necessary," Scot said. "There's nothing fancy to eat. Potatoes, bread—"

"Food of the gods!" she exclaimed. "Look, I meant it about washing dishes, or whatever else I can do. But right now I'm so tired—"

"Sit down," he said quickly. "I've got some potato left from supper. I wasn't very hungry—"

"It's hard being alone," she agreed, collapsing on the couch. "Little things get scary, stupid things."

"Yes." She understood!

"It's worse out in the car. And no facilities."

He brought her the potato, and she ate it quickly.

Now it was almost too dark to see. "Power's off in this district," he said, though he was aware he didn't have to apologize for it. "I have a kerosene lamp, but I don't like to use it unless it's an emergency. Not much fuel." Actually he had plenty, but he didn't know how long he would have to make it last. Probably months, perhaps years. Too precious to waste.

"I understand."

"The bathroom's there," he said, pointing. "We

still do get water, so the toilet flushes okay. Why
don't I just go upstairs, and you stay down here.
Until morning."

"Thanks." She looked and sounded so grateful he
was glad he had let her in. But as he mounted the
stairs, he wondered: would she be there in the
morning? How much of the furniture would be
gone, too?

She was weary and travel-dirty—but she was a
remarkably good-looking woman. Thief or enemy
she just might be, but the thought of her in the
house banished his loneliness. This was an exciting
event, in its way; a change in his circumstance, a
human contact.

She was still asleep on the couch in the morning,
one slender white arm hanging down to touch the
floor, a strand of black hair doing likewise. She had
drawn an old tablecloth over herself as a sheet/
blanket, warding off the chill of night. Nothing had
been taken.[56]

Scot was immensely relieved. Apparently Wanda
was what she said she was: a girl whose car had
broken down.

He checked around the farm outside. Everything
was in order. He saw a stalled car down the street,
one that had not been there before. Wanda's?[57]

He walked down and checked it. In the dash
compartment was a registry in the name of Wanda
Stacey, and several spent candy wrappers. In short,
she was legitimate.

He walked back slowly. He had not gone out
recently and really looked at the neighborhood.
Now he was astonished at the thoroughness of its
decadence. There were no moving cars on the
streets, and all the houses were deserted. The power
company had retreated another stage, so that more

blocks were being demobilized. Like a blight, the dead fringe ate toward the vital center of the city. Weeds overgrew the lawns and sent runners over the curbs.

The human and mechanical silence was abated by increased trilling of birds. Not *all* creatures were leaving!

The sunrise was brilliant, owing to the reduced pollution. There was an unaccustomed lightness to his step.

She was up when he returned. She had cleaned up, and now that she was rested she looked even prettier than before. She was, as promised, washing the dishes. "Your water's not too hot," she remarked.

"It's solar heated," he explained. "I guess you had a shower last night, and that diluted the hot water, so it's lukewarm this morning. That's one of the things about solar—can't recharge it at night."

"Oh—I'm sorry. I didn't realize. I assumed you had an oil heater or something."

"Doesn't matter. It'll heat today, and the heat's free. No point in having it if we don't use it. And it's always possible to heat some extra hot in a pan over the fire. Plenty of wood to burn."

She kept her eyes on the dishes. "You thought I'd be gone with the silver," she said.

"Well—"

"I'm surprised you let me in. And more surprised you let me sleep."

Scot shrugged, though she was facing away and could not see the gesture.

"You're wondering why a pretty woman's on the loose," she said.

"Well—"

"I'm wondering too. I should have stayed with my family."

Scot didn't know what to say, so he remained silent.

"How do you live?" she asked.

"It's my brother's place. He laid up supplies for the winter, more than enough. So it's lasting through spring. When that runs out—I hope the garden comes in."[58]

"I saw the garden last night," she said. "That's one thing that made me choose this house. Aside from the fact that it was obviously occupied. A gardener—well, he's doing something positive, not out looting the neighborhood."

"Yes." Her attractive appearance made him self-conscious and dimmed his conversational ability.

"You ever steal?"

"What?"

"I have. Food from a store. Candy bars, mostly—easy to grab, concentrated. I had to eat. I was ashamed, and I left money—but money's not much good anymore. So it was stealing."

"Oh. No. I haven't needed to."[59]

"I hoped things would be better somewhere else. *Anywhere* else. But I ran out of gas. Is there a station around here?"

"Yes. But I don't think they have any gas."

"And I can't pay for it anyway. So where do I go?"

"Home," he said.

"My folks sold the house to pay off their debts. I was going to emigrate with them, but I—just couldn't. So I inherited the car."

"Couldn't?" he asked, interested. Had she been caught as he was?

"Something about that step—the hugeness of it.
I passed the physical and it was all set up, but at the
last minute—" She made a gesture as of dropping
something on the floor. "The sheer immensity of
space, of actually leaving, not my home, but my
home planet. All my roots, historical, paleontologi-
cal, right back to the slime primeval— I am *of*
Earth. I couldn't leave it, any more than a fish can
leave the water."

"Some fish did leave the water," he said. "They
became the amphibians, the reptiles—"

"And eventually Man. I know. But most fish
stayed in the water, and they are there today. I'm a
stay-in-the-water fish. Some people can't fly. Some
can't use elevators. I can't—emigrate. So I balked,
and now of course I'm on the MT blacklist. When
you're called you *go*—or else. And I dropped it."

"Oh." It was not a feeling he could understand.

"Emiphobia, I guess you'd call it. Fear of emigration. So I stayed, and now I'm alone. I thought I
could find something, somewhere else—far pas-
tures, you know. Not *too* far, of course. But my gas
ran out in more ways than one. The whole Earth's
depleted, for me."

"I wanted to go," Scot said. "But there was a—a
legal complication. So I missed the deadline. I'll
still go—once that's cleared up."

"Bon voyage," she murmured. Then she squared
her shoulders as she put the last dish in the rack.
"What I'm trying so ineffectively to suggest is—
considering it's bound to be temporary anyway,
until you MT —is why don't I just stay here? There's
a lot I can do around a farm, and you treated me
decently, and—"

"All I did was leave you alone!"

"That's what I said. You're a decent guy. And I'm

a decent girl, when I have a chance to be. I—
Suddenly I just can't face going out there again.
When I stop to ask for gasoline or food, you know
what's the first thing the attendant thinks of?"

"I can guess."

"Men don't *leave* me alone. I used to like that, to
play on it. Before MT. Now it's a liability. And I—
I've got to live, somehow. Do I have to spell it out
more bluntly?"

"No." He was uncomfortable with this dialogue.[60]

"I'll be a housekeeper to you, servant, wife—
whatever you say. On a temporary basis. You only
have to be gentle." She glanced up abruptly. "Or are
you married?"

"My fiancée emigrated without me."

"Yes. You have that aura about you. You're
chastened."[61]

She leaned against the sink, appraising him. "I
think I'd be as well off here as anywhere. Better,
most likely. And maybe I could sleep without being
afraid." She dropped her eyes. "Am I embarrassing
you?"

"No," Scot said, feeling the flush on his face. He
had not really believed she was serious. Her suggestion appealed, however. Quite possibly he was
seeing the best of her now, as she made herself
appealing in order to obtain a home for whatever
duration she chose. She might be obnoxious when
he got to know her, or lazy—a pretty girl who was
used to having others wait on her. But perhaps not.
"I'd settle for company and sharing the work," he
said. "I wouldn't— I don't believe in—"

"I knew you'd say that," Wanda said. "That's
why I'd like to stay. I'm so desperate I'll do just
about anything for security—but I'd rather just be

me. I'm really pretty good company. I mean, I can maintain my end of a conversation or I can listen well, and I never fight."

"Sure. Stay," Scot said, hoping again that he wasn't making a mistake. Yet if he were not ready to extend trust, what hope was there?

It was, after all, that simple. Wanda turned out to be an unmitigated blessing. She cooked, she washed dishes, she cleaned up the house, she helped with the gardening—and she was excellent, talkative company who could indeed, as represented, shut up when silence was called for. She really knew how to get along with a man, and this was a much broader thing than simple sex appeal. In fact, after the first day, she dressed in such a way as to de-emphasize her physical attributes.

She moved into Jody's room, and in two days it was as though she had always been there. Scot was aware that his hurt at the loss of Fanny was abating, to be replaced by pleasure with Wanda's company, and that didn't bother him. Of course it would be some time before the process was complete, and he tried to prevent himself from going into any uncontrolled rebound.[62]

He received a letter from Tully, telling of the wonders of Planet Conquest, and in that missive was the key word: FREB. So it was true—the colonization program was genuine. Fat lot of good that did him now! No date had ever been set for his hearing on the auto theft case; the courts were glutted with more important cases.[63]

The mails discontinued soon after that, cutting him off further. The sewer system blocked up and they couldn't unblock it; apparently there was some massive obstruction in a main pipe somewhere under the street, perhaps blocks away. They had to remove the toilet seat and set it on a bucket. Every day Scot emptied the thing into the compost heap and covered it over with dirt.[64]

His parents emigrated to a planet named Heather. Scot was glad for them, and tried to suppress his jealousy. He was now alone on Earth; no near relatives left.[65]

Newspaper delivery stopped. The nearest supermarket shut down. That hardly mattered; he could no longer afford to shop there anyway. The area schools were consolidated into one massive and distant unit; fortunately Scot had no children. But the depletion of this region was spurred on by this. The two million émigré mark passed, and the three million.

But spring was advancing, and the garden was growing. Soon they would have lettuce and radishes.

• • •

Scot stood and stared at the lettuce, impotently furious. A third of the row had been chewed off to ground level by some predator of the night. A number of the leaves had simply been gnawed off and left to wilt.

"Hunger I can understand," he muttered. "But this wanton waste—!"

Actually, he had suspected something of the sort before. Early radishes were supposed to be ready in a month, but somehow they hadn't been. Evidently something had been whittling down their leaves, so that instead of forming good roots they wasted their effort on new foliage. Tully's lettuce had died off; Scot had supposed he hadn't watered it enough, but now he realized that a more active agent was at work.[66]

He stomped back into the house. "It's the slugs and caterpillars," Wanda said. "I used to find them in my flower garden. Only thing to do is douse the lettuce in poison, kill 'em off—and that's hard to do. They're tough."

"But we have to *eat* that lettuce," he protested.

She chewed her lower lip. "That's right. Can't spray or powder lettuce. I remember now.[67] But I sure don't like just handing it over to the bugs. I don't want to seem ungrateful, but I'm getting tired of thawed potatoes."

Scot stewed over it. He was tired of potatoes too. He had put a lot of work into that lettuce. When that crop was wiped out, it wasn't just food, it was all his prior labor, all his expectations. "I've got to do something!"

Wanda pondered. "Maybe ambush 'em?"

"Ha ha," he said sourly.

"I'm serious. Take out the lantern, wait quietly— then turn it on and catch the bugs at work. Stomp 'em. That'll cost you sleep, but it should save the lettuce—and it'll be satisfying."

"Hey, yes!" The solution was so obvious he was chagrined to have missed it before.

That night he did it. In one way it seemed a lot of trouble for nothing. But he simply could not let a bug get away with his crop. Apart from the relief of the monotony of potatoes, he wanted some of the lettuce to carry through to seed, so he would be able to plant a new crop next year. He had no other certain means of obtaining seeds, and wasn't sure whether seed saved for more than a year would germinate. And there were many other vegetables growing; the lettuce merely showed the ravages first. His whole garden, ultimately, was at stake.

He found a place, in sight of the lettuce but not too close. He spread his poncho on the ground and lay down. He wore some repellent so that he would not have to swat mosquitoes. This entailed the risk of repelling the garden predators also, so that he would not catch them in the act, but of course if repellent did the trick he could leave some near the lettuce and save it that way. So it was a worthwhile project. He intended to be absolutely silent.

He worried he might fall asleep and muff the effort. But lying there under the night sky he found there was no danger of that. The stars were brilliant, and now with the elimination of local pollution he could make out the great Milky Way. *How often at night, when the heavens are bright*, he thought, singing silently the final verse of *Home on the Range—with the light of the glittering stars, Have I stood there amazed and asked as I gazed, If their glory exceeds that of ours?*[68]

Where was Gienah, the sun of Conquest? How was Tully doing, and Janice, and Tyler and little Jody, sixty-three light-years distant? And Fanny?

Suddenly he wanted to charge back into the house and make love to Wanda. Not from any overwhelming passion for her, attractive as she was, but to erase the pain of Fanny's desertion. Wanda would do it, he was sure, if he asked her.

But there would be no true relief there. He would only be dragging Wanda into his misery, and she was too nice a girl for that. Let her be—clean.

Strange, that he had always wanted to seduce Fanny, who was unseducible, yet balked at approaching Wanda, who was approachable. What did this indicate about these two girls—or about himself? What kind of double standard did he—

Scot's thoughts cut off. He heard something. Not a bug.

It was an animal or person: massive, clumsy. It skulked around the house, keeping to the shadows. Scot's heartbeat accelerated.

Now it occurred to him that he had been perilously trusting. He had slept inside, fearing no evil so long as his doors were locked. The presence of Wanda had added to that feeling of security. But the house was hardly secure. Anyone or anything could bash in the windows—and how would he and Wanda protect themselves? Here, from the outside, he appreciated how vulnerable the property was.[69]

They would have to put up a fence, he decided. Or at least an alarm system. Trip wires, noise-makers—anything to warn him or Wanda, so that the two of them would never be caught asleep.

The prowler approached the garden—and now, in the starlight, he made it out: human.

The stranger could be up to no good. Otherwise he would have approached openly, by daylight, as Wanda had. What did he contemplate—setting fire to the house?

Terrified by what he knew were exaggerated conjectures, Scot lay still and watched. And finally the prowler left.

He lay still for several minutes, making sure he was alone, letting his heart subside. At last he lit his lamp and checked the lettuce.

Several fat slugs were in it.

He picked them out with his fingers. They coalesced into greater thickness, exuding slime that disgusted him, but he put them in a bag and dumped the bag into the garbage can, setting the lid on tight. Of course there was no longer any garbage collection, but it would do for storage until morning, when he could decide what to do with them. Take a slug, he thought, expand it to one-ton size, and lo! a horrendous repulsive alien monster. All in the viewpoint.

Then he checked the area where the prowler had been. Sure enough, there were footprints in the dirt.[70]

What to do? He could not ignore it. Tonight it had been harmless—but perhaps this was just a scouting mission. Now the stranger knew the layout, knew the farm was unguarded, open to attack.

Scot went inside, prepared to wake Wanda, but she was waiting for him. "It made me nervous, you alone out there, me alone in here," she said. Her face was deeply shadowed in the wavering lantern glow, and extremely lovely. She had a small mole on the side of her chin, but excellent cheekbones.[71] "I kept hearing noises—what were you up to?"

"There was a prowler," Scot said. He rinsed his hands in a basin of water, but the slime clung, refusing to wash off. Next time he'd have to use something to pick off the slugs, not his bare fingers.

She sat down suddenly. "Douse the light!"

"Don't worry. He's gone now." But he turned the wick low, cranked open the lantern, and blew out the flame. The fire flared up as if in protest before expiring in a burst of smoke. Symbolic of what? he thought, as the odor of unconsumed oil spread outward. His love for Fanny, snuffed out but smoking yet?

"We've been too trusting," Wanda said, echoing his own thoughts. "We figured nobody would bother us if we didn't bother them. But times are changing, and people are desperate. All the best ones are going the MT route, so what's left are the crazed and the criminal."

"You aren't," Scot said, still laboring over the resistive slime. "I'm not."

"I mean the proportions are changing. The odds are getting worse every day that passes, especially here in the hinterland. Maybe once we could assume a stranger was most likely okay, but now we can't risk that courtesy. We've got a good little farm going here, and—" She paused. "I mean *you* have. I didn't mean to presume."

"*We* have," Scot said. "It stopped being lonely when you came."

"Well, you know what I mean. It's your farm; I'm just a boarder." But she sounded pleased. "Anyhow, if somebody's scouting us out, it means trouble."

"That's the way I see it. What should we do?"

"If we start standing guard, we'll both be worn to a frazzle in a few nights—and it'll interfere with the farming. That's no good."

"How about an alarm system?" he inquired.

"I wondered about that myself. Seems good, if we can figure out one that'll work. But I think a good scout'd know how to get around anything amateur. We really need to get rid of the—"

She broke off, and he knew why. How would they get rid of the intruder? Club him on the head? Scot had little stomach for it—and might get clubbed himself.

"A deadfall!" Wanda exclaimed. "Dig a big pit, cover it over—right where he was walking tonight. Might not kill him, or even hurt him, but then he'd know this was no pushover. In fact we could booby-trap the whole place. Be better than a guard-dog—though that's an idea too."

"Yes . . ." Scot said, glad for her ingenuity.[72]

"We'll both work on it tomorrow," she said. "I'll feel so much better."

They went upstairs, cautiously in the dark. Wanda felt her way to her room, but paused at the door. He could just make out her shadow in the faint light from her window. "Scot—?"

"Yes?" He paused at his own door.

"I— Don't get me wrong. I don't want to sleep alone tonight."

"I'm shaken up too. Really nothing's happened, but—"

"Could I—put a blanket on the floor in your room?"

"You can have my bed. I'll sleep on the floor."

"I knew you'd say that. But that wouldn't be right. I— We could share the bed, but—" She made an exasperated sound. "I can't say what I want to say! I want company—it's not just the prowler, it's the whole situation. I don't know what the future holds, and I'm frankly scared. I had begun to be reassured, but this prowler— It seems my confidence was just a thin veneer, and now one little tap by fate has shattered it."

She expressed his own qualms so well! "Me too."

She took a breath in the dark. "If sex would make it all right, maybe we should get it over with. Then there wouldn't be any question of propriety—if that matters anymore."

Scot thought again of Fanny, who had always held him off . . . until she decamped via MT. He had been going over this same subject when the prowler

interrupted his thoughts. Perhaps he had pushed
Fanny because he knew she would balk—a kind of
subtle gamesmanship, establishing his masculinity
by her resistance. Wanda wasn't that type, and the
notion of sex with her was exciting. But that would
change their relationship, and he needed to think
about that more carefully.

"I don't want to insult you," he said. "I like you. I
like you a lot, Wanda. But I'm on the rebound, and
I— I have this philosophy, if that's the word. I
don't want sex unless I'm ready to marry—"

"Marry!" she exclaimed. "Now that wasn't
what—"

"I know. And I know it sounds stupid. I don't
want to debate it. So I'd rather just sleep on the
floor. Tonight."

"It isn't stupid," she said after a pause. "You're
one of those guys who won't settle for half a loaf."

"I guess so. I never thought of it that way, and
maybe I *wasn't* that way before. I can't claim to
understand myself, really. But I do know about
being lonely and afraid."

"I have a lot of respect for that kind of guy. I
haven't met many. I'll be back in a moment with
the— No, wait. Can't put *my* blanket on the floor
for you. Not that there're germs or anything you
haven't already been exposed to—"

"It's all right." He was surprised and just a bit
dismayed by his own expressed code. Did he mean
it, or was he merely posturing, affecting sentiments
because they sounded noble? How much of a hypocrite was he?

"It's still not right," she insisted. "You've got a
double bed. It's big enough—no, don't interrupt
me, Scot!—big enough for both of us. I'll just share

it with you. If you just sleep on your side of it, that's
fine, and I won't bother you. If my being there— I
have been with men before, when I was hungry
enough, you know that, and they couldn't hold a
candle to you—no pun!— If you change your
mind, I'll understand. I'm *not* propositioning you!
I'm just saying I know it's not right to lead you on
by getting close at night, and I'll go right along with
whatever you want. No recriminations, no talk of
marriage. I— I don't make a commitment like
marriage unless I mean it, and even then I'm not
sure I could. I mean, if I couldn't MT, maybe I'd balk
at marriage, too. I don't know. I'm like you, I guess.
I won't lie to you by promising anything I can't
deliver. I like you, Scot. I don't *love* you. Maybe
someday I will, but not tonight. I just—want to
know I can reach out and there'll be someone there
to touch. Someone I know, someone I trust. Do you
understand?"

"Yes, I understand." And to his surprise, he did.
She drew the line at a different place than Fanny
had, but it was as real a line. Fanny had evidently
found the sexual commitment more formidable
than the marriage commitment; Wanda reversed it.
Scot differed from both of them in that he considered both commitments to be linked, inseparable.
But rationally, Wanda's way made sense to him.
She would not make any promise she wouldn't
keep. And she, unlike Fanny, regarded love as
sacred. If Wanda ever said she loved him, she would
mean it absolutely.

"I'm not sure you do," she said. "You're generous, so you'll go along with me. But you don't
comprehend my failing. I just can't *make* the really
important commitments, MT, marriage, or any-

thing. I could go common law, knowing I could break it off any time—"

"No."

"Anyway, that's the root of it. I'm sorry."

"Maybe some day you'll make it. An important commitment, I mean. *Any* important commitment."

"You *do* understand! Yes, maybe some day."

And so she came in her nightgown, and she slept beside him. Somewhat to his surprise, Scot found he was able to sleep, too. The truth was, he wanted what she wanted: a companion. Someone to touch when reassurance was needed. That sufficed.

As he drifted off, conscious of her beside him, grateful to whatever Power there might be that they had been able to work it out without sacrificing anything either valued, he recalled something she had said passingly. About not having any germs he hadn't already been exposed to. This brought him one of his quiet revelations: he had sought emigration in part because he wanted to be free of the perpetual risk of illness. Any sick person could transmit his disease, and there was no effective protection against the annoyance of the common cold or related bugs. But—the depopulation of this region had greatly reduced personal contacts, and so eliminated most of his exposure to such illness. One of the things he desired in an alien world had been granted him right here on Earth . . .[73]

• • •

Next day they constructed the deadfall. Scot started digging while Wanda gathered light boards and an old tarpaulin for the cover. When he grew tired, she took her turn digging. She was soon perspiring, and her blouse stuck to her sides. Scot appreciated anew what a splendidly proportioned creature she was, and wondered whether he had done right, last night, in leaving her alone. This was, after all, a changed world, and the old standards hardly applied.

She paused, looking up at him. "I bet I know what you're thinking, Scot!"

He shrugged, embarrassed.

"That's what's so great about you," she continued. "You're a normal male. It wouldn't mean anything if you weren't. You have a marvelous discipline, and that makes you more of a man than if you didn't, if you see what I mean. So look all you want. I'm sort of proud of it, and of you."[74]

He had to smile, though this forwardness embarrassed him. "You're very easy to get along with, Wanda."

"I know it." And she laughed silently, through her nose, and pitched up a shovelful that almost landed on his feet. "See, I make the pitch, but you don't get dirty."[75]

Scot was beginning to wonder what he had even seen in Fanny. Wanda was just as smart and just as pretty—and she had so much more character. And she gave him credit for a strength of character he really didn't have; his actions, or lack of them, derived from a mishmash of uncertainty and hesitation, not discipline. As she probably knew. She really did have the secret of getting along with people: constant flattery.

It was a grueling job, for the pit had to be deep enough to be effective. It took all day, and at the end of it they were worn out, with wrappings around their blistered palms. But when they gingerly spread the last shovelful of dirt over the tarp and sprinkled dry weeds over it, it looked just like a newly prepared patch of garden.

"That's great!" Scot said. "Now let's collapse."

She studied it. "Suddenly I'm not sure it's enough. It might just make him mad, and then there'd be real trouble."

Scot sighed. She *would* think of that—now. "But what else is there to do?"

"We have rope. We could make nooses, and tie him up before he gets out."

"He might tie *us* up."

"Not if we dropped the noose over him fast, and pulled. Like a calf. Did you ever rope a calf?"

"Never."

"Neither did I." She spread her hands. "I admit it's a risk—but I think now that letting him get away, without our even knowing who he was or what he intended—that would be a greater risk."

Scot shook his head, baring his teeth in frustration. "I think you're right. But I'm no hero—the thought of physical violence frightens me."

"Me too. Maybe we should forget the whole thing."

"No, I don't think we can afford that, either. We'll just have to go through with it."

She caught his muddy hand. "Would you mind if I kissed you?"

That startled him. "Yes, I *would* mind. I'm tired and scared and dirty and—"

"Shy?"

"It's not that. I—"

Wanda drew herself up to him, tilted back her head, and kissed him on the cheek. "So am I," she said. Then she went off to find the rope.

How had she meant that? That she was also tired and dirty, or also scared, or also shy? Or all of them? Did it matter? If he didn't watch it, Scot decided, he would very soon fall in love again. On the rebound, despite his best intentions. And was that so bad? Romeo, as he recalled, loved Juliet on the rebound.

And both lovers had died.

. . .

They brought out the poncho and lay down together in sight of the deadfall. They did not talk, afraid that would alert the prowler. Wanda brought out a bowl of potato salad that she had fashioned artistically from the unspoiled pieces of potatoes, spices, and early collard leaves. It was very good, and so was the lukewarm water they had to use in the absence of refrigeration.[76]

The sounds of the neighborhood faded:[77] a distant dog barking, several cars that had gasoline from somewhere—probably the black market that now flourished—voices talking. About half the neighbors within a radius of half a mile had moved out, and the process was ongoing.[78] Wood fires and outdoor privies had become the rule; a number of the nearby houses had been dismantled for these purposes. Scot had laid claim to the houses nearest him, saving one intact as a future barn. This whole area was now a staging place for the uncommitted: those who weren't sure when or whether they would emigrate. Few now believed that it would ever return to municipal status; the effects of the depopulation were too pervasive, too far advanced to be reversed.

The longer he lay there, the more certain Scot

became that there would be no prowler tonight. After all, the man had already scouted this farm. Why should he come again—except for business? In that case, it would be with a gun, or henchmen . . .

Wanda put her hand on his and squeezed gently. This was immensely reassuring. He was not alone; the two of them faced the problem together.

And if the prowler did not come—then there was no risk. That was really best. They would have risen to the challenge, and the challenge would have defaulted.

The air cooled. Wanda had brought out a blanket, and now she spread it out over them both. She inched in close to him, sharing her body heat. The wait became more comfortable.

A crash woke him. Disoriented, Scot scrambled to his feet—and stumbled over Wanda, hunched beside him. They wrestled with each other for a moment before realizing their error. He shouldn't have fallen asleep!

"Tie him! Tie him!" Wanda screamed, thrusting the rope into his hands.

"I can't *see* him!" he protested.

But he could hear! Someone was thrashing in the deadfall. Scot took the noose in both hands and flung it over the sound, then hauled it tight. There was a high-pitched exclamation. The rope jerked— and Scot lost his balance and slid blindly into the deadfall.

Now he was in for it! Desperation gave him strength. He still held the rope in his hands. He grabbed on to the prowler and tried to wrap the rope about him. The man struggled, but Scot hung on, moving that rope. He was afraid that if he didn't get the man immobilized, the man would stun or kill him.

Something raked him down the cheek. A fingernail! Scot grabbed the arm and tried again to loop the rope about it. But in the dark it didn't work, and finally he just hugged his opponent to him with all his strength. If it worked for bears—

Light flared. Wanda had lit the storm lantern. Scot hung on, hoping that Wanda would know what to do next. *He* didn't!

"Say—it's a girl!" Wanda exclaimed.

Scot looked, startled. Sure enough—the face was beardless, and the body soft. It was a young woman, and she seemed to have lost consciousness.

He let go. The girl collapsed.[79]

"Bring her up here," Wanda said. "I think she's hurt."

That was all he needed: to have hurt a girl! Scot unraveled the rope as well as he could and picked her up. She was not heavy. He heaved her to his shoulder, then half-shoved, half-rolled her to the ground beyond the pit. Then he scrambled out himself.

"She's breathing," Wanda said. "I don't think anything's broken. We'd better take her into the house."

Scot picked up the girl again and carried her, following Wanda's lantern. He laid her down on the living room couch.

Wanda got a basin and a cloth and washed off the girl's face. Watching, Scot felt an elusive shock of recognition—but it faded as he concentrated on it. Had he seen this girl before—or merely someone vaguely similar? Probably the latter; certainly he didn't know her.

She was not an attractive girl. Her face was acne-scarred under the mask of dirt, and her hair was mousy. She was almost flat-chested, though that was perhaps the effect of the position. No buxom beauty like Wanda, certainly!

"Skinny as a rail," Wanda remarked. "She hasn't eaten well. Must've been scouting for food, afraid to ask for it."

"And we set a deadfall for her," Scot muttered.

"There was no way to know," Wanda said sharply. "And hungry females can be just as dangerous as men."

The girl turned her head and sighed. She was coming to.

"Take it easy," Wanda said to her. "Can you sit up?"

Suddenly the girl was fully conscious. Her head snapped back and forth like that of a trapped rodent, her eyes now round, now slitted. The whites were bloodshot.

"You fell into our deadfall," Wanda said. "Who are you? What were you doing out here at night?"

The girl's mouth opened. "I— I—" She shook her head. "I'm Lucy."

"All right, Lucy. Are you hungry?"

Dumbly, the girl nodded. "We'll get you some mashed potato," Wanda said, nodding to Scot. He was glad to fetch it; Wanda was doing a much better job of interrogation than he could have.

The potato was not very tasty. They had done what they could, but the last of the bin was the worst, and Wanda used their scant remaining seasoning only for special dishes. Lucy, however, was hungry, and she gulped the mess down appreciatively.

"Now," Wanda said gently. "Why were you wandering around our yard?"

Lucy had begun to relax. Now she stiffened, the cornered-rat look returning. "I—can't tell you."

"You're spying for someone?"

"No—"

"Someone who's going to rob this place?"

"No!"

"Or take over this farm, kicking us out?"

"No!"

Wanda shook her head, turning to Scot. "She says no."

"I heard," he said.

She turned back to the girl. "I wish we could believe that."

Scot wished so too. Had this girl scouted the neighborhood houses before vandalizing them? Was she one of the insane, destroying for the sake of destroying? Harmless she looked, at this moment of captivity—but she had prowled.

"I'll go away," Lucy said. "I won't bother you anymore."

A second time Scot suffered a flash of recognition. Something about the set of her little chin, the way she sat up, turning her head about. But again the positive identification eluded him. He must have seen her somewhere—but *where?*

Wanda caught his expression. "You know her?"

"No!" Lucy cried.

"I don't think so," Scot said cautiously. "For a moment I thought— Maybe I've seen her somewhere, but—"

"She evidently knows *you*," Wanda said. "But she won't tell."

"Where have we met?" Scot asked the girl. "Are

you a neighbor's child? Or—" He brightened.
"College! When I was in college! A coed? Did we
share a class?"

"I'm not a child," Lucy said. "I'm twenty."

Wanda eyed her appraisingly. "It's possible. But
why are you so canny about it? What's wrong with
knowing him before?"

Lucy's lower lip trembled, but she did not answer.

"Let's try this scenario on for size," Wanda said.
"You knew him casually at college. You were a
freshman and he was a junior, so you had no classes
together. You liked him, but he had a fiancée, so you
just saw him around the campus occasionally and
that was all. When he left, you followed him, just
sort of hoping, still not daring to approach him
directly. So you'd walk around at night, peering in
the windows—"

"No," Scot said, embarrassed.

"Yes," Lucy whispered.

"Well, that's interesting," Wanda said with satisfaction. "She says yes, he says no." She shot an
amused glance at Scot. "Love 'em and leave 'em?"

"You know better than that," Scot muttered.

"I sure do!" She faced Lucy. "Who was the
president of the college?"

Lucy stared at her.

"In fact," Wanda followed up, "what *was* the
college? The one you both went to?"

Lucy didn't answer.

Wanda sighed. "Scratch one scenario. Care to
give us the real one?"

Scot had to admire Wanda's efficiency.[80] He had
just about believed the college scenario himself. She
had established more from this reluctant witness
than he would have thought possible. Obviously

Lucy knew him from somewhere, and he had seen her. But where?

"What do we do with you?" Wanda asked Lucy. "You won't tell us about yourself, and we can't have people prowling around at night with dubious motives."

"I promise I won't—"

"Your word is no good; we've just established that."

"Still, after this—" Scot put in.

"Why don't you just tell us the truth," Wanda said to Lucy. "So we can decide?"

For a moment Lucy seemed ready to answer; then she tightened up again. "I *can't.*"

Wanda turned to Scot. "What do you think?"

"We'll have to let her go," he said.

"Where will you go?" Wanda asked her. "Same place you were starving before?"

Lucy was silent.

"We *can't* just turn her loose," Wanda said. "She's hungry, she has nowhere to go, and she knows you from somewhere."

"That doesn't mean I'm responsible for her!" Scot protested.

"Yes it does."

"It does?" Lucy asked, amazed.

Scot didn't follow the reasoning, but Wanda continued to look better in his eyes. What a break for him, that her car should be the one to fail near his door! Another mile one way or the other, and she would have entered some other house, and he would never have met her.

"Suppose we try this," Wanda said. "You stay here, Lucy. We'll feed you and give you a place to sleep. You'll wash dishes, sweep floors, hoe the garden. If you don't like it, you just take off. No one will stop you; we can't take the trouble to watch you. But if you *do* leave, don't come back— especially not at night."

Lucy looked at her, unbelieving.

"And if you stay," Wanda continued, "no tricks. No stealing, no trouble. Just work hard so you'll pay your way. No complaining either. We've got more work here than we can do, and most of it is directly related to feeding ourselves. Okay?"

Lucy nodded.

Scot wasn't sure this was the best procedure, but he preferred to let Wanda handle it. Wanda's own example was the most compelling argument for giving someone else a chance. And it did resolve the dilemma as well as any other course would have.

. . .

The depopulation of Earth continued. Occasionally Wanda walked down the street to pick up an old newspaper. But the lighted zone had retreated another step, and one day she was attacked by a mob of screaming adolescents. Scot heard the commotion and came running, panting, hair disheveled, and with his two months' beard he must have presented a more formidable aspect than he felt, for they faded away. Or perhaps they saw Lucy, following close after him, and didn't know how many more might be coming. But after that, Wanda did not go downtown alone. This cut off another source of news.[81]

They were in a municipal wilderness. Hungry dogs and cats prowled the streets, not friendly. Scot and Wanda and Lucy took to carrying solid sticks and kitchen knives at all times, and they set up many nasty little booby-traps around the house and garden. *They* knew where the traps were; others would not.[82]

Lucy was small, emaciated, taciturn, and she tired easily. But she kept her mouth shut and she did her work. When she was assigned to hoe the weeds out of the turnips, Scot knew that she would take twice as long to complete the job as he would have—but when she was done, there would be not one weed left and not one turnip damaged.

"She's thorough, and she has patience," Wanda remarked. "The plants like that. You can't rough them and expect them to flourish."

"Are people any different?" he inquired, and she shrugged, smiling.

Soon Lucy was doing the evening slug hunting— and damage to the lettuce abated.[83] She started lighting the wood stove in the chill mornings, and that was a blessing for Wanda, who hadn't liked that chore. Scot was now free to do the more challenging tasks, like constructing a proper shelter for the solar water-heater tank. He had done an inadequate job of moving the collector down; the pipes leaked, and the insulation was bad. So he took the metal rim of the old children's swimming pool and cut it into sections to cover as much of the mechanism as possible. Hot water was valuable; insulation from the cold of the night was essential.

Then the area water system failed. Suddenly the pipes were dry. They were thirsty, and the garden was drying up. That meant a great deal of emergency work for all three of them.

Some water had seeped into the old pit that had caught Lucy, and after rains it took many days to sink down. Scot decided to deepen it into an old-fashioned well. So they took turns digging, down and down, then carrying stones to block out the seeping mud and prevent the walls from collapsing inward. It was a messy, frustrating job that they would have given up in disgust, had they not stood in such desperate need of water. Fortunately the water table was not far down, and they deemed a ten-foot depth sufficient. The result was irregular and inartistic, but there were a good three feet of muddy water in the bottom. In a day that cleared, and their supply was assured.

They had a party to celebrate, taking sips of lukewarm water from cocktail glasses and balking at thirds: "No, thanks, I've got to drive!" But the success of this venture was intoxicating; they had met the harshest test of survival.

But dipping it out with a bucket was impractical, as it was hard to get down to the water without tumbling dirt into it and the bucket itself stirred up the sediment. No more than one bucketful could be taken at a time, and that, according to the girls, was no good on laundry days. So Scot had to arrange for a pump. He deepened the well by a couple of feet to give more room for sediment, then set the pipe in the top foot of water so that it would not disturb those depths. He struggled to lay the pipe sections along the ground in a line to the house. Now they had to find proper fittings, searching through the deserted garages and storerooms of their vanished neighbors. Fortunately Tully had had an old hand pump that he had intended to adapt to a windmill —Tully was always working out practical things like that—so that he could have free water some year. Scot was not about to attempt windmill technology, but this pitcher pump would do fine for the free water.

An easy job, fitting pipe and setting up a simple

primitive pump. In theory. But Scot had never been handy with tools, and he knew little about pumps. The girls were as ignorant as he. So he struggled, his temper getting shorter. Wanda stayed near him but quiet, ready to help or calm him on an emergency basis, and Lucy worked outside.

Until about noon. Then Lucy entered. She was breathing rapidly, as if she had been running. She had been eating voraciously these past few weeks, satisfied with the potatoes and early radishes, willing to consume anything remotely edible, and had fleshed out her arms and legs somewhat. She was still a thin girl, but no longer a scarecrow. "We have a visitor!" she cried. "A priest—"

Wanda had come over to see what the commotion was about. "A priest!" she exclaimed. "We don't belong to any church!"

Scot retrieved the wrench he had almost dropped on his foot. "Maybe he wants to convert us," he remarked.

"I think you'd better go out and talk to him," Wanda said.

"Me? What could I say to a priest?"

"We'll *all* go," Wanda decided. "But I think he'll prefer to talk to the head of the household."

Head of the household. That surprised Scot—yet of course he was the legal proprietor. "Okay," he said, disengaging with some relief from the pump. "But you girls stand by to prop me up."

Even Lucy smiled, fleetingly—and he noted, as fleetingly, that this expression did a great deal for her face. They brushed themselves off, though it was a futile gesture: all three wore ill-fitting denims, with dirt ingrained. Frequent washing was too complicated, especially right now in the absence of water and soap. Most of the dipped water that didn't go for drinking or cooking went to irrigate the garden. Cleanliness was a luxury of civilization, Scot thought—and maybe so was godliness. They trooped out, a motley crew.

It did indeed look like a priest. The man was medium-sized but appeared husky under his brown robe. He wore the reversed collar, and a silver cross hung from a ribbon around his neck. A white sash and heavy black shoes completed his uniform. He was a light-skinned Negro.[84]

"Hello," Scot said, feeling awkward. "Uh, I—"

The man extended his right hand. "I am Brother Paul, of the Holy Order of Vision."

"I'm Scot Krebs, and this is Wanda, and Lucy. We're not related, just working together." And why did he feel the need to explain that? There was nothing to apologize for, especially not to this stranger!

Brother Paul smiled. "Of course. I had heard that a community farm was operating here; that is why I came. Did you receive my letter?"

"We don't get mail anymore," Scot said.

"Not even the pony express? But I suppose that's limited to the open country, rather than the surburban fringe." He made a little gesture of unconcern. "I would like to join you for a time."

"Join us?" Scot was too surprised to field the notion well. Wanda had been a lucky accident, and maybe Lucy too—but this man had come seeking them. "We're not a religious group—"

"Neither are we," Brother Paul said. Then he smiled at their expressions. "I shall be happy to explain. But I know you are busy, and I wish to help, not hinder. If you have some task I can assist in, we can talk while working."

"We have tasks!" Wanda said. "But—"

"I don't think—" Scot began at the same time.

"We do not eschew physical labor," Brother Paul said. "What chore have I interrupted?"

"The pump," Wanda said, as though that closed the case.

"I happen to know something about plumbing. Show me your pump."

Scot looked at Wanda, then at Lucy. He found them looking at him. He could not imagine a priest soiling his robes on that ugly job. But he shrugged, as he always did when baffled. "Come on in."

Brother Paul glanced at the kitchen disarray and smiled. He doffed his robe, revealing simple blue jeans beneath, like their own but cleaner. Very soon it became evident that he had not exaggerated: he did know something about plumbing. He manipulated the pipe wrenches while he talked.

"The Order is not a religion; we wear the collar and cross to suggest our nature, but the cross itself predated Christianity. Our members belong to any church, Christian and others. Or to no church."

"An atheist priest?" Lucy murmured, smiling behind her hand.

But Brother Paul smiled too. "Priest no. Brother, yes. I regard myself as something of an atheist— and something of a theist. We really try to embrace all faiths, without exclusion. Even, or perhaps I should say especially, the doubters. After all, doubting is fundamental to existence. The word 'Holy' as we use it does not mean religious, but 'whole.' The whole world, if you will."

Scot's doubts, nevertheless, were increasing. "But I never heard of you before," he said. "No offense."

"We are a small Order, only recently established as these things go. But many of the great movements of the world started small."

"Exactly what is it you do?" Wanda asked.

"We study, we teach, we try to improve the lot of humanity in whatever way we can."

"Like fixing pumps," Scot said, not sure of his own implication.

"Yes. There is honor in any task, provided it serves the need of mankind. We also serve by spreading the message of Paul, as it was at the beginning of Christianity. That message has been lost to many—even many sincerely religious people, unfortunately."

"Saint Paul," Wanda said. "Is that where you got your own name?"

He smiled. "That is more or less coincidental. But yes, I have taken that name, and I do espouse those precepts. I won't preach to you—it is not our purpose to seek converts. But we do not conceal our mission, obviously."

"Just what *is* your mission?" Scot asked, not satisfied with the answer Wanda had received. "I mean, what do you want with us specifically?" He wondered darkly whether this visitor could be another scout casing the joint—with a very ingenious disguise. But why go to so much effort for so little?

"Our world is in trouble," Brother Paul said seriously. "Civilization itself is breaking down—not just here, but all over the world. We don't really understand why, though we suspect it relates to the emigration program. But it *is* a fact. People are going to have to learn how to take care of themselves—just as you are doing here. We believe such community farms, self-sufficient, are an important part of the answer. We want to help you by sharing our expertise with you." He set down the wrench and poured some water into the pump from the pitcher, priming it. "By fixing pumps, if necessary."

"And you want to stay a while here and show us the ropes," Wanda said flatly. She evidently had the same reservations Scot did.

"That's it. Of course I would learn as much as I taught; it's always a two-way process. Perhaps a three-way process, considering the interaction of God."

Wanda shook her head. "Forgive us if we wrong you. But it sounds too simple. All we know of you is what you've told us. You could have put on those robes to lull our suspicions—"

"And instead aroused them," Brother Paul agreed. "A quite natural concern. Philanthropy can be suspicious, especially in these times." He worked the pump handle vigorously, then stopped to make another adjustment with the wrench. "I have taken a vow of poverty, so I have no need of your possessions—but of course you have only my word on that too. I could show you my identification—but that could be forged. I will not force myself upon you; I only make the offer."

Scot spread his hands. "We've gotten where we are by trusting people. We haven't been disappointed yet."

Lucy perked up. "You haven't?"

Scot stretched out his hand and pushed her on the shoulder. "No, we haven't."

Brother Paul smiled. "Those are welcome words. Not as they relate to my situation—as they relate to yours. You are now ready to trust people."

And now that he had said it, it seemed that it had

to be true. And so Brother Paul moved in, converting the cluttered children's playroom to a neat monastic cell.

. . .

Spring advanced into summer, and the population of the neighborhood continued to diminish. The power service was now so far distant it was as though it did not exist, and what had been a great city had shrunk into the size of a backward town. But the farm prospered. Potatoes were replaced by turnip greens and collards, supplemented by whatever they could forage from deserted houses and stores in the area. Even Brother Paul did not consider this theft; the owners were permanently gone, and the canned goods and bottled goods were going to waste. "Use with proper reverence," he said. "Then there is no wrong."

It was becoming evident that they had a viable lifestyle. They would survive, so long as they kept working.

Occasionally news of the outside world filtered in, by way of an old newspaper or word of mouth. A second MT center was completed six months after the first, and so emigration was proceeding at twice the former pace, coming up on a projected ten million by the end of the year. Many other nations were constructing similar facilities, and instituting similar bonus programs; there were riots in those that did not. The roster of planetary colonies was becoming too long to remember. Yet despite this exodus, both unemployment and inflation were out of control. The most educated and capable were the first, not the last, to leave, and businesses were closing down, forcing those other businesses dependent on them to close also. There was such a terrible drain on the world's supply of gasoline that cars were priced out of existence, and at one stroke something like a quarter of the nation's workers became jobless. Thus an irresistible pressure continued for more, not less, emigration, intensifying the effect.

People were starving. But still the world's resources poured into the maw of MT. That was the way the world wanted it.

"Compost's due for turning," Wanda announced one morning, checking her calendar. She was very good at keeping track of necessary tasks; she always knew what to do when, and what the priorities were.

"I'll do it," Lucy said. She seemed to have a compulsion to volunteer for things.

"You've got baking to do," Wanda reminded her. One of the stores they had discovered contained many hundreds of pounds of grain: wheat, oats and corn, the rats ripping open the bags and soiling ten times as much as they consumed. Now those bags were in the farm's pantry, in the lone mouse- and ratproof room of the house, guarded by assorted traps. Bread, pancakes, cereal—it was, Scot had to admit with no affront to Brother Paul, a godsend. Much of the grain he had planted, and some of it was sprouting. "By the time you get done with grinding, heating the oven and all, it'll be too late for the compost. And we don't want you kneading the dough when you have compost on your hands."

Scot had to laugh at that image. "She's right, Luce! Please *don't* compost!"

"And *I've* got the week's laundry to do," Wanda said. "It has to be today, or we'll have clouds and rain and lose all our hot water and have to suffer another week. If you men get the compost turned in time, I'll dump your stinking clothes in the last batch." With the solar heater and the working pump, they had plenty of hot water, and they tended to be cleaner now that Brother Paul was with them, though he had never suggested that anything was amiss. Perhaps it was because he scrupulously washed his own clothes every week, and himself.

"We'll strip down to work," Scot said.

"Okay. I'll dump your stinking *bodies* in the wash."

Brother Paul shook his head in simulated wonder. "What a Mother Superior she would make at the order!"

"A real slave driver," Scot agreed.

"No, the Mother Superior does not compel. But she does organize. Very efficiently. Some might say—I would never suggest such a thing myself, of course—just a mite *too* efficiently . . ." He smiled.

"*Somebody* has to organize," Wanda said, a trifle defensively.

"No question about it," Brother Paul agreed.[85]

They carried spading forks to the main compost heap behind the barn. The barn was actually a former neighbor's house adapted to the purpose, since the neighbor had deserted it for MT. The heap had swelled to an enormous proportion, owing to the voluminous brush and refuse dumped there. It was head-high and twenty feet in diameter.

"I should turn it more often," Scot said. "But I've been so busy—"

"Quite understandable," Brother Paul agreed, removing his shirt. He was a stoutish man, with a fair amount of muscular development: the kind, Scot thought, who might have been good at physical combat. Or was that an unkind thought, considering that this was a man of peace?

"I figure we should move the whole pile to one side," Scot said, removing his own shirt and donning heavy work gloves. His hands now had good calluses, but he had learned to take precautions against blistering. "That way we'll be sure we haven't missed any. And the oldest stuff will wind up on top."

"Yes. I suggest we also form the new pile into the shape of a cup."

"Cup?"

"So that it will tend to collect water and carry it through the center, instead of allowing it to run off. Water is essential to the composting process."

"Beautiful!" Scot said. "I never thought of that! I'll bet you have a compost pile at the Order."

"Several," Brother Paul agreed. "We dislike waste, physical or spiritual."

"Okay. I'll tackle this side, and you start on that side, so we don't get in each other's way."

"We," Brother Paul said. "Pitch in." And he did so, literally.

They labored for half an hour. Scot had not made the pile well. Undigested brush was mixed with garbage from their meals so that he could not get a decent forkful without entanglement and dribbling and wasted effort. "Never again!" he muttered as he yanked out a long branch—and got spattered across the face by gooey half-rotted turnip leaves.

"Those look like carrot greens," Brother Paul said, looking at his own forkful. "You do not consume the leaves?"

"Not in this condition!" Then Scot reconsidered. "The greens of any vegetable should be edible, shouldn't they! Why throw away part of the plant, when we're hungry? We should have been using them all along!"

"Many things are not obvious at first. I had forgotten, myself. Radishes, turnips, carrots, beets —all the greens should be used in salads. I believe there is merit in using the whole plant, just as there is in using the whole animal."

"Yes, I see that now. Waste is the root of all evil."

"Perhaps," Brother Paul agreed, smiling.

If this were preaching, Scot thought, it was not objectionable.[86] So much could be accepted and assimilated in incidental tidbits that would be unpalatable as a lecture. Brother Paul evidently knew this.[87]

As they penetrated beneath the brush, the pitching became easier. Here in the depths of the pile, down where Tully had prepared it—he had evidently had a working arrangement with the neighbor so that there had been no objection to having the pile so close to the house—decomposition was progressing nicely. And at the very bottom it had become fine, crumbly black humus: compost so good that it was a sheer pleasure to see and smell.

"Sometimes I imagine that we shall encounter shards of Babylonian pottery," Brother Paul observed. "Or perhaps even dinosaur bones, if we only dig down far enough in this pile."

Scot laughed. "They'd be composted by this time." Companionship made a tedious job so much more rewarding!

But they had merely gotten down to the base. Most of the pile remained, tiered on either side of the excavations.[88]

They rested again, sweating freely. Conversation was easy in this situation; the strain of muscle exertion broke down intellectual barriers somehow, perhaps because of the camaraderie of sharing a difficult task—or perhaps simply because it offered a pretext to rest a little longer.

"Why didn't you emigrate?" Scot inquired. "Surely you can't really *like* Earth as it is, or you wouldn't have joined the Order."

"I didn't like *myself*, as I was," Brother Paul said. "But your observation is true, to an extent. I am not satisfied with Earth—but I love it too."

"You could love a pioneer planet better," Scot said. "Fresh, unspoiled—there are myriads of worlds out there, each potentially better than this one."

"Yes, that may be so."

"So why don't you go to one of them, as the priests and ministers and rabbis and holy men of other religions are doing?"

"Because my mission is to help those most in need. My mission and that of the Holy Order of Vision. We must go where there is human misery, not where there is joy."

"You would actually turn down paradise?"

"Indubitably—so long as there is suffering elsewhere."

Scot shook his head. "I never thought of it that way! You want happiness for others, not for yourself."

"Our happiness is in bringing happiness to others." Brother Paul paused, reflecting. "Or at least in helping them. Happiness must come from within; we can not provide that directly."

"So you came to help us." Scot eyed the cutaway compost pile, noting the steam rising from the hot sections, and the ugly dry powder composition of the places where the water had not penetrated.

Cup-shaped: by all means! "Were we so miserable, here at the farm?"

"You were willing to be helped."

"Um, yes. I suppose that does make a difference." He remembered what a relief it had been to have that pump working. He looked at the pile again, and decided to talk a little longer. "You say you don't want paradise so long as anyone else is denied it. But suppose *everyone* could emigrate, and it was guaranteed they would all be ideal worlds?"

"Then I suppose the Holy Order of Vision would go too. We could not exist in isolation; that is not our purpose."

"You know, *I* wanted to go—more than anything. But I couldn't—and now I'm not sure I want to."

Brother Paul faced him as if discovering a delightful intellectual challenge. "Let me reverse the question on you. Suppose you could go to the perfect planet, with no adverse elements at all?"

"That's what I mean. That was Conquest, for me. I don't think I would—now. Not without my friends."

"Your friends would go. Everyone you chose."

"They'd have to *want* to, of their own accord. For their own reasons, not mine."

"They *would*. You'd all want to, for a diversity of splendid reasons. And everything would be fine. Guaranteed."

Scot shook his head dubiously. "There would be no challenge. I don't want perfection handed me on a platter. I'm not made that way. I want to *earn* my contentment."

"Well, let there be challenge, then. You and your friends would face new challenges, as many and as formidable as you wanted, and you would always rise successfully to meet them."

Scot sighed. "No, not even then. It wouldn't be real. I don't want anything handed to me, not even my challenges. I don't want to be programmed for success—or failure. I want, if you'll excuse the expression, simply to go to hell in my own fashion."

Brother Paul smiled. "You are saying that you are not made for paradise, after all."

"*Man* is not made for paradise! Or," Scot added with surprise, "for Conquest. You don't want that scenario either. *Do* you?"

Brother Paul spread his hands. "You argue persuasively."

Which was not a direct answer. Was that significant?

"What I want— Right now all I want is—" Scot stopped, surprised again. "Is to finish turning this damned compost pile!"

"Then it must be a *blessed* pile. It answers our needs."

"It must be. Compost is a thing of the spirit."

"It always was," Brother Paul agreed. "Any plant, any roach or worm would tell you the same."

Scot knew the reference to roaches or worms was not disparaging. To Brother Paul, all life deserved respect.

They pitched in with renewed vigor. Now, with every forkful, Scot did not see the toilsome pottage of brush and decaying vegetation. He saw a living process of nature, returning to the soil the things that were no longer needed elsewhere: one of the great rejuvenating phenomena of existence. What better symbol of true civilization in harmony with nature than a functioning compost pile? And he, like Brother Paul, was content to play his part, to make it work. Here was his task: to do with the soil what the Holy Order of Vision was trying to do with mankind. To restore it to its ideal state: heaven in its own terms. His happiness was in accomplishing this significant task.[89]

He paused, in thought and work. "Do you see a parallel between compost and civilization?" he inquired.

"I see a parallel—everywhere," Brother Paul replied. "Just as I see goodness—everywhere."

Scot wondered whether that could be true. *He* did not see goodness everywhere! What about the thief who had stolen his car? Was *she* good?

Irritated that this question should interrupt his rapport with the compost, he asked Brother Paul, after summarizing the episode, "How do you account for it?"

"She needed money for food, perhaps for her children," Brother Paul said. "She did wrong, but we can not call her evil."

"And what do *I* do—after all I have suffered on her account?"

Brother Paul looked up in surprise. "Why, you forgive her," he said, as though that were obvious.

"Forgive her!" Scot cried indignantly. "How do I know how many other lives she's ruined? She doesn't deserve forgiveness—she deserves punishment!"

"Are you sure she has not punished herself sufficiently?"

"Thieves have no conscience! Not so long as they get away with it. You have only to look at our political history to see that!"

Brother Paul did not answer. By that token Scot

knew he had been reproved. He had been offered the chance to forgive—and had been unable to do so.

Well, it was an honest definition of his state. He still could not forgive.

. . .

Brother Paul believed essentially in pacifism: that there should be a nonviolent or nonoffensive way to handle all situations, if one had the proper desire to do so. The others were skeptical, but had no cause to argue the matter.

Then abruptly his philosophy was tested.

Trouble, when it came, did not skulk by night. It marched up in broad daylight. Four tough-looking men came to the door. "We like your farm," the leader said directly. He was a red-haired, red-bearded (or rather beard-stubbled) individual who might have been handsome in better days. His clothes were grimy, and he carried the odor of rancid sweat. In short, he was an average man by the standards of the day. "How fast can you move out?"

It had come, thus abruptly: the time of grim decision. Confrontation by thugs: the very thing Scot had always feared. And he found himself no better prepared to handle it than he had been before MT.

Were they to move out, giving up all they had worked for, exchanging their relatively satisfactory life for that of pure scavenging? Or should they fight to retain the farm, taking the consequence? The demeanor of the intruders made it plain that they were not bluffing.

"We'll have to talk it over," Scot said.

"Thought you might," the man said genially. "Now you just do that—right now—and we'll talk with you. That's the democratic way, ain't it."

There seemed to be little choice. Scot was not a fighter, and he didn't want the girls trying it. The three of them and Brother Paul trooped out to face the four thugs.

"Two girls," the leader said. "That's real nice." He eyed Wanda. "You can stay, for sure. The other—maybe." Then he appraised Brother Paul, who had donned his collar and brown robe. "Who the hell are you?"

"I am Brother Paul, of the Holy Order of Vision."

"Never heard of it," the leader said. He glanced at his companions, who also shook their heads negatively. He returned to Brother Paul. "Well, scat. We don't need your kind here."

Scot knew that their way of life was in immediate peril. But part of him wondered just how Brother Paul would react to this direct challenge to his pacifistic philosophy. If pacifism meant giving up all that one had striven for, could it be a valid answer? This was the test.

"This matter is my concern," Brother Paul said. He did not seem to be alarmed.

"Yeah?" The leader glanced sidelong at one of his henchmen, and inclined his head just slightly. "Brand—move him off."

Brand stepped forward. He was the largest of the four, powerful, with the battered features of a brawler. He grasped the front of Brother Paul's robe with one scarred hairy hand, half-lifting the man to his toes.

"Stop that!" Scot cried. "You can't put hands on a—"

"Peace," Brother Paul said. "He can't hurt me."

With misgivings, they watched Brand march Brother Paul away. It was evident that composure and principle were powerless against blunt force. What was going to happen?

"Now," the leader said. "Discuss: are you moving out now, maybe taking along some of your trinkets—or are you getting moved out our way, and take nothing but maybe some lumps?"

Scot knew he was no hero. He had recovered from his original injury, and the hard work of maintaining the farm had improved his health. But he knew nothing about physical combat, and could never be a match for the least of the four toughs, let alone these three of them. He had no reasonable choice: if he didn't give up the farm voluntarily, he would be beaten up and thrown out. He would lose everything, including his health, just as he had when he lost his car.

His car—there was an object lesson! Had he just stood and watched it go, he would have been out the vehicle, true. But he would have given it up anyway very soon, along with his other worldly possessions, when he emigrated to Colony Conquest with his brother and fiancée. So the car was nothing, really.

Instead he had fought to save it—and lost car, health, emigration, college and fiancée. With the breakdown in communications, he had never been summoned to his trial, so MT was still denied him, by default—assuming he still wanted to go. As he might, if he lost this farm. Lost—all because of that one wrong decision.[90]

Yet he found it was not in him to yield. To let might make right—that was wrong. It was not only his fate at stake, but that of Brother Paul and

Wanda and Lucy. He had to do what was right for them. If he let these men have their way, he would be a vagabond, Brother Paul's effort would have been wasted, and the two girls would be concubines. He would in fact be contributing to the degradation of his world.

Scot was trapped between his physical incapacity and his mental rigidity. He was unable to reply.

"Who do you think you are?" Wanda demanded of the leader. "You can't simply come in here and take over everything we've worked for!"

She had said what Scot should have said. He had failed even at futile defiance.

"Now I've tried to handle it peacefully," the leader said. "But you're making trouble. I gave you a chance to clear out without getting hurt. I was being nice. But I don't mind it the other way." His hand snaked out and caught Wanda's arm. He twisted, and she screamed and fell to the ground.

Scot acted without thinking. He swung his fist at the leader. The blow landed, but bounced off the bull neck harmlessly, and the man only laughed. "Okay, sucker. We'll work you over now. Hold him, boys."

The other two thugs grabbed Scot by the arms and held him upright. The power of their hands was painful. The leader stood before him, fist cocked, eying him as though savoring the moment. A true sadist, he took his time, not acting in the heat of the moment but waiting for maximum impact. Scot had read stories of a man held like this yanking the two in so that their heads cracked together, while he disabled the front man with a well placed kick, but in practice he found himself helpless. He closed his eyes, knowing what was coming, hoping it wouldn't be too bad. He hadn't learned a thing; he had made the same mistake he had with the car thief. Futile action.

"Please refrain."

Scot's eyes snapped open. It was Brother Paul, alone.

"How'd you get away from Brand?" the leader demanded, as surprised as Scot.

"We talked, and he had a change of heart," Brother Paul said. "Now I wish to talk with you. These people have worked hard to build and operate this farm. It is not right to require them to leave. In the circumstances I'll have to ask *you* to leave—unless you wish to take a more constructive attitude."

Scot knew that approach would be met with contempt. The verification was immediate. "Start with him, then," the leader snapped. "I don't like his mouth."

The thugs let go of Scot. "Leave Brother Paul alone!" Wanda cried, stepping forward.

"Yes, we'll have to make a little demonstration," the leader said. "These creeps are slow to get the message."

"Boss, I don't like this," one of the thugs said. "It ain't right to rough up a priest."

"I am no priest," Brother Paul said, and Scot wished the man had not chosen to clarify that point right at this moment. If the thugs were willing to let a priest go—

Brother Paul turned to Scot. "In the face of these men's determination, I don't see what better course I can urge than for you to accede to their demand. If neither side gives way, there may be violence, and this can not be condoned."

Wanda was still rubbing her arm where the thug had twisted, but she was by no means cowed.

"Brother Paul, I think I understand your position," she said. "But I hope you'll understand when I say it is sometimes hard to see the distinction between pacifism and cowardice." And she faced away from him.

Brother Paul was unperturbed. "This is true. It can also be difficult to perceive the distinction between pacifism and courage." He turned to Scot. "The bravest thing you might do would be to walk away from this house. I will, if you choose, bring you to the nearest station of our Order, where you may stay as long as you wish. The girls also. You will not need to join the Order. We seek only to help."

Scot realized that here was his way out. They would have a place to stay, with food and comfort, and comparative security. It probably would be better than the farm.

Yet there remained that core of stubbornness in him that simply would not give over, however reasonable the alternative. He didn't understand it, as he had never been this way before, but he was subject to it. "I can't do it," Scot said. "I'm sorry."

"I'm with Scot," Wanda said. "If we don't fight for what we believe in, what use is there in living? Maybe we'll go down—but these beasts will know they paid a price. Maybe next time they won't be so eager to raid what isn't theirs." She turned to Lucy, who had been standing white-faced throughout. "How do you feel, Luce?"

But the girl just shook her head mutely. She was obviously terrified, almost literally petrified. She had her hands cupped together at her chest, as if suffering internal pain. There would be no help from her!

"You will not take the reasonable course?" Brother Paul asked Scot. "I urge you again, for the sake of peace—"

"Not that sort of peace!" Wanda flared.

"Listen to the preacher," the leader said. "He just may save you a broken skull."

Scot felt cold all over. The choice Brother Paul had proposed theoretically at the compost pile was now literal. He could have a good life at or near the Order station, merely by agreeing. The alternative was not merely neutral, it was highly negative. Heaven—or hell.

"I—can't," he repeated, again resigning himself to what was coming. Not only for him, but for Wanda. *Why couldn't he have been sensible and yielded?*

"That was very interesting," the thug leader said. "I thought for a minute he was going to make you see light. Well, where were we? Oh, yes: we were going to see you out so you won't forget. Go to, boys."

The two thugs advanced a second time on Scot. But Brother Paul stepped in front of him. "Since this man will not yield, I am forced to intercede. You gentlemen will have to go."

"That does it!" the leader exploded. "Do Brother Nosey first—and hard."

This time one man hesitated, but the other moved in on Brother Paul. Wanda tried to interfere, game to the end, but the leader grabbed her by the shoulder and flung her back.

"I wish you would be reasonable," Brother Paul said. Scot was amazed and dismayed by the man's foolish persistence. Surely he realized that anything he said at this point would only make things worse. Yet the lead thug did pause. "I must ask again that you depart," Brother Paul continued, "and leave these people alone."

The leader laughed harshly, evidently always ready to spin out an enjoyable hassle, cat and mouse. "And what are you going to do about it?"

Scot wondered whether there would be any chance of disabling at least one of the thugs by jumping on him just as he grabbed Brother Paul. The situation was beyond saving now; what did he have to lose?

"The way of love and peace is always best," Brother Paul said. "Yet for any action there is a necessary consequence."

The first thug shot out his arm to strike. But suddenly Brother Paul was inside the man's reach, whirling around, heaving—and the man tumbled headfirst over Brother Paul's back and landed hard on the ground.

Scot gaped, not comprehending what had happened. But the second thug was already on the robed man, foot swinging in for a brutal kick. Brother Paul stepped nimbly aside, caught the foot, and levered the man down.

"I want you to understand I hold no animosity for you," Brother Paul told the men on the ground. "Allow me to help you up—" And he lifted the second man back to his feet.

The leader was openmouthed. "The creep can fight!" he exclaimed.

Brother Paul made a formal little bow to him. "I tried not to hurt your men. Please leave now—all three of you."[91]

For a moment the leader seemed ready to attack. But he thought the better of it. Brother Paul's motions had been too sure, too effective, and his

poise was too great. The action had been no fluke;
he could very easily have put the men down unconscious or with broken bones. "Come on, boys."

The three left. They just turned away as if they
had lost interest. Wanda whirled on Brother Paul.
"You never even hinted you could fight like that!
Why did you keep it secret?"

"In my youth I was a student of judo, the
so-called 'gentle way' of self-defense," Brother Paul
admitted. "It is not a talent I regard with pride, but
rather a legacy of my past, and I'm sorry to have
used it."

Scot shook his head. "All the time you knew you
could take them, but you reasoned and backed off
and tried to talk us into leaving peacefully—"

"And I called you a coward," Wanda said, chagrined.

"I was," Brother Paul said. "I took a somewhat
violent way out, because I was afraid of the consequence if I didn't. Perhaps there was a better way,
had I acted correctly. I shall have to meditate to see
where I went wrong."

"Where you went wrong!" Scot exclaimed. "You
saved the farm! Would your Order condemn you for
that?"

"Oh, no, not the Order. Individual Brothers and
Sisters have differing standards. Some would not
hesitate to use such a tool, or feel guilty about the
manner of handling the situation so long as the
results achieved significant growth and realization.
There should be no hesitation in using power as
forcefully as needed in each experience. It is always
the Vision that prompts all motivation and subse-
quent actions—in conjunction with thorough understanding of the divine laws, the universal

principles. Eventually this brings about the perfected state. But there were complications here, and
I do not know my own code well enough to be sure
that I applied it correctly."[92]

"But we were about to get beaten up," Wanda
protested. "Maybe raped, killed—"

"The alternative might have been worse," Brother Paul said. "Men might have been killed needless-
ly, and the conscience of a young woman could
have been severely tested. I felt I could not permit
that."

Both Scot and Wanda made gestures of confusion. "We might have *tried*," she said. "But we
never could have—"

Brother Paul crossed to Lucy, who remained
frozen as she had been all along. "Sister, permit
me," he said. He put his hand gently on her right
arm, drawing it out from the clasp of her other
hand. And Scot and Wanda gaped again.

Lucy's right hand held a tiny gun.

"I am sure she would have used it in your
defense," Brother Paul said. "Lucy is completely
devoted to your effort."

Numbed, Scot examined the gun. It was no toy; it
had a clip of four bullets, yet was so small it had
been completely concealed in her hands. He realized that she had kept it pointed at the thug leader
throughout.[93]

Brother Paul took the gun from her hand. "Would
you like me to pray for you?" he asked her. "You
have been through a terrible trial."

Big-eyed, stiff-faced, she nodded.

"Pray for us all," Wanda said. One tear trailed
down her cheek. "We didn't know . . . anything."

Brother Paul dropped the gun on the ground,
held Lucy's hand, and reached for Scot's. Scot took

Wanda's hand, and she completed the circle by taking Lucy's free one. They all bowed their heads.

"In the name of that Vision we all share," Brother Paul murmured, "we ask the understanding and compassion of the Divine Spirit, by whatever name we know it. We ask that we shall become better able to handle the problems we encounter, and to arrive at more compatible solutions. We ask that we learn what it is we can do to help this girl achieve her own perfected state, and never to face the prospect of such violence again. For we love her."[94]

And Scot felt an almost tangible power in Brother Paul's hand, like an electric charge but with no shock. It passed through him and on to Wanda. He knew she felt it too, for she squeezed his fingers in response. It was a strange, wonderful feeling. He wondered whether this was what faith was like.

After a moment of healing silence they separated. Scot looked up—and saw one of the thugs. Oh, no!

Brother Paul turned about. "Why hello, Brand," he said pleasantly.

"I thought about what you told me," Brand said. "I don't need no more time. I'm ready now."

Scot looked from one to the other. "What did you two talk about?"

"Brand would like to join the farm," Brother Paul said.

"He—join?" Scot asked incredulously.

"As a productive member," Brother Paul continued. "He is sorry for any inconvenience he caused you, and is willing to lend his strength to tasks that might otherwise prove difficult."

"Yeah—that's it," Brand said. "He says it better'n I could."

Scot spread his hands. This must be what Brother

Paul meant by finding a more positive solution. Not merely driving off the invaders, but converting them. "Why not?"

...

Brand joined the farm—and once again it turned out to have been a fortunate addition. The man *was* powerful; he could hoist a log weighing 150 pounds to his shoulder and carry it without seeming to notice. When he took the sixteen-pound sledge-hammer and had at the big gnarly chunks of wood, the pieces fairly burst apart. When he pitched compost, the pile was turned in rapid order. He was like a tractor or a team of work horses: no great amount of imagination, but force that seemed able to move mountains.

He was illiterate, but that didn't seem to be much of a disadvantage. And there was another surprise.

"Listen," Wanda said one afternoon to Scot.

He listened. Someone was playing a piccolo in the back yard, by the sound. The thin melody was absolutely beautiful.

"Perfect pitch," she said. "Every note true."

It was a melody he had heard before, but now it seemed much lovelier than he remembered. "Who?" he asked.

She drew him to the window. They looked out. Brand was stacking split wood and whistling while he worked. "Beethoven's Ninth Symphony," Wanda said.

"Classical music?" he asked, amazed.[95]

"He doesn't know it by name, and of course he can't read music; he just knows what he likes," she explained.

They listened for some time to a medley of

classical and popular music, all expertly rendered. It was the finest whistling Scot had ever heard, and it was hard to believe that this big, dull man was doing it. Yet it was so.

"Shows you never can tell," Scot said. "If he has a soul, it comes out through his music."[96]

In the evenings Brand and Brother Paul practiced judo, bowing to each other formally before reviewing the holds. Now the others began to see how the thugs had been subdued so readily. Brother Paul could flip huge Brand over his shoulder to land crushingly on the straw, unhurt. And soon Brand was able to do it too. It was a matter of timing and balance and leverage. Brother Paul offered to show the others how to do it also, but Scot and Lucy declined, afraid of the violent falls. Wanda tried it for a while, but discovered it was necessary to get quite close to a man in order to make a throw work—chest to chest, belly to belly, thigh to thigh, with hard contact—and was afraid this could be misconstrued. She tried to talk Lucy into working with her, but Lucy wouldn't, so Wanda dropped out.

Prompted by Brand's whistling, they began to sing while working. No one had a good voice, but in harmony the rough edges tended to fade, and it became an uplifting experience. They sang anything anybody knew—folk songs, hymns, popular songs, even *Emigrate With Me,* though that usually ended in laughter. None of them intended to emigrate, now.

It rained, and the roof leaked. Scot and Brand hauled up the spare roll of roofing paper and a bucket of tar on the next sunny day and went to work. And now Scot had a chance to find out something he had been curious about for some time. "Just what did Brother Paul say to you, the first time?"

"Nothing much," Brand said. "Just how you were nice people who maybe could use a strong man."

"But you were with—those others. Why should you change?"

"Didn't make much sense to me at first," Brand admitted. "But then I saw the light."

"The light?" Revelation hardly seemed the style of this man, despite his whistling. "When— Where did you see it?"

Brand laughed. "In mid-air."

"What?" Humor wasn't his style either.

"When he threw me."

"Brother Paul used his judo on you? I thought he always took the peaceful way."

"I guess he forgot, for just a moment. When I tried to bash in his head."

"Oh."

"I always did understand a good bash," Brand said. "Funny thing was it didn't hurt. He flipped me over and put me down so gentle, and then he put a little armlock on me. I knew right off I couldn't touch him in a hundred years. You ever feel an armlock?"

"No."

Brand shook his head. "Take my word: It don't matter how much muscle you got, when you're in an armlock, you're finished. I thought maybe he'd teach me some of that stuff."

Now it came clear. Brand had had an ulterior motive. "Suppose he hadn't?"

"Then I wouldn't learn it. I like it here anyway. I was getting tired of raiding anyway. He was right—

you're nice people. You like my whistling, you don't laugh 'cause I'm too dumb to read. Maybe I'll be like you some day."

"Aren't you afraid of what your former pals might think?"

Brand rolled back his right sleeve and bunched his biceps. The muscle bulged hugely. "Naw. They'll never come here again." But then he reconsidered. "Still, I don't want to fight. Brother Paul says peace is harder to learn than fighting."

"I guess it is." They were having, in their fashion, a philosophic discussion.

"Them girls," Brand remarked.

"Wanda and Lucy? What about them?"

"I got a feel for women. Been with a lot, in my day."

Suddenly Scot liked the conversation less. But he was curious to know what the man was getting at. "If you like a girl and she likes you—"

"Naw. Not my type, neither one. Wanda's 'fraid I'll feel her up in judo, so she won't do it, but she shouldn't worry. I like 'em—" Brand paused to describe an elephantine female shape in the air with hammer and nail.

If Wanda was too slender for this man, he had grandiose tastes! "What about them, then?"

"They both work hard. The one sets things up, the other grinds."

"Lucy won't let anyone else do the grinding! I'd do it myself—I know how hard it is—but she—"

"Let her grind. It's good for her."

Good to let a small, weak girl struggle with an extraordinarily fatiguing chore, while a muscular man like Brand stood by. Scot had seen Lucy striving to keep that handle turning, panting, collapsing for five minutes at a time, then resuming the effort. Probably it was a form of self-torture, in expiation for some inconsequential error in her past. Apparently that didn't bother Brand, who claimed to understand women. "Then what's your point?"

"I'd wait."

"What?"

"You don't have no feel. No offense."

The man was trying to be diplomatic. He wasn't good at it, but Scot appreciated the effort. "No offense, of course: I never did know much about women." Certainly not about Fanny!

"Yeah. I mean you'd make a mistake now. Maybe in two, three months you'll know."

"Know *what*?"

"Which one."

"I don't think we're getting anywhere," Scot said, exasperated.

"Like peace. I can't learn it right off. Gotta take my time, watch, listen, pick it up natural. One day it'll come."

"And one day I'll learn about women—if I wait, watch and listen?"

Brand smiled. "Right."

Scot returned to his work. He was amazed at the presumption of this oaf, seeking to educate him in the facts of life. Yet he had a nagging feeling that Brand had had a kernel of substance to impart. Whatever it was.[97]

Brand commenced whistling. The sound was fine, so evocative, that Scot was unable to hang on to his irritation. He wondered whether the other members of the thug squad would have turned out to have similar assets—had Brother Paul been able to convert them as he had Brand. How difficult it was to judge a person by the first experience with him!

. . .

Fall, and the woodcutting tools were getting a heavy workout. Scot, Wanda and Brother Paul were doing a major sharpening while Lucy worked in the garden. Scot used a whetstone on the axes while Wanda held the long two-man saw for Brother Paul's careful, patient filing. These were jobs that had to be done properly and could not be rushed.

Ten million people had now emigrated from America, and the informal word was that two more MT units were being readied.[98] The colony planets, according to the printed circulars the government released, were all doing well. Better, it seemed, than Earth.

But the disappearance of the adjacent city had alleviated the ravages of vandals and thugs. Now isolation and the coming winter were the main hazards for the farm. Yet they had discovered that though their neighbors were now one to three miles away, these distances became less than next door had been in the city. There were the Browns to the north and the Smiths to the south, sturdy, durable families, willing to help in an emergency, willing to be helped. When the Smiths were sick, Wanda had gone to pick up their three small children, boarding them for a week. The Smiths had responded with the gift of this fine saw they were now sharpening: invaluable for felling and preparing new wood. Wood loomed large in the concerns of the neighborhood; it was the only source of heat for the winter.

"Is Paul your original name?" Wanda inquired. "That is, it seems almost too apt."

"I was given that name when I joined the Order," he admitted. "I chose to cast aside my prior life, and so it was appropriate that the old name be cast aside too.[99] I have never regretted it—and I often meditate upon the significance of the similar change in the original Paul, and its relevance to both Christianity and the Holy Order of Vision. Indeed, at times it seems we are one—Saul, Christianity, Vision and me, a fourfold and infinite unity.

"Saul?" Scot asked.

"Paul and Saul are the same. The Bible refers to him first as Saul, and then in Acts XIII, Verse 9 mentions that he is also called Paul, and thereafter he is Paul. Actually, it is merely the Roman version of Saul—but I like to think that the apparent change in name actually derives from his change of heart when he became a Christian, as I did. In fact, it helps me to feel an identity with him."

"That must be very important to you," Wanda said.

"Yes, frankly it is. May I tell you about Saul?" He paused in his filing to look askance at them. "We meet him in Acts VIII, when the unbelieving multitude stoned the prophet Stephen, and laid down their clothes at a young man's feet, and that man's name was Saul. This was part of Jewish custom: Saul had instigated the stoning, and this ceremony was acknowledgment of this fact. Of course there are many more levels to it than that. There was a great persecution against the newly forming Christian Church. Saul committed the men and women of this church to prison, and many were scattered abroad through all the area."

Brother Paul smiled. "Actually, this was like trying to put out a fire by scattering the burning embers through the parched countryside. Each em-ber ignites a new fire, and what was a contained phenomenon becomes uncontained. So perhaps Saul was acting on behalf of the nascent Church even when he was opposing it."

"That's why you don't seek converts!" Wanda said. "Outsiders can do your Order as much good as members."

Brother Paul shook his head. "No, we are not interested in converts. We accept them gladly—but those of our spirit will come to us without urging, and others will not. We merely try to serve our purpose in the world, helping mankind."

"Oh, of course," she said. "I didn't mean to belittle your motive." Scot knew she was thinking of the time she had called Brother Paul a coward, and learned he was not. She had been more careful since.

"I know that." He made a little gesture, as of patting a puppy on the head. "At any rate, the Church was spreading like wildfire. Stephen was dead, but another prophet appeared from among the people, Philip, and he preached as effectively as Stephen had. And Saul—do you mind if I quote directly from the Bible? It is written there so much better than I can say it."

"I'm agnostic," Scot said. "I don't believe in the Bible—not as the ultimate authority on everything, not literally—but I don't mind listening to it." He glanced at the others, and there was no objection. Brand had come in, and stayed to listen.

"'And Saul, yet breathing out threatenings and slaughter against the disciples of the Lord, went unto the high priest,'" Brother Paul quoted, his voice assuming the special timbre of one repeating poetry. "'And desired of him letters to Damascus to the synagogues, that if he found any of this way'—he meant Christians—'whether they were men or women, he might bring them bound unto Jerusalem.

"'And as he journeyed, he came near Damascus: and suddenly there shined round about him a light from heaven:

"'And he fell to the Earth, and heard a voice say unto him, Saul, Saul, why persecutest thou me?

"'And he said, Who art thou, Lord? And the Lord said, I am Jesus whom thou persecutest.'"

Brother Paul shook his head. "That was the vision of Paul, and this is the origin of our name, the Holy Order of Vision. Paul was blind for three days, and did not eat or drink. Then a disciple named Ananias came and put his hands on Paul, and his sight returned at once, and he arose and was baptized. And the course of Christianity was changed."

"No offense, but I would be suspicious," Scot said. "Here is this persecutor, jailing Christians and even killing them—and he suddenly turns about and starts preaching Christianity! I'd figure that for some kind of trap."

"So did the Christians," Brother Paul agreed. "They even plotted to kill Paul, watching at the gates to catch him. But his friends learned of the plot and let him over the wall of the city in a basket. Now he was in trouble with both sides. But in time he convinced them by his actions and words. This, ultimately, is the only sure way to judge a person."

"I wonder about that conversion for another reason," Wanda said. "That vision is very like a mental breakdown, or even a migraine headache. He saw a light and heard a voice and fell to the ground, and was struck blind—could it have been an obstruction in the brain, a tumor? If so, what is the significance for Christianity?"

"I have meditated on that also," Brother Paul admitted as his file approached the end of the saw. "I have tentatively concluded that God works in mysterious ways—mysterious to *us*, not to Him— perhaps even through tumors on the brain.[100] Perhaps Paul was fated to die of cancer, and it affected his personality adversely, made him increasingly rabid, and his newfound faith was responsible for regression of the growth. That would not invalidate his message. Ultimately it is Paul's message, not the man himself, that moves us, his willingness to admit all men, not just Jews, into the new Church. I believe in that message; it needs no apology, and cannot be negated by criticism of the precise nature of the man's conversion. The Holy Order of Vision believes in that message: that God, and the worship of God, is whole, Holy, not circumscribed or partial. The very word 'Holy' derives from the Anglo-Saxon *hal,* meaning whole." He stopped. "Sorry—I was preaching. I didn't mean to do that."

"Shucks, we're used to it," Brand said.

"No, it's good to hear true belief," Wanda said. "There is so little of it these days, so little real belief in *anything*."

And Scot wondered whether she was speaking for herself, for her inability to make any definite commitment, whether of emigration or marriage. Commitment should follow true belief.[101]

• • •

Winter. Fifteen million people had emigrated, and with the accelerated MT program the total would soon pass twenty million. But there was little local change; this area had already been depleted. Scot's own greatest changes had occurred with the loss of electric power and the arrival of Wanda; the progressive regression and addition of people to the farm since had been routine. Was it really this way all over the world?

"I've primed and pumped and pumped," Wanda complained. "But the water just won't come up."

"I'll have a look at it," Brother Paul said. They were eating a breakfast of cracked wheat cereal, actually quite tasty and filling, cooked on the wood stove.

Efficiently he dismantled the pump. "Bearings are worn," he said. "Washers are shot. It can't develop the necessary suction. I might make replacement washers, but they wouldn't last long and probably aren't worth the effort."

"So the pump's done for," Scot said grimly.

"As a practical matter, I believe so. We lack the technology to maintain it."

"But we have to have water," Wanda said.

"We'll simply have to regress another step," Brother Paul told her. "Carry water from the well in buckets."

"Can't do that," Wanda pointed out. "We covered over that well to protect it and the pipes from freezing, and now it's all frozen dirt above the water. Under the regular snow and ice. We might clear it out—"

"Not worth it," Brand objected. "I could do it, but our shovel's rusty. It couldn't take the beating."

"We can melt snow," Lucy suggested.

"Smart girl," Brother Paul told her, and she flushed with pleasure. What an impact a passing compliment had, Scot thought. "Collect clean snow in pans, put them on the stove, or merely in the kitchen. It'll melt. In spring we'll locate a spring, no pun, and carry water in buckets. Or re-excavate our well for the purpose. In any event, an ancient and honorable system."

Wanda sighed. "Women carrying jars of water on their heads."

"Gives 'em good posture," Brand said. "Chests out, hips square."

"And nude too, if you had your way," she said. "Back to the Saxons, back to the Stone Age."

"Oh, the Saxons weren't Stone Age," Brother Paul said. "Medieval yes, Neolithic no. They conquered Britain after the Romans collapsed."

"The Angles, the Saxons, and the Jutes," Scot said. "Ancient history lives again."

"And others," Brother Paul agreed. "But mainly the Saxons. Actually, I believe they were originally imported from Gaul to Britain by the Romans, to aid in the defense of the island. Or by the Britons remaining when the Romans departed, early in the fifth century A.D. 425 or so—history does not record the date. But—"

"You're a historian too?" Wanda asked, interested.

Brother Paul chuckled. "Not at all! Edification of the mind is one of the disciplines of the Order, and we don't confine our studies to the Bible. We study all religions, as well as philosophy, psychology, practical ministry, stewardship, healing, science—"

"Faith healing?" Lucy asked.

"Scientific prayer, yes. Prayer *is* scientific; it has to be, or it fails.[102] But we also go into physiology, causes of disease, methods of treatment—we do not eschew modern knowledge and practice, but we do not depend on them, either."

"Modern science too?" Wanda asked.

"Physics, chemistry, mathematics, astrology—
we try to obtain a good working understanding of
the laws of creation as taught in the New Testament
and as they reveal themselves in the several sciences
of Man."

Astrology? Scot wondered. Well, why not? It was
no doubt every bit as valid as the economics that
had postulated MT as the solution to Earth's problems of population and resources. Now so many of
the congressmen who had approved MT had emigrated themselves that no quorum remained to
reverse the directive, and so MT continued like a
rampaging elephant, unstoppable though the Earth
be depleted to extinction.

"At any rate," Brother Paul concluded, "I picked
up a bit of history, and don't regret it."

"Certainly not now," Wanda said. "We're living
history—backwards. Every month brings some
other regression. We'll be seeing real Saxons again
soon, I'm sure."

"Well, the Saxons were civilized in their fashion.
They came as warriors, but after about the year 600
when their conquest of England was more or less
complete they settled as useful citizens. Many of us
derive from them: Anglo-Saxons. No shame in
that!"

Many of us, Scot thought, glancing at Brother
Paul's dark skin. A man without even racial consciousness, let alone prejudice.

"No shame at all," Wanda agreed. "Or any other
derivation."

She's aware, Scot thought.

"We are all of one flesh," Brother Paul said.

"Even the Saxons!" Wanda added.

And Scot suffered another revelation. "As our

population declines, our civilization recedes!" he said. "The two are linked!"

It was one of the few times Brother Paul was startled. "There may be something to that!"

Wanda, too, was awed by the notion. "Cause and effect? Could our whole progress toward civilization have been governed solely by population pressure?"

"Well, it is said that large animals are more complicated than small animals," Brother Paul said. "They are not larger to handle complication; they're complicated to handle the largeness. It takes a more sophisticated breathing system to process the volume of oxygen needed by a large creature, and a more complex nervous system to handle those refinements. Why couldn't it be the same for societies? Perhaps not on a straight-line basis, but as an underlying principle that manifests inevitably if not counteracted, like gravity or entropy. We five don't need a formal government—but a nation of many tens of millions *does*. It is more complicated —because it is larger. If it does not achieve those special refinements we call civilization, or if it neglects them, it fragments and loses its identity."

"Fall of the Roman Empire," Wanda agreed. "First it degenerated, then it collapsed."

"That's true of all empires," Brother Paul agreed.

"We've always supposed that larger population was the result of civilized improvements," Wanda said. "Farming, pottery, metalwork, mass production. But of course when you have a city, sophisticated communication, transportation and production—and of course the rule of law—these aren't luxuries, they're necessities. The city goes haywire if civilization breaks down. But as we have seen, depopulation also guts civilization. Out here in the sticks we're reverting faster than anyone. It could be coincidence—but I don't think so."

"And we've taken such pride in man's progress!" Scot said. "This makes it no more than a muscle twitch—a side effect of our numbers."

"I wouldn't say that," Brother Paul said. "If the population enforces change, it is still man's individual decision that determines the nature of that change. It is a challenge, and only those who rise to it can survive. When lemmings overpopulate, they march into the sea and drown. *That's* muscle-twitch reaction.[103] So I think some pride is deserved, in that we have converted our crisis into a benefit. Few other species have managed that."

"You have a generous way of looking at things," Wanda said. "It does you credit. But it still puts us in our place. We're losing population, and we're losing civilization, despite all our experience and knowledge. If the Saxons had been as numerous as modern man, they'd have been as civilized."

"We *are* the Saxons," Scot said. "And the Angles and Jutes and Normans and Celts and Romans, all merged and multiplied."

"But if population really controls civilization," Brother Paul mused, "what will continued emigration lead to for those of us remaining? What of Earth? Is it to be another Atlantis, sinking out of sight?"

They all exchanged glances, having no answer. Space was being conquered—but what of Earth?[104]

. . .

Winter passed, spring came. Their nearest neighbors were now their only real contact with the world, and the neighbors themselves were isolated. Occasionally travelers passed on horse or foot, exchanging news of far places for a night's lodging. It was a private, peaceful, harsh, rather satisfying life.

As the summer heat waxed and the garden began to produce, Brother Paul approached Scot, hand extended. "It is time for me to go," he said. "It has been a year, and I have fulfilled my mission here."

Scot had known the man's stay was temporary, but this came as a shock. "Already? You have shown us so much, and there's so much more—"

"You'll survive the winter, as you did the last. You've become independent of Earth's technology. You can cope. But feel free to call on the Holy Order of Vision if you have need."

"I don't know what to say," Scot said. "You're like part of the family."

"The family of Man. We are all brothers." Brother Paul paused. "I'm afraid that what I have to say next will be awkward. But—"

"I'll say it," Wanda said, coming up behind Brother Paul. She took Scot's hands in hers. "Scot, I know there has been an—an understanding between us, and I think it would be fair to call it love. But I have come upon a greater understanding, and I have to go. I'm sorry—but I'm glad too. I hope you'll understand."

Scot was stunned. "You're going too?"

"To the Holy Order of Vision," she said. "I think that is what I really want in life."

"Oh—with Brother Paul?" Oddly, he felt no jealousy.

"No. He will take me there, but only to introduce me. It is the *Order* I want. I'm finally ready—to make a real commitment. To be a Sister. It's a wonderful moment in my life."

"I'm afraid I have, in a very real sense, taken her

away from you," Brother Paul said. "Your loss is the Order's gain. I hope there are no regrets."

It was what she wanted . . . "It will be empty here without you—both of you," Scot said. How empty he could not yet imagine; he held the import at bay, away from his immediate consciousness. Wanda! How could she?

"Perhaps one day you will rejoin us," Wanda said. "Brothers and Sisters do not have to be celibate, and I know you'd be good in the Order." The invitation she was giving him was quite plain, and it was far more substantial than the one she had given at their first meeting. She would marry him if he joined her in this. She had found her point of irrevocable commitment at last.

But so had Scot. He shook his head. "Not my type of thing."

"There can be as much conscience in the negation as in the acceptance," Brother Paul said, understanding. "This farm is your life, and that is good and right for you. But it would be kind of you to visit the Order."

"Yes. I'll do that." They were being so generous, so understanding; could he be less?

Wanda approached him again, holding out a length of something. "This may be in improper taste," she said. "But considering what you have done for me and what we have meant to each other, I'd like you to have it. Will you wear it, Scot?"

It was a little silver cross on a fine chain: symbol of the Holy Order of Vision. "Is it all right, Brother Paul?" she asked.

"I believe so," Brother Paul replied. "This is not usual procedure, but somehow I feel it will do him good."

She reached up and put the chain over his head.

Numbed, Scot observed the flex of her bosom with the motion, and wished she were embracing him instead of leaving him. The cross was a poor substitute for Wanda! But he had to accept it.

. . .

They were gone. The ache of Wanda's absence was terrible. Scot could not condemn her; she had done what she had to, openly and honestly, and unlike Fanny she had faced him with the news and given him a chance to accompany her. He had turned her down—why, he could not quite explain to himself. But where could he rebound—from the rebound?

He kept himself busy, trying to forget the ache through hard work. With Wanda and Brother Paul gone, there was more to do; the gap was more than emotional. Lucy took over the cooking and Brand whistled sadly as he built a huge stack of wood for the winter. It would be months before snow fell, but the wood had to be seasoned or it would not burn properly. They left Scot alone.

But he found he could not mourn forever. It was not as though Wanda was dead, any more than Fanny was. She had merely found a new life, perhaps a better one. He could not begrudge her that. His sadness was selfish—and foolish, because nothing barred him from rejoining her except his own obstinacy. Why had he balked at joining the Order?

They started the harvest. The first early potatoes were ready, grown in the compost he and Brother Paul had turned: civilized compost, he called it. It was important that the crop be handled promptly, so that there would be no wasteful rush later. These small potatoes had to be treated gently. Scot and

Lucy took spading forks and began digging up the plants and sifting through the dirt for the brown treasures. This could not be rushed; they did not want to spear any potatoes on the tines, or miss any.

The day started cool, but the sun and their continued efforts warmed them both. Scot removed his jacket and Lucy her shawl. Still it was hot, and in due course they stripped down some more: he to his bare chest and she to her homemade halter. Manufactured undergarments were now too much of a luxury for routine use; clothing, like the rest of society, had regressed.

They shook off as much dirt as feasible and packed the potatoes carefully in bushel baskets. It was a fine crop: they had learned something in the past year about gardening, and they had kept the weeds and bugs out and brought buckets of water faithfully all summer. These plants had been coddled, and they had responded splendidly.

Lucy leaned over to pick up the basket as Scot placed the last potato. "I'll carry it," he said. "It'll be too heavy for you." He could not have managed anything like this before he became a farmer, but he had put on muscle steadily. In fact, it was clear that his brother Tully had owed much of his physique to his lifestyle, rather than to heredity. Scot was by no means comparable to Brand, but he was much more powerful than he had been. It was a healthy life.

"One way to find out," she said. She caught hold of the two wire handles, braced herself, and heaved the basket up.

Scot stared. She had shown him more than her strength. Her halter, not close fitting, had fallen away somewhat so that he had a plain view of her breasts—and he was amazed. He had thought of her as flat-chested. She was not; she had extraordinary pectoral development, as nice as he had ever seen.

After that, he watched her covertly as they worked. Lucy's face had cleared, and her skin was now tanned. She had a healthy glow about her. Even her hair had thickened, and it flung about her shoulders in lithe brown hanks as she moved. Her legs and arms were slim yet well fleshed: the tonus of healthy muscle. Her torso was supple. In short, she was a remarkably comely lass, not at all matching his mental picture of her.[105]

How could he have missed the change? He knew part of the answer: Wanda. When Wanda was at the farm, he had had eyes for no one else. He had hoped to marry her, when she was able to make the commitment. He had been willfully blind. Lucy had changed little by little, like a child growing up, unnoticed.

They finished the potatoes by noon and went inside for lunch. Brand came in, shedding bits of bark and sawdust. Lucy went out to pick some fresh tomatoes and turnips for salad; they never took things early, as there was no effective way to store them in summer. By planting in successive stages, they had things ripening all summer and fall, not all at once: another hint Brother Paul had provided.[106] Except for things like the main potato crop that they intended to store for the winter; those had to be timed for cool-weather harvest.

The two men munched the hard rolls she had baked. Originally they had used yeast to make the loaves rise, but it had run out and they had adapted to unleavened bread. It was possible to keep a yeast culture going indefinitely, using a little for each baking, but it hadn't been worth the effort.[107] The hard bread wasn't bad; they merely had to chew

with more authority. Many of the necessary rever-
sions turned out to be suitable after all, like this.

"Ain't she somethin' in that halter!" Brand exclaimed genially.

Scot nodded. Obviously Brand had been aware of
the change for some time, and now knew Scot had
observed it too.

"I told you she was worth watching. Doll who
packs a derringer and looks like that—" He broke
off. "But not my type, you understand. I got no
ideas about her."

Implying that Scot *did?* A light dawned. "You
tried to tell me way back when, on the roof. Not to
choose the wrong woman!"

"Yeah." Brand tore off another hunk of bread
with bared teeth. "I knew Wanda was getting hot
for Vision. Idealistic type, you know. Luce ain't like
that."

Brand had had excellent foresight. Too bad Scot
hadn't understood. Maybe the man would know
about a more practical detail. "Lucy didn't look
this way, before. How did she change?"

"Good clean livin'," Brand opined. "Clears up
the skin, takes off flab, builds muscle. Same's
happened to you."

"It wasn't exactly muscle I was thinking of."

"No? You know what it takes to grind that
grinder?"

"Chest muscle!" Scot said, remembering where
he had ached in the early days, before Lucy took
over the grain grinding chore.

Lucy—grinding—chest muscle. "What do you
know!" Scot exclaimed, completing his realization.

"Yeah, I figured it would happen. Makes a difference, don't it?"

"Considerable."

"Yeah. I remember this floozie I knew. Went from a 32 to a 36 in four months, doing chest exercises. When I tried that grinder, I knew it'd do."

And Brand had encouraged Scot to let Lucy do the grinding, callous as that seemed. He *had* known! All that struggling to turn the wheel, building a substantial layer of muscle—not self-torture but self-development. And what development! "But there's more to a woman than a bust!" Scot exclaimed, ashamed of his interest.

Brand ran his tongue over his lips as if savoring something. "Sure there is. But it's like money. Sure sweetens the pot!"

Scot shook his head ruefully. "Brand, you're one smart bastard."[108]

"Naw. I just know muscle and women. Got to go out and find me one, one day."

"Why *don't* you?"

"Not my farm."

"What has that got to do with it?"

"I can't just go bringing my friends here. They might not fit in."

Brother Paul must have cautioned the man, way back at the beginning, to prevent the toughs he had originally associated with from moving in at a later date. Brand had honored that restriction scrupulously. "Well, we're short a woman now," Scot said. As if there were a quota! "If you find one you like, bring her in."

"Hey, thanks!"

So easily was a problem solved. For Brand.

Lucy returned. "We was talking about you," Brand said.

"Really?" She sounded pleased. Scot was not.

"Yeah. We like your—"

Scot cleared his throat.

"Cupcakes," Brand finished, gesturing with his bread.

"Thanks. Thought it was about time I showed them off."

Scot glanced at her, surprised. Was this the pale, thin, frightened girl he had trapped in the deadfall? She was *enjoying* Brand's clumsy humor. As though there could be any confusion about the cupcakes he referred to.

"Women're like that," Brand said. "You got to jolly 'em along. Lie to 'em. Tell 'em how pretty they are."

"Have a radish," Lucy said, jamming a huge carrot-shaped white radish into his mouth.

Brand bit into it. "Hot stuff," he remarked, and Lucy smiled.[109]

It was incredible to Scot, but apparently Brand was right: women did like to be jollied along. At least Lucy did. She could not have had much experience with men prior to her arrival at the farm, but she had come alive after Wanda left. It could only be in response to the elimination of competition. She had known she could not compete with Wanda, so had never tried.

In the afternoon Brand busied himself with more splitting and stacking. He had to get enough done so that he could go north to the Browns for a couple of days to help them with the same chore. He would bring back a hundred pounds or so of their excellent dried corn in exchange. Brand was the finest firewood handler in the area, and this labor exchange was mutually profitable. Scot suspected the big man

would be looking about for a suitable woman, too.
At any rate, the sound of the sledgehammer was
loud, signaling his location.

Scot and Lucy worked on the potatoes, carrying
them down to the cellar and transferring them
carefully to the bins. They didn't want to bruise any
by dumping them; that could lead to early spoilage.
Potatoes were their security against starvation.

It could have been a tedious chore, in the cool
gloom of the cellar. But it wasn't. "You know," Scot
said, "I've been working with you for months, and
never really saw you."

"Fifteen months," she agreed. "Why should you
have? There wasn't anything of me to see, and
Wanda was there."

No illusions on that score! "I guess you know I
never would have noticed you, if she had stayed."

"I know." Not even any girlish ploys, demurrals,
or artifices. Lucy was talking business.

"I never thought of myself as fickle. But when I
have my eye on one girl, I just don't—"

"That's not fickle, that's loyal," she said.

"Well, what I'm trying to say—"

"I know what you're trying to say."

She had a bit too *much* confidence now! "Oh.
Well—"

"I'm not sure you'd want me."

"I've gotten to know you pretty well, considering
I wasn't looking at you. I don't really expect you to
believe this, but maybe the reason I wouldn't go
with Wanda was—"

She reacted as if stabbed. "Don't say that!"

This was something unexpected. "I'm trying to
be frank with you. It's only fair. I wish you'd be
frank with me."

"You really want to know?"

"Whatever it is, yes."

She took a deep breath, girding herself, and even in the gloom this had an eye-popping effect. "I stole your car."[110]

At first Scot thought he had misheard, preoccupied as he was by the legacy of the grinder. It didn't make sense! He had no car. He'd had a car once, but it had been stolen.

He stared at her, this time not seeing her bust. "Oh, no!"

"I was hungry," she said. "I never took a car before. But my folks were broke, and I couldn't get a job, and my brother had shown me how, and I just had to try it. Then you came out too soon. And I panicked. I never meant to hurt anyone."

Scot remembered the handful of material he had gotten. What a price he had paid! "Do you realize what that cost me?"

"I was afraid you were dead. That I was a murderess. I couldn't sleep. Finally I looked up the address the car was registered to—and you were gone. It took me a long time to trace you down, and then I still wasn't sure. Maybe you were crippled or blind. So I'd skulk around at night . . ." She shrugged. "You know the rest."

"I lost my future!" Scot exclaimed. "My fiancée, my chance to MT—"

"I know. I'm sorry. I'd make it up to you if I could—but I can't. But I had to tell you the truth before you—said anything more. If you didn't go with Wanda because of me—well, now you can go."

He thought of his college education. But MT had destroyed any conventional future anyway. He thought of Fanny—and hadn't it been best that he learn of *her* fickleness before he married her? She had not loved him, only used him. He thought of his health—and knew that it was better now than it had ever been. All that he had really lost was his chance to be a pioneer, to colonize a new planet. That one loss had been appalling—yet he had already realized that he no longer wanted to emigrate. As he had told Brother Paul, he didn't want his challenges handed to him on a platter. "You're right. You can't make it up."

For she had changed his whole life—for the better.

"But I would try," Lucy said.

Now he remembered how she had held a gun on the thug leader. She had been terrified, but determined—to make it up. She would have killed to save him from another beating. Would Wanda have done that? Or Fanny?

"What's done is done," he said.

"Do you want me to leave now?"

He halted with a potato in his hand. "Leave?"

"The farm. Now that you know."

"What use would there be in that?"

"You must hate me."

Old, old feminine ploy! But she seemed serious. Now he remembered how hard she had worked all year, never complaining, never shirking. The weight she had put on was proof of that! He remembered Brand's opaque advice: choose the right woman. Obviously Brand felt Lucy was the one. And Brand seemed to have pretty good judgment about that sort of thing. Yet not until today had Scot ever thought of Lucy in that connection.

"I don't know," he said. "Let's give it a try."

He put his potato in the bin, brushed some of the

dirt off his hands, took her in his arms and kissed
her. She met him with surprising eagerness. Fanny
had never shown such enthusiasm. Neither, for that
matter, had Wanda.

He let her go and pondered the matter. Fanny
would never have slept with him. Wanda would
have, because she thought it was right in the
circumstance—but that had been an intellectual
acceptance, rather than an emotional one. Wanda
had always done what she felt was right. Lucy was
quite another type. She was his—mind and body—
if he wanted her.

But wanting wasn't enough. He had wanted
Fanny—and Wanda. More than either had been
able to accept. Lucy's change of appearance was
miraculous, but he could not afford to let that lead
him astray, as it had twice before. What he *really*
wanted—was to be wanted.[111]

"If you feel guilty about the car, forget it," he
said.

"I *can't* forget it."

"I mean put it out of your mind, just for a
moment, and answer me this: if you had no guilt, no
experience with me before the farm, nothing but
the two of us as we are now—how would you feel
about me?"

"I don't have any right to say it," she whispered.

"Say *what*?" he demanded roughly.

"I love you," she said almost inaudibly. "Or I
would—if you'd let me."

"*Let* you?"

"I don't have the right—"

"You have the *right* to do what you damn well
please! But that's not—"

"If you'd forgive me . . ."

Forgive her. She too had been listening to Brother Paul. As he should have. This was the woman he had not been able to forgive. "How long would you stay with me? If."

She spread her hands. "How long would you want me?"

"That isn't the point! Twice women have walked out on me! When would you walk out? When you figured you'd paid me back for the car?"

"When you sent me out."

"I just want to settle down!"

"So do I." But when she said it, it sounded like a prayer.

"With me? For life?"

"Yes."

Here he was bargaining for something that could not be bargained for! "Well, I can't say I love you. But I can forgive you—now. Now that I understand. And if you're serious—well, the time will come. I seem to have been able to make a similar transition before, and I suppose I can do it again. I know that's not much of a bargain for you—"

"It will do," she breathed. She came to him, put her arms around him, and simply hugged. And he knew that time would get him there.[112]

• • •

He came well outfitted with hiking shoes and backpack. "What'll you take for a night?" he inquired.

"News," Scot said.

"Done!" And the traveler entered. News had become a commodity second only to food in value, since the pony express had failed. Here and worldwide.

They fed him on what they had, and let him wash in their precious hot water, and gave him a spare room. In return, the visitor talked. His name was Donald—no one bothered with formal surnames these days—and he was on leave from government service, wrapping up personal matters so that he could emigrate.

He told how the worldwide exodus had now passed one and a half billion people, for there were now over a hundred MT units scattered across the planet, all exporting bodies at full capacity. He described the way the world was being impoverished in order to provide the necessary energy, but there was no way to stop it because the people demanded their continued right to emigrate. At first they had thought atomic fusion plants would generate the energy, but these had been caught by the squeeze of regression: there were not enough sufficiently-trained atomic engineers to set them up. Thus there was greater dependence on the old-fashioned radiation-polluting fission plants, and accumulating wastes such as plutonium—the most toxic stuff in the universe—had forced a number of shutdowns. The oil fields had been drained dry, including the vast American shale deposits; the mountains of spent shale seemed to rival the Rockies. Now they were back on coal, with monstrous strip mines tearing it out of the ground, leaving a literal wasteland and countless tons of sulfur pollution in the atmosphere. "And if this industrial depletion continues—and it will," Donald assured them, "pretty soon we'll be back on wood. And when that's gone—well, I'm emigrating now, before it's too late."

Scot was shocked, but he did not comment.

There was, after all, nothing he could do about this savaging of his home planet. Earth was consuming itself, like the fabled snake eating its own tail, and it could not continue indefinitely. And all this man wanted was to get his share of the spoils before the end came!

The traveler was a technician for MT. He explained how he calibrated the transport capsules for orientation on each new colony planet. Fifteen hundred worlds had now been colonized, so changeovers were frequent. The computer ran the program, but there were always unpredictable variations in the subspace that these instantaneous transmissions traversed. "We dummy it up with radiation calibrators," he said. "Little checkers of metal like this." He showed them a cylinder hardly thicker than his thumb. "This emits radiation at a standard rate. But conditions in subspace change it slightly. The computer interprets that shift, and adjusts the orientation of the capsule to compensate. Otherwise there would be a drift each time, only a tiny fraction of a trillionth of a percent—but we mattermit across light-years, and it's cumulative. Know what would happen if a capsule came in skewed beyond tolerance? I'll tell you," he continued without pause. "If even one corner of one capsule overlapped the wall of the capsule building, you'd have matter superimposed on matter. Boom —near total conversion of the surplus to energy. Know what that means? Make the H-bomb look like a firecracker. Even a fraction of a gram means trouble; as it is, the walls get scoured because we can't make a perfect vacuum in the chamber, and a few molecules of air always superimpose. Once there was a last-minute leak, letting in about a cupful of air, and when the capsule phased in the whole building shook. So this calibrator—"

He glanced down at the device and took another gulp of the precious goat's milk they had traded from the Smiths. Too bad, Scot thought, that they had never brought in any animals—but none of them knew enough about animal husbandry to risk it. "No, I didn't steal this one! It's worthless. It's a shade out of tolerance. Put this one in a capsule during an orientation run, and the computer would correct for an erroneous amount and put the next capsule four feet out of tolerance. That means about a foot of overlap with the wall. Like shooting fish in water: that refraction throws you off, if you don't adjust for it right. Sometimes I think how easy it would be to sabotage our whole MT program: just use the emergency entrance in the back of the transport chamber building, go in and put this in place of the proper calibrator." He made a gesture with his two hands. "Half an hour, then boom!"

He talked well into the night, and they listened raptly. This was news of the world! At last he took a lamp to his room.[113]

Suddenly there was a raging fire. They were able, later, to reconstruct how it might have started. The visitor, unused to kerosene, had set the lamp on an insecure perch so that it gradually tilted and finally fell. Or maybe his arm had knocked it over as he slept. Foolishly, he had not extinguished it before retiring. It had crashed to the floor, its glass base shattering, the fuel splashing out over the wooden floor, and the fire had leaped from wick to spillage.

They fought valiantly to save the house, but it was old and dry, and this was fall, and they had little water. The task was impossible.[114]

The three of them lined up, stunned at the

enormity of their loss, watching the terrible blaze.

"Where's our guest?" Lucy cried suddenly.

"He didn't get out!" Scot cried. He launched himself at the house.

"You can't go in there!" Brand cried, grabbing him.

"There's a life at stake!" Scot cried, shaking him off. He plunged into the great orange maw, wrapping his wetted coat over his head and shoulders.

And his memory cut off there.[115]

. . .

Brand returned from his spring News visit with grim news of his own. "Not only did I not find any good woman, all our neighbors to the west are gone," he reported. "Their crops and stock too—nothing left."

"Without message to us?" Scot asked. "They wouldn't do that. We have trading debts—"

"Not voluntarily," Lucy said. "But if something wiped them out—"

"They weren't vandalized," Brand said. "Just wiped out. Like the folks just up and left."

"They MT'd?" Lucy asked, surprised.

"I don't believe that," Scot said. "They were diehards, like us. And a lot of them *couldn't* emigrate."

"Unless MT changed the rules . . ." she said, frowning.

"They'd still tell us. News is paramount. They wouldn't cut and run without spreading the word."

"Unless MT *really* changed, I mean," she continued. "Suppose they ran out of people to ship, what with all their restrictions, and had to do some hard recruiting?"

"They'll never run out of people! Not in the first

few years, anyway. Too many *want* to go, so long as it's prepaid. All they have to do is lower the recruitment standards a notch."

"Suppose they ran out of good worlds, then? Found some tough planets nobody wanted to go to—"

"With super-energy sources on 'em," Brand said. "Right there to be mined, cheap."

"So they *had* to colonize them," she said. "What would they do then?"

Scot nodded slowly. "Press gangs, could be. Send out troops, take everybody in a given area, MT them to the mining world. No word to anybody, so there'd be no panic. No warning, no reprieve."

Brand agreed. "That's the way a good raider works. We must've been just out of their range."

"So far," Lucy said.

The two of them looked at Scot, and he realized that another crisis of leadership was upon him. "We've got to find out for sure," he said. "We've checked the west. Now—today—we'll check north, east and south. If our neighbors are there, spread the word. If they're gone—"

"And stay out of sight," Brand said. "Watch for traps."

"I always do—now," Lucy said, and smiled at Scot. At moments of moderate crisis she became so fetching he had to take her in his arms, and he did so now.

"Got to get me a woman," Brand muttered.

"Brand, you go south," Scot said. "Lucy east. I'll go north. We don't need to check more than two or three homesites each way. We can do that within three hours. Let's go!"

"Will you be okay?" Lucy asked.

"That fire only burned me, it didn't cripple me!"

he snapped, and then was sorry. "*You're* the one to be concerned about. I was forgetting. Maybe—"

"I'm not crippled either!" she snapped back.

"Gee, it was such a nice romance while it lasted," Brand said. They laughed and kissed. They fought often, and made up often, and liked it that way.

They went. Scot trekked north, taking advantage of cover, moving through the mounds of rubble and wood that were the former houses of suburbia. It had only been three years since the onset of MT, but it seemed like a generation. Soon the ravages of termites, rats, weather and salvage operations would reduce this to a bumpy plain. Already the vegetation was prospering, overgrowing the old highways and concealing much of the wreckage.

Neighbor Brown's farm was several miles distant. Scot remembered the last time he had visited there. Lucy had picked up a splinter that inflamed her foot, and had been irritable, and had worked herself into a tantrum. He had had to tote her away, picking up several scratches in the process. His quarrels with Fanny had always been subtle, and he had always given in at the end. Wanda had never quarreled at all. But Lucy—she was a spitfire! Yet her love was certain. After they got clear of the Browns' she had fallen into his arms and they had made love tempestuously.

That had been the trouble with both Fanny and Wanda: they were too controlled. Lucy let go, expunging her emotion, and it was better. She had changed, once relieved of the burden of guilt about the car. Once she had goaded him into hitting her, and the odd thing about it was that she was pleased. He had reacted in a way she understood. But during the fire—and now he remembered one of those blanked-out fragments of that experience that had left him so ill—Brand had had to use a judo holddown to prevent her from charging in after him. This was a face of love that was new to him—but it *was,* indubitably, love.

Now he closed in on the Browns' farm. His caution was justified—for there was activity here. Men were moving about, strangers, armed with swords and bows. They were methodically cleaning out the Browns' stores of food and hides, loading them on a wagon drawn by two fine horses.

Scot knew better than to walk right up. He was seeing the scourge in action! He skulked about, observing, knowing he could not help the Browns without giving himself away and putting his own farm in peril. He owed the Browns a lot, and hated to see them in this predicament—but there was a standing agreement in all the neighborhood: first warn others of the threat, *then* help friends. Had that agreement been honored before, his own farm would have been warned already—and probably the Browns' too. In this framework, violation of this common-sense rule could mean disaster to the whole area. Perhaps *had.*

These were not MT personnel. They lacked the MT insignia, and were too primitive. They were members of some kind of tribe, disciplined but of a low order of technology. Regression seemed to have a positive survival force. The most primitive seemed best able to cope.

"The Saxons!" Scot breathed, remembering his conversation with Wanda and Brother Paul. "The Saxons have come!"

And why not? They had known that eventually a regression like this would manifest. Organization still beat disorganization, and primitive grouping was the way of the future. Savage conquering tribes had formed from the remnants of that civilization[116] they had originally merged into, hardly more than a thousand years before. These restored tribes were now laying waste to the settled areas.

He saw Mr. and Mrs. Brown and their child seated against a wagon wheel. Each had a collar of heavy rope, and the collars were anchored to the wagon. They were captives, soon to be slaves, most likely. His friends—and he could not help them!

This had to be a large tribe, for obviously it was cleaning out all the farms of the region, methodically. His own would be next.

Scot backed off, found new cover, and moved silently home.

"The Saxons!" Lucy said wonderingly when he told her. "I thought that was a joke."

"Well, I didn't really know who they are," he said. "But Saxons is what comes to mind."[117]

"It will do. Like raiders, only worse. What can we do?"

Brand shook his head. "Brother Paul would say to—"

"Forgive them," Lucy said bitterly. "Love them."

"Well, it worked on me," Brand pointed out.

"And on me," she agreed. "When Brother Paul said, 'Help this girl, for we love her'—when he prayed for me, knowing how imperfect I was, I—" She shook her head. "I felt something go through me, something wonderful." She glanced at Scot as if expecting him to challenge this. "But I was lonely, in need of love. Somehow I don't think the Saxons are that vulnerable. They're not criminals. They're —businessmen. No conscience."

"Tribesmen, not businessmen," Scot said. "But

the principle's the same. They're acting for the good of their tribe, following orders. We settlers are the enemy—or at least we are the harvest. They're probably suffering from underpopulation pressure —not enough tribesmen to maintain the level of culture they like. So they recruit new members. We can't blame them for that."

"You've already forgiven them!" Lucy said. "Brother Paul had more effect on you than I thought."

Brother Paul had removed Wanda—and so paved the way for Scot's true love: human, not idealistic. What greater effect could there be than that? The forgiveness, too, was important. But of course she was only teasing him: she believed in forgiveness. "I understand their rationale," he said. "That's not the same as forgiving them. I understand lots of things I don't like."

"Do you understand me?"

"No."

They embraced. "Maybe we could raid a woman from the Saxons," Brand said. "A nice, fat, juicy one."

"We can't fight them," Scot said. "They'll come in force. Maybe we'd better hide out at the Order." Brother Paul had left directions for locating the nearest station.

"When would we come out again?" Lucy asked sharply.

And Brand shook his head negatively. "She doesn't want to take you to where Wanda is," he muttered.

"That's *right*!" she said.

"We're not joiners, we're loners," Scot said. "That's our style."

"So lets *live* our style," Lucy said. "I like it here."

"Maybe we could negotiate with the Saxons," Scot said. "Find the peaceful compromise. Brother Paul would approve that."

"Maybe so," Brand agreed dubiously.

"Do you think they would honor a flag of truce?" Brand shrugged. Lucy shrugged.

"All right. I'll try it," Scot said. "I'll go alone. If I don't come back, you two go to the Order—fast."

But both shook their heads. "I'll never leave you," Lucy said flatly. And Brand added: "We're in this together."

"But they could simply lay hands on us all!"

"Not me," Lucy said. "I bite."

Scot eyed faint marks on his forearm. "I know."

"We might have to fight," Brand said, as if testing the water. "Band together with other settlers. United front."

"No! There has to be—" He broke off, unable to convince even himself. "Anyway, the others can't leave their farms for any such campaign."

"Brother Paul fought," Lucy argued.

"Naw—not the same," Brand said. "He never fought me—he only showed me." But he brightened. "I could show a Saxon, though—the same way."

"Single combat," Lucy agreed. "Only gentle, Brother Paul's way. You could do it, Brand. He taught you how."

"Yeah." Brand smiled. "He wouldn't say no to that."

Scot realized he had overlooked a subtle but pervasive change in the man. Brand really cared what Brother Paul thought. Brand was now a convert—not to the Holy Order of Vision, but to at least part of its philosophy. He was sincerely trying to practice nonviolence. "Well, we can try it," he said.

"First we got to alert the neighbors," Brand said.

They did that, then went north. Finding the Saxons was no problem: a party was already heading south, following Scot's prior trail. Another primitive skill: sniffing out faint trails. He had not thought to erase his tracks.

Scot halted, waiting for them to come up. The party consisted of two horse-drawn wagons and three outlying horsemen. The men wore cloth trousers, heavy leather slippers, sleeveless shirts and thick woolen capes, each a different color. The leader had a horned helmet, and a two-foot scabbard hung at his side.

Twentieth-century America! Who would have believed it!

"Saxons, all right," Lucy murmured.

The horsemen reined in smartly, their steeds trampling the earth very prettily, the picture of animal health and vigor. Nomads took good care of their animals.[118]

Scot raised his right hand. "We come to parley," he said.

The wagons drew up. They were simple wooden-sided affairs with spoked metal-banded wheels. From one of them descended an older man garbed in a gray tunic, with a brass collar around his neck. The gaze from the shadow of his hood was piercing.

"A Druid!" Lucy whispered.

"We have come to take you into our culture," the Druid said.

Scot shook his head. "We do not wish to enter your culture, no offense intended. We want to be left alone."

"We are prepared to take you by force," the Druid said without animosity. "But we hope you will see the advantage of joining us, once you understand our system."

"We would like to parley with your leader."

The lead horseman put his hand on his sword. But the Druid, the evident commander of this party, stopped him with a gesture. "It is your right. We are governed by law."

I hope so, Scot thought. "May we accompany you to your leader—in peace?"

The Druid smiled. "You may. Flag of truce. Please join me in my wagon."

And so, nervously, they rode in style along the overgrown highway to the Saxon camp. Their host turned out to be a former professor of law, an intelligent and knowledgeable man. He called himself simply the "Priest of Lugus," explaining that Lugus was the Celtic God of the Harvest—very important.

He was able, in this guise, to draw upon his legal expertise to settle quarrels and assist in organizing their growing tribe: a better life than he had before. The arthritis that had made him ineligible for emigration had now largely abated, and he attributed this to the satisfaction of his present mode.[119] "With the exclusion of the sick, the insane and the criminal from emigration," he remarked, "the country should by this time have been overrun by nuts. But the average person is healthier in every respect than before. Like me. Like, I am sure, you." He was not embarrassed to call himself a Druid, practicing magic in the service of one God among many. "Each culture develops the system that suits it best," he said. "Lugus and the other Gods serve us as well today as the Christian God served us five years ago. I believe in Lugus; when I invoke his name he answers. Without him we would have no harvest. We must change with the times; we are closer to nature now."[120]

Scot decided not to debate such points. If the man really believed in a pagan God—well, that was his business. Why shouldn't religion regress along with everything else?

"We think of your tribe as Saxons," Lucy ventured.

"We regard ourselves as closer to the Celts," the priest said. "But it really does not matter, so long as we have a functioning system. We stand as a bulwark against the burgeoning chaos fostered by the depopulation of our sphere."

"There is no chaos here," Scot argued. "We live at peace with our neighbors." Like the Browns . . .

"Not for long," the Druid said. "You have not yet encountered the Huns or the Scythians."

"The Huns!" Lucy exclaimed.[121]

"I assure you, you would prefer life with us," the priest said. "But we must have the strength of numbers, or we—and you—shall fall to more primitive societies."

Scot didn't like to admit it, but the man was making some sense. It was, it seemed, impossible to prevent the cultural regression—but the worst aspects of it could be staved off by choosing sides wisely. Still, he preferred independence.

They approached the Saxon camp. This was built up with huge earthworks topped by a log-and-mudplaster wall that looked quite formidable. It would be difficult indeed to storm that from outside —and once in, the intruders would be unlikely to get out, unless allowed. Armed sentries paced the ramparts, and bowmen peered from the embrasures.

Scot was amazed at this substantial evidence of the onset of the past. This was a primitive walled city, here within twenty miles of his farm. History had become tangible.

"You are not conversant with our code of laws," the priest said. "Would you like me to represent you before the King?"

So Saxons—or Celts—had kings! But of course they had to have a leader of some sort, whatever the nomenclature. Democracy was a comparatively modern system. And anyway, this was not the literal restoration of history, but an adaptation to the needs of the present, influenced by the most convenient examples available. Those who heeded the past were doomed to relive it . . .[122]

Scot wasn't used to snap decisions, but he recognized that indecision could be hazardous. Should he trust this educated neo-pagan? Part-way, maybe. "We would appreciate your counsel, but must represent our own interest."

"Well put," the Druid said affably.

The guard at the gate challenged them, and they halted. "Three settlers for parley," the priest said. "Safe conduct."

"They must have supervision," the gate-captain said.

"Present."

"Pass, then."

It was, indeed, a small city. Chickens fluttered out of their way, and goats followed them inquisitively. All around, men and women were at work. A blacksmith hammered on the metal rims for new wheels. Women sewed hides together. Children plaited thatch for the roofs of the simple wooden cabins. A group of wild-looking dogs set up a clamor from a pen: those would be vicious hunting canines. No, no escape from this stronghold!

"There's Brown," Lucy said. Sure enough, their former neighbor was sitting on the ground, staring dully into it.

"Don't look like he's enjoying his new life," Brand muttered.

"Involuntary recruits are put on thirty-day captive status," the Druid said. "After that they are allowed limited freedom. In a year they can be granted tribal citizenship, depending on their attitude. Then they can rise in the hierarchy. The process is faster for voluntary recruits, and the captive status is dispensed with."

"Relax and enjoy it," Lucy said. "So what if it's rape?"

"Your tongue could lead you to what you fear," the Druid warned her.

Scot knew now: he had to help their friends the Browns out of this mess. But how?

They approached a burly man who had the air of authority. "Your Highness," the Druid said, "these three settlers want to parley. They are here under flag of truce."

So this was the King! He seemed to have no special court or finery. But perhaps this was for the best.

"Parley? *What* parley?" the King demanded irritably. "I sent you out to incorporate 'em, not debate with 'em."

"We met them on the way, coming to us," the Druid said. "Thus by action and expression, they came to parley. We are bound to honor that, for we are civilized."

The King puffed out his red cheeks. "If you say so, Lugus," he muttered. "But don't push your luck past the harvest." He turned to Brand. "What's on your mind?"

"This one leads their party," the Druid interposed smoothly, indicating Scot.

"Well, let 'im speak his piece!"

The King evidently owed his position to factors other than diplomacy, Scot realized. Blunt talk might be best. "We only want to be left alone," he said. "We'll be happy to trade with you and exchange information, but we don't want to be part of your tribe. In fact, all the settlers of this area, like the Browns, should be freed."

"So? How you figure to defend against the Huns?"

"We'll parley with them too."

The King burst into laughter, not humorous. "Look over there," he said, pointing with a dirty fingernail.

On the window-ledge of his cabin-palace was a row of human skulls, their eye-holes like windows. "Those are the folks *we* sent to parley," he explained. "We raided 'em and recovered our dead— but that's all. Their lines are within fifty miles of here, and they're getting stronger all the time. Anybody we don't recruit, *they* will. We tried letting some settlers go—and now they're Huns."[123]

"Nevertheless," the Druid interposed again, "we are more civilized. We prefer not to use coercion. We feel sure you will see the logic of our position."

"There is logic in ours, too," Scot said. "We have a functioning farm and a workable neighborhood society. You could make more profit in honest trade with us than you could by enslaving us. Free enterprise is still the best incentive."

"We can't tolerate enemies in our midst," the King said.

"They are not enemies," the Druid pointed out. "They merely wish to have the status of allies, rather than serfs."

"Allies can fight," the King retorted.

The Druid turned to Scot. "Are you prepared to take up arms in support of our defense against the Huns?"

A trap! "No. Only in defense of our farm and friends."

"I thought so," the King snarled. "Druid, take 'em in."

"They are here under flag of truce, Sire."

"Then see 'em back to their own farm—*then* take 'em in."

The Druid spread his hands. "I'm afraid that's it," he said to Scot. "If you will not join us voluntarily today, we shall have to use force tomorrow. But I must advise you that the lot of involuntary recruits is worse."

"You said. We saw," Lucy said.

"We prefer to settle the matter by single combat," Scot said regretfully.

The King's interest perked up. "Now?"

Scot swallowed and nodded. "Our champion to meet yours. Unarmed combat, no bloodshed." And Brand stepped forward.

But the King waggled his forefinger. "*You* issued the challenge; *we* choose weapons. Swords—to the death."

Brand faltered. "I can't kill," he said. "I swore—"

"Uh-huh," the King said contemptuously.

But again the Druid stepped in. "The oath of nonbloodshed is valid, particularly in these times of inadequate personnel. After all, a dead serf is a useless serf. We could arrange a combat to terminate with yield."

The King scowled. "Priest, you're pushing!"

The Druid held up his left hand, the fingers curving into an odd configuration. It did not seem to be a threat, but the King stepped back. Scot decided it was a magical gesture—and the King believed in magic. Just then a cloud covered the sun, bringing sudden shadow and a cold breeze.

"All right, all right," the King muttered. He turned to Brand. "All right, this one time. A yield-fight."

The Druid let his hand drop, and the sun came out again. Of course it was a trick of timing; the Druid must have observed the progress of the cloud, and known exactly when and for how long it would intercept the sun. But it was an impressive maneuver.[124]

The King clapped his hands loudly, and suddenly all the tribesmen ceased their labors and gathered in a great circle. Primitives loved a spectacle!

"I never in my life used a sword," Brand said to Scot.

"Feint," Lucy suggested. "Make him parry you —then slip under and throw him with your hands."

"Hey, sure!" Brand agreed, brightening.

A Saxon retainer brought Brand a gleaming two-foot blade, double-edged but with a blunt point. "We're in luck," Scot said. "No point on it. They don't thrust, they just cut. Much easier to deal with."

Now the Saxon champion entered the makeshift arena. He was a huge man, larger than Brand, and his bare arms were tautly muscled. That was not encouraging.

The King clapped again. "Go to!" he cried.

Scot had increasing misgivings as he watched. Brand was obviously uncertain, while the Saxon was confident.

Brand tried gamely. He stepped in swinging.

The Saxon danced nimbly aside and whacked Brand on the posterior with the flat of his blade. The assembled tribesmen laughed appreciatively. The blow could readily have been fatal, had it been fatally intended.

Lucy shook her head. "Snowball in hell," she muttered. "These people have really trained in the sword."

Brand faced about—in time to see the Saxon's sword whistling toward his head. He jumped backward, falling to the ground, his heels going high. There was more laughter.

This was no fight—this was entertainment. And they were committed to join the tribe when Brand lost.

Brand got up and stalked the Saxon again. He swung. This time the Saxon parried, sliding his blade down along inside Brand's and twitching expertly. Brand's weapon flew from his hand and landed in the dirt to the side.

The Saxon, smiling, cuffed Brand with his left hand. That was his mistake. Brand caught that hand, turned, and ducked—and the Saxon tumbled over his left shoulder to land heavily on his back. There was a gasp of surprise and pleasure from the audience, and Lucy clapped her hands.

Brand followed up immediately with an armlock on the Saxon's sword arm, putting pressure on the elbow until the man yelled and dropped his weapon. Scot remembered seeing Brand and Brother Paul practice such holds—always reiterating the caution that they should be released the instant the opponent yielded, for it was indeed possible to break an arm.

"And there it is," Lucy said. "Brother Paul strikes again."

"A bloodless victory," Scot agreed. What a relief!

Brand let go and stepped back. The Saxon sat up, rubbed his arm, and looked about. Then he snatched up his fallen sword and launched himself at Brand.

"Hey!" Scot and Lucy cried together.

Brand, caught completely by surprise, was overwhelmed. The Saxon bowled him over, whacked him with the flat, and finally put the blade to his throat. If he moved, his neck would be cut open.

"He yields," the Druid said.

"Well, so much for that," the King said. "Does this count as voluntary or involuntary membership? Well, assign 'em quarters and go clean out their farm. We'll work out the details later." He turned away.

"You can't do that!" Scot cried, running into the arena. "It was a foul. Your champion yielded!"

"I did not!" the Saxon snapped, backhanding Scot across the cheek. The blow was like the thrust of a car fender. Dazed, Scot tumbled to the ground and sprawled there ignominiously.

The Druid came over to help him up before Lucy could get there. "You must not evince bad sportsmanship," he murmured. "That's a sure ticket to captive status." Then he stared. "You wear the Cross?"

Scot's cross had flung out in the course of his fall, but the chain was unbroken. "Yes," he said, not caring to explain further. What did these treacherous Saxons care about Wanda and her conversion?

"A crucifix?"

"No. Holy Order of Vision. But about that battle—"

"Which Brother?"

"Brother Paul. Look, we *saw* your champion yield! That's why Brand let him go, instead of breaking his arm. He—"

But the Druid was moving away. He caught up to the King. "Your Highness, there is a new factor. This man—"

"Oh come *off* it!" the King snapped.

"He wears the Cross of the Order of Vision. His protest must be heard."

"Not by me, it mustn't!" And the King stalked into his cabin.

"Still, it must be heard," the Druid said. He returned to Scot. "We retain reciprocal conventions," he said. "I know Brother Paul. Tall blond man, very thin—"

"Forget it," Scot said. "Obviously a different man. Ours was chubby and black."

"Merely testing," the Druid said. "I wanted to be sure the Cross was legitimate."

"It's not. I never joined the Order. This was given me by a friend who did."

"But it came from Brother Paul?"

"Ultimately, yes. But—"

"As a matter of professional relations, we must uphold its validity. I would not want the Order of Vision to think the Order of Druids was remiss. Some of our neophytes train there. Very good schooling. You shall have your hearing."

"All I want is justice!" Scot said. "Brand plainly won, and—"

"You have a grievance. Obviously your man subscribed to a different code than our champion, and I failed to so advise you. He supposed that a cry indicated surrender rather than mere pain. Hence the confusion."

"I guess that's it," Scot agreed. "Brand could have broken his arm—"

"Since the King declines to listen, you must use another avenue of redress. You must sit outside the house of the one who wronged you."

"Sit outside his house?" Scot asked, confused.

"Without food or drink. Until he accedes."

"Why would my sitting and starving make any difference to him?"

"It is a matter of honor. He will not take sustenance himself so long as you remain."

"Oho!" Scot saw the relevance now. It amounted to a personal challenge to the warrior. Or to his sense of honor.[125]

"What are you going to do?" Lucy asked. "Remember—"

Remember that he wasn't strong, after the fire. He wished she'd stop reminding him! Scot turned to the Druid. "While I do this—what about my friends, my farm, my neighbors?"

"All will be held in abeyance, on my authority," the Druid assured him. "But beyond this I cannot go, even for the sake of reciprocity. I *am* a Saxon, as you put it, subject to my King."

"Thanks," Scot said. "Where's his house?"

"Here." The Druid stopped. "I suggest, however, that you wear your Cross where it can be seen."

"The cross means nothing! I never joined the—"

"If I were you, I would reconsider that statement. The Cross is serving you well in need."

"You, a pagan, say that?"

"The Cross is holy to us too. Do not dishonor it."

Brother Paul had commented on that. The cross

predated the crucifix as a holy symbol, and was not specifically Christian. And apparently it gave him a special status here—not because *he* was anything special, but because *it* was.

Scot sat cross-legged outside the Saxon champion's door, and waited. It seemed rather ineffective as a protest, but what else was there?

After a while the Saxon came out, glanced at him, wrinkled his nose, and went back inside. So much for this matter of honor.

The sun was hot, and very quickly Scot became thirsty. Part of it was psychological, he knew—but most of it was real. He had not anticipated anything like this, and had not eaten heavily.

The tribesmen of the camp gave him only passing glances. Lucy and Brand were given bread and milk and allowed to settle not far off. Scot could talk to them, but it occurred to him that it might be smarter not to; perhaps his silence would be binding on his adversary also.

His legs went to sleep, but he dared not shift position. He was not sure of the rules of this challenge, the fine print, and could not take a chance. So he jiggled around just enough to restore some painful circulation, and waited.

At dusk the Saxon emerged. He stared down at Scot. "Exactly what grievance do you have against me?" he demanded.

Was it safe to answer? It must be! It was only right that the accused be advised of the charge. "Our champion had you helpless and in pain, disarmed. He thought you had yielded when you screamed and dropped your weapon, so he let you go. Then you attacked him, and knocked me down when I protested."

"To you I apologize; I acted impetuously," the man said. "But as regards him: I never yielded. The scream was but a ruse."

"Brand did not yield either. The Druid yielded him, not us—and the Druid did not have authority to do so."

"He yielded him—else I would have slain your man."

"Not if Brand had broken your arm, when he had *you*. No one could have escaped that armlock."

"Ridiculous!" the Saxon snorted. He stomped into the house.

"Do you sleep?" Scot called after him.

The Saxon whirled, scowling. "I do not sleep!" He stomped back to Scot and sat cross-legged before him.

So it was true! The aggrievor could not partake of any refreshment his aggrieved eschewed. A fitting contest!

Night set in. The stars appeared, and it became cold. Scot's thirst abated, but now he was shivering. He had not dressed for this either!

"What do you hope to gain from this?" the Saxon asked him from the darkness.

"The freedom of my farm," Scot said. "And of my neighborhood. I owe debts to friends like the Browns."

"If you wanted freedom, why didn't you emigrate?"

"I belong on Earth. Why didn't *you* emigrate?"

"Bum rap."

Meaning the man had had a criminal background —or something similar. "Me too, actually," Scot admitted.

That might account for the rapid reversion of

American culture right back to this tribal society.[126]
Subtract most of the healthiest, soundest, motivated people, let the rest scramble for survival amid
inadequate supplies and energy—and here he was,
fighting for his dwindling rights via the advice of
the priest of a pagan Harvest God. The thugs Brand
had come with had wanted property; the Saxons
wanted people. That was another measure of the
status of the world.

They conversed irregularly as the chill night
dragged on. This was as much to verify alertness as
from sociability.

"Look—I only did what the King ordered," the
Saxon said at last. "Your beef is with *him*."

"Can the King be called to account for this?"

"The *King?* You kidding? You *ask,* you don't *tell*
him."

"That's what I thought. The King is inviolate.
But you're his champion. I must deal with you."

"Look, man—I've got to keep fit for combat! I
need my food and drink and sleep. What if the
Huns should come?"

"I sympathize. I'd like to see you in top condition
for the Huns. All you have to do is admit you were
beaten. Then we'll go home and you can feast."

"I wasn't beaten!" the man roared.

"Well, admit there was a misunderstanding, then.
It's little enough, considering that our whole livelihood is at stake, not yours. Maybe we could run the
fight over."

Luckily, the Saxon objected. "To run it over
would be admitting I didn't take it the first time. It
would smirch my status, and could make the King
appoint someone else as Champion. Then I'd have
to go back to the fields."

Scot didn't answer. He saw that more than the

warrior's pride was at stake, and that made it harder.

Somewhere around midnight, by the rotation of the stars, a person emerged from the house with a stone lamp. By the wavering light Scot saw it was a young but hefty woman. "Want a blanket, Fred?"

Fred? Well, a Saxon warrior could have any name he chose!

"Bitsy, you know the code. Not unless *he* takes one."

Hospitality? No—merely equality. Honor forbade the Saxon's taking advantage of such a comfort alone; it would be construed as a prejudicial weakness. Scot was coming to appreciate the Saxon code more and more. It threw the burden of decision on the person most strongly motivated. The one in the right.

The girl came to Scot. "Blanket?"

Why not? The Saxon could probably withstand the cold better than Scot could. "Thank you."

She gave it to him, then went for another.

"Wife?" Scot inquired when they were alone again.

"Sister." Then, as if appreciating the small comfort that had been allowed, the Saxon amplified, "Nice kid. Never done wrong in her life. Our folks MT'd, but she had a man who couldn't, so she stayed. Then it broke up, and she was stuck. I've been seeing after her."

"I know how it is," Scot agreed. "My fiancée MT'd without me. But later I found a better woman. Your sister should have no trouble."

"She's big, like me—some say fat. But it's not fat, it's a big frame and muscle. She's twenty now, in her prime. I could make somebody take her, but she won't have it that way. Oh, if I lost her as spoils of war she'd go—but she won't take it as charity. She's near as stubborn as I am. So she cooks for me, and washes. Good at it, too."

"I'm sure," Scot agreed politely. "The pretty ones always go somewhere else, always get a man, even if they can't do a thing."

"That's for sure!" the Saxon said emphatically. "Lot more to a woman 'n looks! Bitsy can carry a dressed hog. Where's the pretty girl can do that?"

Scot visualized the increasingly large wild pigs that roamed the countryside. Many would weigh over a hundred pounds, slaughtered and dressed. Brand had brought a couple down with the good bow they had traded from another neighbor, as well as a few of the migrating wild bovines. "Mine could, maybe," he said. "She's a small girl, but she's got chest muscle you wouldn't believe."

"I believe," the Saxon said. "I saw her. But who else?"

"Not many."[127]

The man grunted affirmatively, and there was another long round of silence.

Morning came, and still they sat. Scot felt the need to relieve himself, but of course could not. The Saxon looked uncomfortable, and now Scot realized that his own lack of a big meal and drink was a net advantage.

He fought off waves of sleepiness, determined not to relent. The Saxon camp came alive, ignoring them. The Druid passed by and nodded affirmatively. "There is an easier route," he said. "If you would agree that some justice lies on either side, and exchange tokens of compromise, this becomes unnecessary."

"We must be free," Scot insisted.

"You *can* be free—within reasonable limits. Deliver the pinch of incense to the altar of Baal—I speak figuratively, of course; Baal is no Celtic God—swear fealty as vassal to the King—and perhaps he will be disposed to return you to your farm. You would pay seasonal tribute to him in return for his protection from the Huns. Is that unreasonable?"

"It's one way of doing it," Scot said.

"And you," the Druid said persuasively to the Saxon. "Could you not spare some token as a sign of amity? This man has challenged you honorably, and he bears the Cross of the Holy Order of Vision—brothers in spirit to we Druids.[128] You would sacrifice no honor in this gesture—"

"I never sacrificed any honor!"

The Druid returned to Scot. "I can virtually guarantee that the King would accept your vassalship.[129] I have reasoned with him, pointing out the significance of your association with the Order of Vision. We want no quarrel with them."

"They don't quarrel," Scot said. "Their whole philosophy—"

"Ah, but the King does not realize that."

It was too smooth, too ingenious. Scot distrusted it. This man spoke of religion, but he lacked Brother Paul's fundamental integrity. Scot remained sitting, though his tongue ached for water. "I will not practice deceit," he said.

"One must accede to the times. When in Rome—"

"I'm in this challenge because I'm *not* in Rome," Scot said firmly. "And not in the Saxons, or Celts or whatever. I intend to be my own man, on my own farm, with my own wife and own friend. And I must help my neighbors, who have helped me in the past. If I start compromising now, where will it end?"

The Druid shook his head and turned away. "If you should change your mind, it can still be arranged," he said.

When the Druid was out of hearing, the Saxon spoke. "For what it's worth, I agree with you. These smooth operators can twist things about so you don't know which end is up, but what's right is right, and you sure told him."

Scot was surprised. "Even though I'm opposing you?"

"Well, I'd go along with some deal, just to get this over with—but I won't compromise my honor. Why should you compromise yours?"

"I'm glad you understand," Scot said.

He had survived the night fairly well, thanks to the blanket. But now the rising sun came down directly in his face, and his thirst intensified. He lacked the sheer mass of the Saxon; how could he outlast this man? But how could he quit, giving up his freedom?

"You see, my wife is pregnant," Scot said, as much to distract himself from his discomfort as to inform his opponent.[130] "I don't want my child to grow up in a commune."

"If it were up to me, I'd let you go," the Saxon said. "But I can't say I lost a fight when I won."

"No, of course not," Scot said. Impasse, again.

"Your champion—you called him Brand—where's his woman?"

"Brand has particular tastes," Scot said. He had to lick his mouth several times to wet it enough for clear talk. "He wants a woman, but—well, most are too frail and small."[131]

"He doesn't know beans about sworded, but he can sure use his hands."

"He's very strong, but really very gentle too."

The conversation lapsed again. Toward noon Scot's head seemed to heat up, and the thirst became ravening. He screwed his eyes shut and hung on.

"Do you sleep?" the Saxon inquired hoarsely.

Scot's eyes popped open. "No!"

Eyes open, he suffered. The image of the man ahead of him wavered, turned color, became a shimmering flame. Like the fire of his house, that had wiped him out—but for Lucy and Brand and the Browns and the community of neighbors. His hair had grown back, and so had his skin, but he had never recovered full vigor. A second time, a stranger had devastated him—and would there be some redeeming later development, as with Lucy?

He blinked, and the flame abated. Eye fatigue, he knew—and brain fatigue too. He had been awake thirty hours—not an undue period for an active man, but much harder for a tired, hungry, thirsty, stationary one.

Was it really worth it? The Saxons were not a bad tribe, as he understood them. They had honor and a degree of culture, and life with them would in many respects be easier and more secure than life on the diminished farm. As Earth continued to regress, such tribes would become increasingly important. Why buck the inevitable?

Yet he would not yield. He had always capitulated to Fanny, and she had left him. He had gone along with Wanda—and she had left him. He had fought with Lucy, and she remained. A poor parallel, suspect as both example and analogy—but his fevered brain clung to it. He did better when he resisted to the bitter end.

If only the regression of Earth would stop, so that life could settle down and civilization resume its

forward progress. But that could never be, so long
as MT continued to empty the planet.

MT—empty! A pun, hideously funny and unfun-
ny. Earth was dying in that sad mirth. *I am Earth
whom thou persecutest* . . .

So many idealistic colonists, like his brother
Tully, setting out to make brave new lives on brave
new worlds, while all the time the mother planet
needed their energies most. The same enthusiasm
and techniques they used to tame wilderness
spheres would restore this planet too, if only applied. The windmills, water wheels, solar collectors,
gardens, respect for wilderness ecology. There was
wilderness enough right here! Why couldn't these
colonists see that the fittest planet to colonize was
Earth itself?[132]

"The fittest planet for man to colonize is Earth!"
he exclaimed, snapping out of his reverie. The
revelation was like a gentle light surrounding him.
"There is the answer!"[133]

"How's that again?" the Saxon asked.

"My quarrel is not with you. It's with MT," Scot
said.

"There's a mouthful!" the Saxon agreed. "All
those dopes thinking they'll do better somewhere
else, when they're the ones fouled up Earth. Drawing off all the gas and coal for the machine, leaving
us nothing. They ought to stay home and clean up
their own mess."

Scot struggled to unkink his legs. Pain lanced
through them and he fell over.

"Take it easy," the Saxon said, rising easily and
helping him up. "You've had a rough night."

Lucy and Brand hurried over. "What happened?" Lucy asked worriedly. "Is it your burns
again?"

"We don't want to fight the Saxons," Scot said. "I will proffer fealty as vassal to the King, asking only that he grant my neighbors the same opportunity."

"Very good," the Druid said, arriving at the scene. "I am so glad to discover this difference resolved." He turned to the Saxon, raising one fine eyebrow. "And you—have you some gesture?"

"A blanket?" the Saxon inquired.

"They have blankets at home. Would you want to be considered less than generous? Have you nothing that would portray your magnanimity in victory, unmistakably?"

"Let him alone," Scot snapped. "He's a good man. He did right, the way he saw it. He doesn't owe me anything."

"I like you better every time you open your mouth," the Saxon said to Scot. "I would like to give you something—not in payment for anything, but because you are a man I can respect."

"Thanks," Scot said. "I respect you too. But all I want is to go home."

"With your wife and unmarried champion," the Druid said. "Isn't it too bad he never found a good enough woman, while on the other hand—"

The Saxon's mouth dropped open. "You clever swine! You don't mean—?"

"Why not try it?"

"All right, I will!" The Saxon turned to Brand. "Sir, you fought well, considering that you have no experience with the sword. Though your friend has withdrawn his protest, I respect the courage of his stand and concede that there could have been some misunderstanding in the course of our encounter. I ask whether you will accept, as a token of amity between us, my sister." He drew Bitsy forward by the elbow.[134]

Brand's mouth dropped open. So did Scot's.

"It would be discourteous to decline such a well-intentioned gesture," the Druid said to Brand. "Unless you find her unappealing . . . ?"

Brand remained speechless, looking at Bitsy. Scot looked too, observing how much more substantial she was in daylight. Pretty in her way, but of heroic proportions.

"This is very sudden," Lucy said. "Why not let them talk it over—Brand and Bitsy? By themselves."

"Come, eat, drink with me," the Saxon said to Scot. "You and your woman. They can talk meanwhile."

But Scot could tell by the way Brand was looking at the young woman that she was exactly what he had waited for. And Bitsy was already flushing her appreciation of that gaze. Like Scot himself, she wanted to be wanted. Very little discussion would be required.[135]

It was a good meal and a good deal. They stayed another night, and departed for the farm with Bitsy in the morning. The Browns and three other families were granted release on similar terms, after the Druid and the Saxon champion described Scot's notions of integrity to the King. His oath of fealty could be trusted.

* * *

Life returned to normal. They built another sod house for the new couple, and shared food and work as before. Bitsy was a workhorse of a girl with a gentle nature, a fitting companion for Brand. Her presence also made for amiable relations with the Saxons, for she kept in touch with her brother.

In due course there were children, and Scot

thought his happiness was complete. But something gnawed at him. How could he settle for his comfortable existence as a farmer, while MT continued to decimate Earth? It was not enough to secure his own welfare, when that of others suffered.

What *was* civilization, anyway? Was it each family for itself, and to hell with the world? He remembered his conversation with Brother Paul while pitching compost. The Holy Order of Vision would not take the comfortable, self-serving route; it sought out the problem and put its energies and knowledge there. Without Brother Paul's help, Scot's farm probably would have failed. It was a philosophy Scot had benefitted from. Was he to ignore it, now that—

Now that his turn to contribute had come?

He talked to Lucy about it. She argued—but would not directly oppose him. "I'm with you—whatever you decide."

And Brand: "Brother Paul would say do it. Myself, I'd do it. But I don't want Bitsy or the kids getting involved . . ."

He checked it out with the Druid and the King. Both gave astonished approval. "It just might work," the Druid said. "Three to one you'll die in the attempt—but what an adventure! To get even with MT after all these years . . ."

So at last it was decided. Scot would undertake his mission to save Earth.

Bitsy took the children to visit her brother, freeing Scot and Lucy and Brand for the mission. Once the location of the MT transporter had been secret, with the émigrés brought in by sealed trains, but now the disappearance of the civilized communications network had changed all that. Every potential émigré had to make his own way to the station, usually by horseback. All roads, almost literally, ran to MT; the population and resources of Earth were still being drained into this maw. MT—the maw of Baal, consuming Earth's families.

Scot and his party walked. Horse farms were no longer adequate to the need, and even ponies were too expensive for the common man. But the MT trail was still well trodden.

Five years had made a phenomenal difference. Once the area had been built up with houses, small business and industry. Now only the shells of the buildings remained. Most had been gutted by fire, some by vandalism, others by neglect. Some stood partially dismantled, with pipes and chimneys projecting up like alien architecture.

The people were gone. Scot knew that no more than half could have been accounted for by the MT exodus; it would take ten years at full capacity to deplete the full population of Earth. The rest had gone in a lesser migration: to the larger metropolitan areas, where electric power remained, or to the more open country where it was possible to farm or range with the Saxons or Huns. Or they had died. He didn't like to think how many had gone that last route—but it had to be an unconscionable percentage. There had been the thug ravages of the expanding fringe, and the Saxon/Hun wars, and then the Beaker People incursions in America, and similar campaigns elsewhere in the world. So many families had been unable to maintain themselves amidst the disintegrating society. Scot's farm had been lucky, socially and geographically. Survival was a primitive business, and fitness was as much a matter of fate as capability.

The grass of bygone lawns was tall, though the snow was not yet off it. The reedlike stalks of it thrust up through the slush. Small trees were rising, the hardwoods bare, the evergreens hearty. The occasional large stumps showed the fate of the full-grown trees as heating fuel had become scarce. But as if in compensation, hedges had become walls of brush, narrow inlets of wilderness. Pavement was overgrown, grossly cracked where the concrete showed. Here and there the street had collapsed, eroded from below by the sewer system.[136]

But the people's loss had been the animals' gain. Dogs skulked, hairy, gleaming-eyed wolflike creatures, no longer the friend of man. Rats peeked out from the rubble. Cats had gone wild too—it had not been much of a change for them. Birds were everywhere—not the pigeons and ducks and chickens associated with man, but true wild species, including owls and hawks. More striking was the resurgence of forest and meadow life—deer, bear, porcupines, weasels, beavers, and a number of newly-wild cattle, horses and swine. They used the remaining intact houses for shelter and migrated as far south as they needed to each winter to find food.

The animals, while not unduly shy, tended to stay clear of the small human party. But the occasional human remnants did not. More than one ragged group had approached brandishing crude stone-age weapons, only to retreat in the face of Brand's sword. They could not know that Brand would not actually use that sword on a human being.

Lucy stopped. "Deadfall ahead," she said.[137]

"I don't see it," Scot said, peering about.

"I've had experience," she reminded him, and smiled. She was so pretty in that instant that he had to kiss her. As always, she accepted the gesture not graciously but eagerly, then continued. "The snow is smoother on that one patch. Elsewhere it is tracked up, uneven. But there they cleared it off, made a level surface, and waited for snowfall to cover it over. The animals detour around it, see— no tracks. That trap is for *people*."

Scot saw it now. A square about eight feet on a side, too even. "I don't like traps set for people," he said.

"Let it pass," Brand said. "Nothing to gain by violence."

How much they had changed! Scot had once set a trap for a person—and caught more than he anticipated!—and Brand had once lived by violence. Brother Paul's influence seemed to be running a long, cumulative course, though they had never seen him again. Or perhaps marriage and family had provided other values for both men.[138]

They skirted the deadfall. They moved on at the rate of about thirty miles a day, as they were seasoned walkers and campers. They brought down occasional animals with bow and arrow, no more than they needed to eat, carefully skinning them and salvaging the hides for future processing and use. Along the way they made hidden caches, as they could not carry these hides all the way to MT. Not while they were curing. To be a primitive hunter was to avoid waste, for the interaction of nature was of overwhelming importance. They always made token offerings to the nature gods, for these were now much more important than that distant God of civilization.

As they neared the MT complex, civilization upgraded. The houses were in better repair, and more and more of them were occupied. The wildlife retreated, and tame animals reappeared. Fifty miles out they passed the electric perimeter. Now there were cars on the road, and then buses, and even a train cruising along the adjacent tracks, smoke and steam puffing from its stack.

Ten miles out the traffic was thick, with stoplights glaring and horns honking. A factory chimney spewed foul smoke into the atmosphere next to the lovely cut-glass facade of a church. What remained of the snow was stained gray. Beer cans littered the fringe of the street, and waste paper and cigarette butts clogged the drainage vents.

Scot halted abruptly, stung by an unexpected misgiving. "This—this is civilization," he said wonderingly.

Lucy laughed. "I almost forgot what it looked like."

Brand scowled. "It looks like sh—" He cut himself off and kicked at a can.

Scot looked at him. "Is it really worth saving, this ugly mess?"

The big man shook his head. "I dunno."

"Well, *I* know!" Lucy flared. "This is the heart of what's wrong with the world. The single-minded waste. What did you expect it to look like— heaven?"

"Destroy MT—this will disappear," Scot said, as though convincing himself. "Beneath the squalor of this prison of rampant technology, there has to be some basic pride and nobility of the human state. Our action may seem harsh at first, but it will free the soul of these people. They will have to seek gainful employment, return to the soil, to renew their ties with the land . . ."

"And in order to develop this technology again," Lucy agreed, "they'll have to abolish waste— because there simply isn't enough left here on Earth to do it wastefully. So we'll either have a primitive culture—or a truly civilized one, unlike what we had five years ago."[139]

Scot put an arm around her. "I think you understand it better than I do."

"I understand the criminal—I mean civilized—mind."

"You know, if we could steal a car now, short out the ignition—"

She trod on his toe. "That's not funny!"

"Hey, don't fight," Brand protested. And he was serious; violence upset him increasingly, and he didn't understand their brawls. He and Bitsy never fought.

Lucy relaxed. "All right, seeing as there's a gentleman present."

Nevertheless, they had to borrow a parked car for the night, for they had no better place to stay.[140] They could not camp in the street, and had no money for formal accommodations, and could not afford to call attention to themselves. They located a lushly upholstered antique in a private parking space and curled up on the seats for four hours' slumber: enough to see them through the day ahead.

Well before dawn they advanced on the MT complex. This was a huge compound, girt with wire mesh fence. Guard dogs roamed between that fence and the fortress-like main building.

Brand surveyed it. "We ain't getting in *there* without a hassle," he said.

"Of course not," Scot agreed. "We aren't going to attempt any violence. We have to use our brains."

"And our nerve," Lucy said.

"I can't even read," Brand reminded them.

"You've got conscience," she reminded him.

Conscience . . . Scot mulled over that word, that concept. He had returned to it again and again. Could he really justify what he was about to do, on any ethical basis?

That will be for others to answer, he thought. Was he contemplating a "consequence" that Brother Paul would have approved, or an "aggression"? The line was fuzzy.

Lucy jogged his elbow. "Don't start reasoning it out now, love. We have to trust our considered decision."

Scot sighed. "Yes."

They walked up to the entry building and joined the line there. Scot was mildly surprised that there was still enough business to create a crowd. Apparently the predominant urge of most of the remaining population of Earth was to get away from Earth. How would all those people react—when that exodus was terminated? Hardly with gladness . . .

But he had to distrust these last-moment doubts. They were pretexts for inaction.

The office was very like the one Scot had entered so many years ago, with his brother Tully and Fanny.

Fanny—that thought still caused a little twitch somewhere in his gut. The feeling he had for her was gone; now it was more a sensation of irritation and wonder. Though Lucy had cost him Fanny, he had long since learned how he had profited in that exchange. Fanny had been the dream, and she was where she belonged: on the dream-world of Conquest. Lucy was the reality, and she was where *she* belonged: here on Earth. And the reality was better than the dream.

And he realized a fundamental parallel, his conviction that Earth was ultimately better than any colony derived from his certainty that Lucy was better than Fanny. Even Lucy-on-Earth, against Fanny-in-Heaven. Fanny had seemed perfect to start with; his mere touch would have defiled her. Just as man's touch defiled the perfect alien planets. Lucy was imperfect, a thief, combative—yet she had grown with the need and become a woman more truly lovable than any other. As *Earth* could grow, given the chance—unpretty, criminal, combative Earth, with immense potential being dissipated among the stars.[141]

He put his arm around Lucy, there in the office, and brought her in for a kiss. "You've had another chain of thought," she murmured.

"For Earth," he responded. "You are my Earth, my everything."

"Always."

"Very touching," the man at the desk said. "Are you two quite sure you want to *leave* Earth?" And the people in the line sniggered.

Scot straightened his face. "I am Scot Krebs. I was denied emigration five years ago, because I was accused of attacking this woman."

"You don't seem to have changed your ways," the officer remarked, punching the computer console for the name.

"I married her," Scot said.

The console flashed its verification. "That charge is still outstanding," the official said.[142]

"But I told you—this is the woman. She will testify that she has withdrawn the charge."

"Anyway," Lucy said mischievously, "I *like* being attacked."

The people in line laughed, but not the officer. "This is not my responsibility. You'll have to have it cleared by the secretary."

"What's there to clear?" Scot asked. "All you have to do is verify her identity."

The official stood. "This way, please." He glanced at Brand, next in line. "I will be with you in a moment, sir."

"I gotta go to the bathroom," Brand muttered. "Make it snappy."

The official didn't answer, but Scot could tell by the set of his jaw that he meant to take his time.

As they followed the official down the hall, Brand complained again about the delay and his need for a rest room. "Oh, go ahead," the man behind him said. "I'll hold your place in line. We've all got a long wait coming."

And in a moment Brand would go off looking for the bathroom—and blunder into the wrong section. Perhaps even the wrong building. With luck he might even make it back to his place in line before the official returned, after untangling Scot's problem.

They entered another office. "Mr. Blount, there is an irregularity," the official said. "This man has an unresolved charge on his record that he says no longer applies."

"Very well, Bill," Blount said. "I'll take it from here."

"Right." The official left.

Oh-oh, Scot thought. Brand couldn't possibly complete his mission before the official made it back to the desk. That was bad.

Mr. Blount was businesslike and efficient. With the aid of the computer records he established

Scot's and Lucy's identities, their common-law marriage registry, and the separate charges against them. Scot dropped his complaint of car theft, and Lucy voided hers of attack. "After all," she said, "spouses can't testify against each other."

"Unless they want to," Scot said.

"Don't contradict me, or I *will* testify against you, you bra-snatcher," she said. And smiled.[143]

"I believe the matter stands resolved," Blount said. "I will authorize your entrance for emigration on an alternate basis. Should two approved transportees fail to appear on schedule at the time your turn comes, you will go in their stead to whatever colony planet is then current. You understand, you have no choice of colony."

"We understand," Scot said. His mouth felt dry. Here he was, approved for emigration, his years-long dream—and he had no intention of taking advantage of it. "Where's the physical?"

The man raised an eyebrow. "We dispensed with the physicals two years ago. Insufficient trained medical personnel."

They returned to the waiting room and got in line again. Brand was not there. Lucy squeezed Scot's hand nervously. Had Brand failed—or was he still trying?

The line moved along, and this time Scot and Lucy were approved for emigration as Alternates, and given numbers 451 and 452. The head of the line now stood at 429, so their chances of receiving an early opportunity were good. Too good; if Brand didn't reappear, they might be trapped.

"Six vacancies on Sylva, Lot 4" the loudspeaker announced. There was a scramble as numbers 429 through 434 rushed to the second MT desk for verification. Here a difficulty manifested: 433 and 434 were two members of a family of four, and they did not want to be separated. If there were two vacancies on the next Lot, the other two could catch up, and they would be reunited fifteen minutes later. But it was purely chance; six Lots might go by, or a dozen, without vacancy. Then the next two could be sent to a different colony planet. That was not to be risked! Since none of the four ahead would yield their places, the two finally had to give way to the next in line: 437 and 438. "But we'll be on the next Lot," the man said grimly. "We're at the head of the line."

"Another Lot in only fifteen minutes," Lucy murmured. "Sixteen numbers . . ."

"I can hardly wait," Scot replied nervously.

They waited. With the clockwork that had proceeded virtually uninterrupted for five years, draining the planet Earth, the Lots went out at the rate of four an hour. Each Lot contained 256 people, with the overwhelming majority showing up on time. Sometimes a last minute illness or accident caused defaults, and then the Alternates got in.

Sylva Lot 5 was unusual. "Seventeen vacancies," the speaker said. That carried it through 451: Scot's. But not Lucy's.

"I'll wait for my wife," Scot said, waving number 453 on. He hoped his hand was not visibly shaking. This was getting way too close for comfort—and where was Brand?

But two Alternates were missing. Suddenly there was room for Scot and Lucy after all. If they balked, it would be suspicious, and of course they would have to go home. If they didn't balk, they would wind up as colonists on Planet Sylva.

Horrified, Lucy stared at him. There was no time for temporizing; they were already shuffling toward the transport chamber.

"We're here!" a man called. "Numbers 444 and 445! We were in the bathroom! Never thought it'd be so soon!"

Lucy staggered to a chair and sat down so suddenly Scot was momentarily afraid she had fainted. "But now we're at the head of the line," he whispered. *"Where is Brand?"*

"Do you think he came back in line—and got shipped out before we returned?"

Scot dismissed that. "He'd wait for us."

"But they don't give you any choice! You go, or you get blacklisted."

"He'd take the blacklisting. He wouldn't leave Bitsy."

"Then he isn't back yet. Or—"

Or he had been caught. "I don't feel so well," Scot said. "Maybe I'd better go to—" He paused. "Could he be there?"

"Better check," she said.

He moved down the hall to the bathroom. It was empty. What had happened to Brand? Only ten minutes to find out.

He returned to Lucy. "Not there."

"We can't proceed without that manual."

Tensely they waited while the minutes ticked off. When the openings for the next Lot came, they would have to balk—and then their plan would be spoiled, for they would be blacklisted and subject to immediate arrest if they returned to MT.

Lucy squeezed his arm shakily. "Would—would it be so bad to emigrate? Sylva—that means forest. It sounds nice . . ."[144]

"They *all* sound nice," he snapped. "It's all promotional. Hell itself would be named 'Fireside Soul.'"

She burst into a titter that sounded halfway like a scream. "I want to go to Fireside!"

"We'll face hell on Earth if you give us away," he gritted.

An officer entered the room. "Does anybody here know a man named Brandon?"[145]

Startled, Scot looked at Lucy. Should they admit acquaintance—or sit tight? They had not anticipated this wrinkle.

Then he shrugged. What did they have to lose? "He came with us."

"He has been arrested. You will have to testify."

"Arrested!" Scot exclaimed with unfeigned shock. "Brand wouldn't commit any crime!" *Except one: trying to save Earth.*

"Four vacancies on Sylva, Lot Six," the speaker said.

"That's us," Lucy said worriedly.

"Sorry," the officer said. "You'll have to take another Lot. We'll issue a deferral. We need information on this man."

With mixed apprehension and relief they followed the man down another hall, to another office. This one was manned by a uniformed policeman. "Your friend broke into an office and stole a manual. Why would he do that?"

So Brand had succeeded—partially. He had gotten the manual—but hadn't gotten away. And what was Scot to say?

Lucy spread her hands. "He's illiterate."

"Illiterate! What use could he have for a manual, then?"

"Maybe he thought he could hock it," she suggested. "Don't those books have all sorts of secret information?"

"No. Only technical instructions and ephemerides. Astronomical tables locating the exact positions of the planets we ship to. Only computer and transport personnel have any use for such information." He paused thoughtfully. "And why would he want money—if he were about to emigrate?"

They were in trouble. This was an intelligent official who had Brand in custody and was suspicious, perhaps, of them too. Yet—they had done nothing. Yet.

Lucy, as she had promised, was better at lying than Scot. "We hoped to get him away from Earth, where he wouldn't be tempted," she said glibly. "He's something of a kleptomaniac. Fascinated by official-looking things. Does your manual have complicated diagrams or different kinds of type?"

He'll never swallow that! Scot thought.

Incredibly, the man did. "Yes, that's a good description of the manual. With different colored pages and tabs. Actually it has very little material value, and outdated copies may be obtained for a very nominal fee. But I can see that it would be impressive to an illiterate." He shrugged. "Nevertheless, your friend has committed a crime, and must be denied the privilege of emigration. You may proceed without him if you wish."

Lucy shook her head. "I don't know. We want to go, but—what will happen to him?"

"He'll be turned loose at the gate and told not to return. Should he return, he would be jailed." *Blacklist* was a taboo word.

"But without us, he would have no way to make a living."

"That is his concern. No one has to emigrate. Personally I feel that Earth itself has a lot to offer—if only people would take advantage of it."

Scot was amazed. This man had aptly expressed his own thoughts—yet he worked for MT! Or was it a trap? If they had learned that Brand was married and had a baby, two babies—

Lucy looked crestfallen. She certainly was good at lying, even by mute expression! "We wanted so much to go! But now—could we take some time to think it over?"

Does the end justify the means? Scot thought. *Here we are stealing and lying in the name of a good cause . . .*[146]

The policeman smiled. "We'll issue you a 24-hour extension on your Authorization. Then you can go or stay, as you decide. But that decision will be irrevocable."

"Thank you," she whispered.

As they returned to the waiting room, Scot relaxed partway. "Nice going—but without Brand, what can we do?"

"He got the manual—and they didn't recover it," she said. "He must have hidden it somewhere—"

"The bathroom!" he exclaimed.

Sure enough: tucked behind the tank of a corner toilet was the thick leatherbound Operations Manual. Brand had done his part.[147]

Lucy obtained the Extension Permit at the desk while Scot concealed the manual in his shirt. They still hadn't seen Brand, but could not risk looking for him, much less trying to free him. The authorities just might be giving them enough rope to hang themselves, waiting to discover how they were going to sabotage the MT unit.

Outside, they walked until they found a large blank building, circled around it, and settled in the privacy of the back wall. Eagerly they perused the manual.[148]

"I wish I were an engineer," Scot muttered. "This thing's a monster!"

"We don't need to understand the details," Lucy said. "Just locate the time and place."

"The place we know. But the time—I can't make head or tail of these technicolor tables!"

She closed her eyes and poked her finger at the page. "Then," she said as it touched.

"We can't go into it randomly! We'll either miss the mark or miss the capsule entirely. We won't get a second chance."

"It's not random," she protested. "It's intuition."

Scot made a derisive noise. "Intuition!"

"Well, what's wrong with that?" she demanded. "The nature Gods approve it."

Too late he read the signs: she was tired and nervous, ready to blow up when balked. "Nothing's wrong. Only—"

"Only you can't read the manual, and Brand's in jail, so it's all wasted! What will I say to Bitsy? We might as well have stayed home! You and your big ideas! Save the world! Blow up MT!"

"Pipe down," he cautioned her. "Someone'll hear."

"I will *not* pipe down! We left a perfectly good farm for this idiocy! What do you think you're—?"

So it was to be a full-scale tantrum. He couldn't afford that! Not here, not now. But only desperate measures would cut her off.

He swept his arm out, scooped up a handful of snow, and thrust it down her bosom. And quickly covered her mouth to muffle her piercing shriek.

His action had the desired effect. Lucy went into a frenzy of contortion to relieve the cold mush in her clothing, and didn't even bite his hand. He helped as well as he could. Then she started laughing. Then they made love. And finally they talked it out and deciphered the manual's coding system.[149]

They had just two hours to plant the radiation coder, when the MT program shifted from Planet Sylva to Planet Oceana. If they missed that, they would have to wait another month for the shiftover to Planet Zephyr. "We can't risk that delay," Scot muttered. "If we don't emigrate, and hang around beyond our permit extension, they'll arrest us too."[150]

They took another thirty minutes to study the MT complex layout by the wan light of the storm lantern, then proceeded. Scot kissed Lucy: "In case we have to part suddenly, and I don't see you again." Immediately he amended himself. "Soon."

"Oh, Scot—do we have to?"

"I promise: this is my last world-saving mission."

"That's what I'm afraid of!"

"Okay, darling—I promise it's *not* my last."

She hugged him close. "Without you, I'm nothing at all."

"Uh-uh. Without that *grinder* you'd be nothing at all."

She twisted so as to strike him with her right breast. "Just a thief."[151]

"First my car—then my heart."

"I gave back some, you know."

He kissed her again. "I love you."[152]

She pushed him away. "Do your job, then come home, and I'll give you such a reward!"

It was now 5 A.M. by the huge outdoor clock above the capsule building.[153] The changeover to Oceana was to occur precisely at 6 A.M. with a double dry run for fine-tuning orientation. The calibrator had to be in that first shuttle.

"You understand what you may have to do," Scot said grimly.

Now she was deathly solemn. "I understand. Forgive me."

"You I can forgive. Myself will be harder."

"Sometimes you're so sweet . . ." she said.

He was aching with love for her, but they had to proceed. They had a very narrow span of time to utilize. They moved back up the street toward the MT center.[154]

Thanks to the manual, Scot now had a clear picture of the layout. The capsule chamber was adjacent to the processing building, connected by a series of air locks. They had to reach it deviously. They entered the processing building, went down the hall to the bathroom, and each entered the appropriate one. Scot's was empty. He forced a back window open, then returned to the door. Lucy was waiting for him.

"Mine's clear," he said. "Come in."

She came in with him quickly. He boosted her out the window, then followed. Now they were loose in the maintenance section of the complex. They walked briskly toward the rear of the capsule building, just as if they belonged there.

There was the emergency lock, just as shown on the chart. Dawn was developing, and the increasing light made Scot nervous. "Take my watch," Lucy said, handing it to him. "I synchronized it with the MT clock, maybe a second fast."

He took it. The time was 5:56 A.M. Right on schedule.

Scot took hold of the wheel that released the air

lock and turned it. The thing was stiff but it gave under their joint effort, then became easier. At length the lock swung open, like the door of a giant safe.

"Okay," Scot said. "Wish me luck."

"What kind?" she asked, then kissed him quietly, desperately. "Now quit dawdling!"

Inside there was a second wheel. He took hold of it, but it wouldn't budge. "It's an air lock, dummy," Lucy called. "Fail-safe. You have to close the outer one before the inner one will move."

"Oh." Embarrassed, he closed the outer one. Then the inner one did move—but he had wasted several precious seconds.

The portal swung outward, and he stepped into —an accordion-pleated tube crossing a narrow passage. This was the space between the building and the capsule, maintained as a vacuum; the tube extended itself automatically when either air lock was activated, and would be folded out of the way when the locks closed again. A sophisticated emergency access, seldom used.

He played the beam of his little flashlight over his watch. The time was 5:58. He was taking too long! He spun the wheel of the capsule lock, and this was much better; the door popped open as the mechanism released it. He jumped in, drew it closed, spun the inner wheel, and turned to the next. This was like traveling between spaceships! He rotated the wheel just enough to be sure he could open the portal on demand, then shone the light on his watch—*Lucy's* watch—again. It was ten seconds before 5:59; he had recovered his schedule.

He put his ear to the panel and listened, trying to make sure the interior was clear, but no sound penetrated. Well, the chances were the personnel were gone; they wouldn't play it too close! That was why *he* was playing it close.

Precisely at 5:59 he spun the wheel, opened the portal, and stepped inside the capsule proper. He was vaguely disappointed as he played his flash about; it was merely a big, empty chamber with numbered squares marked on the floor.

Why was he concerned? It was empty as it should be, *had* to be! The timing was ideal, so far. But he now had only forty seconds to complete his mission and get out. If he ran late, he would get shipped to Planet Oceana—or get caught in transit between capsule and building. Either way, *finis*.

The calibrator sat in a holder near the main entrance; his light reflected off its polished metal. Scot ran to it—and found it locked in place. He needed tools to budge it, and didn't have them. Thirty seconds.

Could he leave both calibrators? No, surely the computer would get a dual reading that would trigger an alarm. Then the human personnel would investigate and correct the error. Everything had to seem in order.

Tools! There had to be some near! Why take them all the way back to the depot when they'd be needed again in just fifteen minutes? Scot's light and gaze swept across the room—and he saw the toolbox. He let out his breath and ran for it, found a wrench, ran back to the calibrator assembly. He turned the main nut, loosened it, got the checker out of its clasp, dropped in the other, tightened, and looked at the watch.

Ten seconds remained.

No time to put away the wrench! He slid it down toward the toolbox, hoping the workmen would think someone had been sloppy.[155] He sprinted for the lock, hearing the satisfying clang as the wrench struck the box. He dived through the aperture, yanked it closed after him, spun the wheel, jumped out the next. Four seconds—no time to close the capsule's outer door properly! He slammed it, leaped through the accordion tube, scrambled through the next lock, hauled it shut and spun the wheel as the watch's sweep hand passed the six o'clock mark.

Panting, he waited. He should be safe now.

Nothing happened.

Had he mistimed it? Or failed? He started to reopen the lock, then caught himself. These capsules were precisely phased, and the walls of the containing chamber were heavy. Operation should be silent. Probably the capsule had phased out on schedule, and now there was the alternate capsule in its place.

He emerged—and Lucy was not there.

Less than four minutes—but it meant that in that time someone had come, and she had had to distract him—any way she could. So long as she kept suspicion off Scot. And she had. *What have I done to you?* he thought in momentary anguish. He had prayed this would not be necessary!

He closed the lock and hurried away. He could not remain in this area, for his very presence could arouse fatal suspicion.

Now he had half an hour to locate Lucy and Brand and get them out of the MT complex. Fifteen minutes for the test capsule to return; fifteen more for the "corrected" one. Both empty, so that there would be no loss of life. With luck.

He turned a corner—and almost collided with a

guard. "Hey—you're not мт!" the guard exclaimed. "Where's your badge?"

Oh-oh. "I'm looking for my wife," Scot said. "She ran in here somewhere—we're on the alternate list." He shook his Authorization and Extension.

"Well, get back to the processing area," the man said irritably. "You've no business here."

That was what *he* thought! "But my wife—"

"All right, we'll check in at the security office. She must've been picked up for loitering out of bounds."

To Scot's immense relief, she had been. She had not had to do what he had been afraid of.

"This woman tells me your friend was arrested," the sergeant said to Scot. "You're emigrating without him?"

"No," Scot said. "We'll take him home. Will you release him in our custody?"

"You understand, none of you will be able to come back, ever," the man said. "You only get one chance to emigrate."[156]

"Yes. But we really have no choice."

The man shrugged. He spoke into the intercom on his desk. "Bring out the prisoner; he's going home."

Beautiful! Evidently these personnel didn't have much trouble, and were lax. They waited.

But the mills of a lax bureaucracy moved slowly. Ten minutes passed, fifteen. They dared not protest —but now hardly ten minutes remained before their deadline. What would happen if they were still here when the second capsule returned?

Well, they had known there was risk in this venture. They might be incarcerated as traitors to their culture—but the job would have been done.

Lucy squeezed his hand, understanding. She was ready to die with him.

Another alternative was worse. Suppose he had failed, and no disruption occurred?

At last Brand appeared. Scot stepped forward, frowning. "I hope you realize, friend, that you have cost us our chance to emigrate!" he said. "What on Earth did you want with a manual you couldn't even read?"

Brand looked properly abashed. "Gee, it had such pretty colors . . ."

Scot shook his head in affected exasperation. "Well, let's go. Too bad you weren't color-blind too."

Then the policeman who had first investigated the case entered. "A very pretty scene," he remarked. "But I think too pat. I believe these people are up to something. We'll just give them a lie detector screening first."

Oh, no! Five minutes to go—and now this! Scot had no idea how to foil a lie detector apparatus. And in any event, once the MT blew—

"Take 'em to the interrogation office," the officer said.[157]

This, as it happened, was set apart from the main complex. They got into a jeep and zoomed across the city, to debark at an unpretentious building. "This is all routine," the officer said as they entered. "If your story checks out, you'll have our apology and maybe another chance to emigrate. So don't—"

There was a shudder, as of an earthquake. One wall of the building collapsed. Dust billowed up to mix with the snow from outside.

Amazed, they looked out through the open wall. A monstrous cloud was rising over the MT complex two miles away, like an old-fashioned hydrogen-bomb follow-up, but somehow more authoritative than any film from this vantage. Already bright flames were licking at the base.

Gazing upon it, feeling the awful heat of an explosion a thousand times as powerful as he had anticipated—if he had ever really believed in it!—Scot felt a sudden surge of *déjà vu,* the sensation of having been here before. Unbidden, his mind retreated into an experience that had been buried.[158]

. . .

Into the great orange maw of his flaming house: now at last he remembered. He had wrapped a wet coat about his head and shoulders, brief, insufficient protection from the intolerable heat, and charged ahead. Falling, blazing timbers dropped beside him, but he kept on, choking on the roiling smoke. It was like a descent into hell, and in the heat-seared agony of his vision he thought he saw the dancing demons of his torture.

He found the guest room on the ground floor, pawed at the bunk. But his hands fell only on the visitor's traveling pack. Donald was gone.[159]

So it had been for nothing, this charge into the holocaust. The visitor had decamped without informing them, lacking the courage to face the victims of his carelessness, or even to warn them about the fire he had started. If they died because of that neglect, or lost their home and livelihood, too bad. The true MT philosophy![160]

Disgusted, Scot turned and staggered back, carrying the pack. But now a rising wall of flame cut him off. He turned again, casting about for the window, but the inferno was everywhere. Bright, bright! *And suddenly there shined round him a light from heaven* . . . He could no longer open his eyes; the smoke was too thick.[161]

Think! he told himself. Find the bunk. The window is beyond it.

The floor gave way beneath him and he fell to hands and knees. The heat was less intense here, but still too much. Blindly he crawled until he struck an obstruction. A wall? He felt along it and grasped—a piece of broken glass. The lamp!

Therefore, the bed was near. No more time. He lurched to his feet, braced his arms with the pack in them, and dove across the region where the bed should be. His shoulder struck something hard. Debris fell around him. *Who art thou, Lord?* He lurched again, thrashing—and suddenly there was air.

He rolled into that draft, extracting his body from the fiery wall. His coat hung up and he had to tear free of it; it was burning anyway. Then strong hands were on him, hauling him forward. His hair was singed, his skin scorched, his watch broken, but he was out!

The fire spread to the surrounding brush and burned out the entire block before being balked by the "natural" barrier of the surrounding streets. Scot faded in and out of consciousness as Lucy took care of him. They carried him to their neighbors several miles to the north, the Browns. There Scot recovered, contemplating the little metal calibrator that was all they retained of their visitor. What a price they had paid for their hospitality!

In that period of infirmity, depression and near-blindness Scot had time to do much thinking, and when he could function again he asked the Browns to stand witness for his formal declaration of marriage to Lucy. There were no priests, ministers or rabbis in the region, and they regarded it as a civil ceremony: fitting for the times, and binding as marriages of pre-civilized times had been.

They returned and rebuilt on the cellar of the original house: a cabin made of sod. It was merely a matter of cutting oblongs of turf like large flat bricks, with the grass roots holding the soil together so firmly that it was a viable construction medium. *The living roots strengthen the soil,* Scot thought as he worked, *as living friendship strengthens the soul.* If compost were civilization, soil was soul. Brother Paul would appreciate that![162]

The turf house was dark but substantial—and fireproof. Space was cramped, but since most of their belongings had been wiped out they had less need of space. They consumed roasted potatoes from the cellar, and then the snows came and preserved much of the rest. Nature's freezer—better and cheaper than man's poor mechanical imitations.

They adopted a hunter-gatherer mode of life, bringing down the increasingly plentiful wild game with bows and home-made spears and even thrown stones. The beauty of stones was that they didn't have to be carried or recovered; they were everywhere.

Brand's supply of firewood had been wiped out by the blaze, and that was a critical loss. But he was able to gather more from the neighborhood. Their solar water heating system had been damaged beyond repair, the copper tubing melted. But Lucy's grinder remained, and that pleased Scot because of what he knew to be the wrong reason: not that they would have bread to eat, but that she would retain a beautiful bosom.[163]

Other neighbors shared, providing corn and milk and blankets. Hardly a day went by without a Brown or a Smith or someone else stopping by to "exchange news"—actually checking to make sure the crippled farm was surviving, and to help as required. Cultural regression, Scot realized, did not actually mean barbarism; in many respects it meant a closer, warmer, more meaningful relationship with one's neighbors.

"Do you know," Scot remarked one day in spring, "we're actually better off than we were. That wooden house was an anachronism. Now we're closer to nature." He glanced at their house, noting how the grass was growing tall on the sloping sod roof. They had a living house!

Then Lucy told him about their coming baby.

Next month the Saxons came, and Scot remembered his debt to his neighbors.[164]

Now, gazing on the magnificent blaze following the MT explosion, Scot knew that America would follow his own course, and after it, the world. The anachronism of MT had been destroyed, and though there would be much pain in that loss, the long-range result would be beneficial. Now man would indeed colonize his own planet, and inevitably Earth would prosper—and perhaps learn to avoid its past mistakes.

The officer still stared, oblivious to all else. Scot knew what that shock was like; he had been through it himself. A lifestyle had been destroyed; few people could anticipate the better one that would replace it.

Scot linked hands with Lucy and Brand and

started walking.[165] No one tried to stop them; no one would. They had a long hike ahead, but their families were waiting: Scot's little boy, Brand's twin girls. Families with better futures than they had had a moment ago.[166]

Man's colonization of the fittest planet was commencing.[167]

Notes

1. I had a dedication which did not appear in the book: "Dedicated to the anonymous real-life counterparts of Brother Paul and the Holy Order of Vision. Perhaps you will know them when you meet them." The dedication page is missing from the manuscript as it was returned. By what right an editor deletes a dedication I don't know. The copy-editor's job, as I perhaps naively understand it, is normally to correct spelling errors and typos, to mark hyphenations for the typesetter (who is presumed to be too dull to do it properly otherwise), change the author's -- dashes to — — — dashes (it is of course correct the way the author does it; fortunately the typesetter always changes it back to --) and the like. Frankly, I regard it as make-work so that there won't be too many unemployed girls tramping the streets of Parnassus. But

copy-editors—let's just call them copyeds—
invariably have delusions of literacy, and cannot
restrain themselves from rewriting the text itself.
Normally the editor goes over the manuscript after
it has been copy-edited and STETs out most of the
changes, and then the author eliminates the rest
when he sees the galley-proofs. But in this case the
Editor was evidently sleeping, and no galleys were
sent to me, so we have here a clear example of the
consequence of allowing copyeds to run amuck.

My manuscript was marked in several colors, as
one person after another went over it. I believe that
two, possibly three, were at the New York office,
and two were after the manuscript went to the other
writer for reworking. I know from my own experience that the frame of mind used to edit a book
differs from that used to write or rewrite it. Editing
is a critical process, while writing is a creative
process, so that though one copyed may in this case
also have been the Writer, I choose to distinguish
between them. It's a Jekyll and Hyde case: the
writer is a nice guy, while the copyed is an arrogant
little tyrant. This is of course true of every writer
who edits, not merely this one; check with any
writer for confirmation. Thus my Rogue's Gallery
calls out five copyeds and one writer. Here, then, is
the cast of characters in this ugly little drama,
personified as I perceive them. (I, being a writer, am
naturally creative, so my interpretation reflects
that.)

PENCIL—Evidently the first copyed to have at
this text, female. She means well but does have her
feminine hangups.

BLACK—She must be the new copyed who was
hired; she is really out to prove herself. That kind is
dangerous.

BLUE—an occasional dabbler, perhaps someone who happened to pass through the office on the way to the subway.

RED—Argumentative male; he remarks on everything, regardless whether he has any basis.

PURPLE—Androgynous copied who sometimes resembles Red and sometimes Red's wife. Two hands with but a single pen?

WRITER—I judged his actions by checking the published text.

EDITOR—The person theoretically in charge, who contacted me periodically on the phone to assure me that all was well.

And here I must make a disclaimer: some of the language quoted is intemperate. Readers may think I am making up some of the remarks; I assure you that this is the nonfiction section of this book, and that the following copied remarks were indeed made, either directly on my manuscript or on a separate sheet associated with it. This presentation is not a joke, even though I feel that much of the copy-editing was. It seems to be easy for some to sit on the sidelines and second-guess the one who is doing the work, using uncouth language, as we shall see here. Now *I* am the one second-guessing *them*—and believe me, it's a pleasure!

One other thing: though there are a number of notes called out here, there were many more on the manuscript. Not one page escaped unscathed. I have merely made a sampling of the juicier ones, to avoid becoming unduly tedious. The situation was in fact more extreme than this presentation shows. Few, if any, of my original sentences were actually published in pristine form.

Remember, in the Introduction, I mentioned that Editor had asked for a Prologue, Epilogue, and some technical material. I don't feel any of that is necessary, so I am running none of it in the novel proper. But for those who are interested, here is the Prologue, which did appear in the published version of the novel:

A man performed an experiment on white mice. A few pairs were given the freedom of a large, well-appointed cage. The climate was maintained at a pleasant level for the species; there were no predators and no diseases or natural hazards, and food and water were limitless. The mice were left to their own devices in this simulated paradise, while the man, like a beneficent but aloof God, watched.

The mice bred. Soon the few were many, and the many became a dense throng. Yet there was still food for all; only the space was limited. With the increasing press of bodies, the mice became irritable and asocial, fighting with each other over trifles. Some were neurotic; others ceased activity and just lay like vegetables. Babies were neglected, left to fend for themselves in an increasingly violent situation. Many were trampled to death, and those that survived were not sweet and gentle. Paradise had become hellish.

What had happened? The basic problem seemed to be the man's interference with the natural order. Mice depend on certain selective forces for the overall health of their species. Predators constantly cull the weak or slow or stupid or old or merely unlucky. Disease thins the population. On occasion starvation wipes out large numbers. The mice must breed prolifically in order to survive these hazards. All

these killers are cruel on an individual basis—
but not as cruel as the alternative of
overbreeding without concurrent elimination
of the surplus or expansion of the living area.

A mouse, looking at Earth as a planetary
cage, might see distressing parallels to man's
present condition. The human population of
our world has been increasing phenomenally
—but its resources are being exhausted, and
the habitable area is limited. We show the signs
of the approaching end, as war and crime,
disillusion and suicide and juvenile wildness
increase. Already segments of the world's population are starving, and the threat of nuclear
or biologic holocaust hangs over us all.

We cannot continue this way. The day of
reckoning is inevitable, and it is not heaven but
hell-on-Earth we face.

Unless there were some other avenue. Suppose it were possible for man to be freed from
his cage, so that he could emigrate painlessly to
other worlds?

A remarkable breakthrough occurs. This is
instant matter transmission to other habitable
planets. Suddenly the cage has been sprung,
and man's great adventure commences . . .

2. Red penned in the margin of the manuscript,
"Rewrite the entire opening" and "Describe the
participants." Accordingly, Writer did so, and here
are the first three paragraphs as the novel was
published:

As the drama on the giant screen in front of
him worked its labored way into one of the
obligatory love scenes, Scot's arm almost auto-

matically tightened around the shoulders of
the girl beside him. Instead of responding by
leaning against him, however, she wriggled her
shoulders in annoyance.

"Stop it, Scot," she said. "I came to see the
movie, not to experience it."

Scot relaxed his grip in mild irritation. Fanny was a lovely girl, but she did have this
evasive nature. She resented any distractions
from whatever occupied her attention at the
moment. To be fair, he conceded this did have
its compensations; when she made love, she
devoted herself to the act with the same single-
minded purpose she now displayed in watching
the screen. But Scot wasn't in much of a mood
for being fair, so he settled back under the
steering wheel in annoyance.

Very well, back to my comment: Writer did a
decent job here, generally, but he changed my
characterization of the girl. Instead of being a
"don't paw me!" type she became an "everything in
its time" type, who *does* make love outside of
marriage. If I were young and single again, I'm sure
I would prefer the latter type of girl—but this is not
the one I had in this novel. The "will she or won't
she?" question is fundamental in characterization,
and important in this novel specifically, and I
object to a change of this nature being made here.

Writer reworked the remainder of the opening
similarly; his text covers the same territory as mine,
in different words. Readers who are curious about
the extent of the differences throughout the novel
will have to locate a copy of the published edition
and compare in detail. It seems pointless to do it
here. Thus most of my notes will be on the notes the

copyeds made on the manuscript. Writer was required to honor these directives, contrary as some of them are; he was in a difficult position and should not be judged too harshly. (How do you obtain a copy of the other edition? That is a challenge; I am naming none of the other participants of this mess here. So you would have to locate a complete listing of my published works, and run down a "collaboration" under this title, then see if one of those out-of-print specialty stores will locate a copy for you. I really doubt this is worth the effort.)

3. Miss Pencil inquired at this point "Cut?" and Miss Black responded "Yes!" Note the exclamation point. What was there about this innocent passage that so offended these copyeds? At any rate, it was deleted.

4. Miss Black, on her sanitary separate sheet, says "Fanny can't imagine leaving earth." Purple responds "Keep—but. . . . ." Note the five dots in the ellipsis; that formation does not occur in nature.

5. The entire reference to Philip Nolan was cut by the Pencil–Black combo.

6. Miss Black crossed out most of the technical detail (I suspect she's a woman like Fanny), but Writer restored some of it.

7. Pencil marked most of what remained of the foregoing hundred words for italicizing. Miss Pencil was very free throughout, demanding italics: I would like to hear her speak! But Writer had the good sense to ignore most of those directives.

8. At this point a chapter-break has been inserted. I don't object to this chapterization; I had avoided it solely to save space, and would have chapterized myself had I had room. It turned out

that 55,000 words was meant to be the *minimum* length; I could have written to a more comfortable length after all. Ah, well. I'll skip future references to chapters, and just render this novel as I wrote it.

9.   Writer changed Scot's grab from her bra to her hair. Now I object to this; hair is no necessary distinction between man and woman, as a look at contemporary fashions shows, but a bosom remains a pretty solid indication.

10.   Pencil shifted the reference to her age from just before her speech to just after it, and Blue changed the words "the early" to "her"; Red marked this paragraph and said "Do something about that." So Writer cut the whole thing. I don't know what set them all off; maybe they just had nothing better to do.

11.   Miss Pencil decided to rewrite this: "Scot shook his head—and a quick searing stab of pain shot through his temples. Now pieces of the scene began to fit together:" Remember, I commented how copyeds aspire to become genuine writers. Miss Pencil shows definite promise; I like this bit, alliteration and all—but Writer, perhaps jealous of his prerogatives, changed the whole thing.

12.   Black asks: "He was knocked unconscious —but still had a bra in one hand and a pamphlet in the other?" To which Red responds: "Make it lying underneath him, then. But he could still clutch the bra, since he seems fascinated by teats anyway." But as already noted, Writer avoided the whole issue by having him grab her hair instead. (Note the cultural indication: where I would use the term "breasts" Red prefers "teats.")

13.   Black objects: "His car is stolen—and he's in danger of a court case against him—unbelievable." You think so? There was a news item

in real life about a family who parked their car with their daughter sleeping in the back seat. Two men stole the car, raped the daughter, wrecked the car and damaged other property in the process—and the *owner* was legally liable for damages. There was another in which two men engaged in a holdup; the police killed one and put the other on trial for murder though he hadn't fired the shot. Because the law said that anyone engaged in a crime involving a gun was guilty of any damage done by a gun— something like that. The law takes some funny turns! But Red, heeding this spurious objection, deleted the reference, saying "Drop—not enough police protection for them to bother with it." Now you might be wondering why I had such a devious way for Scot to get in trouble, when there could have been something that made more sense. Well, it was deliberate. I am showing that Earth really does not have much to offer Scot, in any respect. He can't even get justice. That's the kind of person who would really like to try a new and possibly better world. Fanny, who has never been abused by fate, doesn't understand. This sets things up for the irony that is to follow—for the course we might reasonably anticipate does not become reality.

14.   Blue deleted the last sentence, whereupon Pencil and Black deleted the whole paragraph.

15.   Pencil and Red had different problems with this paragraph. Pencil's were of the usual pointless shift-words-about variety, just to show that some-one was on the job. Thus the first sentence was changed to: "In general terms, it described Con-quest, an uninhabited planet that circled the star *Gienah* in the constellation *Cygnus*." Red said: "Something about getting better descriptive terms, than constellation, since that is not based on actual

proximity but on apparents [sic—obviously spelling is not this person's strong suit. Try "appearance"] as seen from Earth." Well, this is a pamphlet for popular consumption, and for that purpose the constellations are just fine. Red is simply nitpicking. He goes on to circle the words "making the overall climate more vigorous" with a question mark. Sigh. Very well, Red, I'll explain: it is Earth's oceans of water that stabilize its climate; land gets hotter and colder, so a planet with more land and less water is apt to have savage extremes of climate. Writer understood this, and kept the reference. Writer also explained about the use of "constellation" for Red. I believe I have mentioned the superior comprehension that creative writers possess.

16. Blue changed "God" to "How." I feel that people take God's name in vain frequently in real life, and should be represented, as far as is feasible, as they are.

17. Pencil wanted to change "indigence" to "bills," so Black cut the paragraph entirely. So Writer had Scot watch TV after all, inserting a rationale: the government, in an attempt to reduce violence, had guaranteed a TV set for every household. Writer was doing yeoman service, trying to compensate for the damage done by the hatchet-wielding copyeds, like a surgeon trying to rebuild a butchered body. How much better it would have been simply to muzzle those animals!

18. Here Pencil attached a pink slip, saying: "How could the MT program be otherwise than free? If colonization was the aim, it is illogical to charge $6M. God help the 'Filles de Roi' if they'd had to pay." To which Black replies: "Easy to solve— instead of saying how much it costs—have Scot

worry about the price." Well, I can offer an even easier solution: just leave my text alone. I set emigration up as a privilege so precious that no one could afford it—then offered this special bonus deal, so that the average man would jump at it without counting the other costs. It's sound marketing policy; people grab eagerly for bonus deals, thinking they're getting something for nothing. Naturally the MT Agency inflated the original price, though not as high as Miss Pencil suggests, so that the bargain would seem that much better. I saw clearly how this operated when I went to buy a package of dried milk and discovered that it cost 30 cents more than the prior week, but was now listed as a bargain: "20 cents off!" People buying that bargain would pay 10 cents more than they would have for the non-bargain package, the week before. No, I didn't buy it; I shifted to a cheaper brand. I try to learn from every experience, and so perhaps that company had done me a service of a sort. If private companies misrepresent figures, believe me, the government is worse! I am convinced that this is the way such a program *would* be presented, and that people would react to this "bargain" exactly as represented in this novel.

19. Pencil corrected my spelling to "pedalled" from here on. This shows another aspect of the arrogance of copy-editing: my spelling was correct. Writer ignored this change.

20. Red circled and questioned the two references to General Mills, so Writer deleted them. Well, this reference was based on something that actually happened to us at the time I was writing the novel: our daughter brought home General Mills literature that had been distributed at her school. Now I come from a health-conscious family

—Tully's lifestyle mirrors much of my own, tandem bicycle and all—and the pronouncements of the likes of Dr. Stare and the sugar-merchants are ludicrous to me. A case can be made for sugar being one of the more dangerous substances circulated in our society. I happen to be diabetic myself, so I am sugar-conscious, and I avoid it wherever I can. But regardless of the merits of General Mills products, this *is* the way such a family would react; my portrayal is true. A deep ire gnawed in me when that happened to us. Maybe all the copyeds munch on sugar doughnuts while trampling on my manuscript, but they have no right to substitute their tastes for mine, and I don't want them diddling in my fiction like this.

21. Black says: "They have a home and a bike shed— + the mail arrives somewhere else." To which Red responds: "At a rural mailbox—straighten this out for confused copy-editors." What do you know! Red must have been exposed to some aspect of reality, somewhere along the way. Rural mailboxes *do* tend to be somewhat removed from their houses; sometimes you can spot a cluster of twenty of them at the mouth of a dirt road. I really didn't think I needed to explain *all* the facts of real-life to the city folk; perhaps I erred. Then Red adds: "No—small P.O.?" Yes, that too, Red; you're learning.

22. Red challenges this: "woodlot that close to a city? Put in explanation." Earlier, Red had a problem with the country being only ten miles out of the city. Well, I now live in a forest—ten miles out of town. Red seems to assume that all cities are the size of New York. Writer, who lives in a more rural setting, ignored this.

23. Purple says: "Scot is a first-class Male Chau-

vinist Pig—leave him that way, but modify it a bit." Writer left it, barely modified. I suspect Purple is on occasion a Female Chauvinist Pig.

24. Red inquires: "Do people really talk like that?" Yes, Red, the literate ones do. Those who say "breast" instead of "teat" when talking of a human female.

25. The last 27 words were cut by Blue.

26. Black protests: "Scot surprised they had a phone—yet he'd arranged to come by phone—but forgot. Incredible." Well, actually it was Scot's father who made the arrangement, though Scot knew of it, obviously. Such peripherals do on occasion get misplaced. Evidently Black never had a miscue of that nature, but that sort of thing happens to me often enough. Intelligent people tend to have a number of things on their minds, so they make minor errors that simpler-minded folk don't. Thus the "absent-minded professor" syndrome. But Red, evidently of Black's persuasion, agreed, curtly: "OUT." So out it came.

27. Black says: "Wherever the mail comes has a phone near it—ANOTHER PHONE." And Red says "Back at the house—explain in one-syllable words?" Writer simply deleted the whole business about the phones. Sigh—it's hard to know where to start, in addressing this copyeditorial preoccupation with minutiae. The scene made sense as I wrote it; why go through such contortions to revise it?

28. Pencil started crossing out sentences, but Red circled the whole paragraph, curtly saying "Rewrite." Writer simply cut it out entire.

29. Black says "Scot forgot he was banged by a car last week so he can't pick the girl up—he's just ridden 10 miles on a bicycle in one hour!" To which

Red responds: "Change." He circles these two
paragraphs, saying "OUT--give the kid a thrill." So
Writer changed it to "piggyback ride" and made it
possible. Here we go again! I was in a rollover in my
car in 1956; the roof was dented in six inches, and
the clearance for my head was six inches, so I figure
I came that close to never having a writing career. I
was lucky; I escaped with no more than a moment's
unconsciousness and a bruised shoulder. I was for
some time unable to lift that arm above head-
height, but below that level it was okay; I needed no
medication and wore no sling, and in several weeks
it healed. I gave Scot that injury, because I know its
nature. Riding a bicycle is feasible, especially when
the other party is doing the pedaling. Picking up a
child is not—but it's easy to forget until one makes
the attempt. This scene needed no modification.

30. This six-hundred-word sequence of the
child's problem was deleted by Black, who says:
"Neighbors on same block? Is this a farm or a house
on a city street? This whole scene with the kids and
the neighbors is silly." Now this is a very interesting
deletion. I had been asked to do a novel that was
rooted in conventional matters, remember, rather
than far-out space-opera stuff, so I kept it very close
to home—closer than any other I have done. But
Miss Black pronounces it silly. I think her attitude
is silly. First, farms *do* have neighbors, and acreage
is platted in large blocks. We do live in the forest
now—the forest we were making ready to move to
as I wrote this novel—and we do have neighbors,
who also live in the forest. Distances tend to be
greater than in the city, is all. Second, though Black
may feel the sequence is unrealistic, it is taken
directly from life: it was my own younger daughter
who got hit, and I was the one who went with her to

unravel the problem. I feel very strongly about the welfare of my daughters; we lost three babies before we had two we could keep, and they are all we will ever have. I am a peaceful man until my children are threatened; then all bets are off. I acted with restraint, considering the fury I felt. To have my little girl dash out with such joy of anticipation, to share her food and her home-made toy phone—and be treated like that, hurt and humiliated—well, it is evident that the copyeds did not understand, but I trust that those who care about children do.

31. This whole scene, too, was deleted. Pencil attached another pink slip, saying: "This whole incident makes no sense—is pages on a child's fight that appears to have no connection to the story—perhaps a vague comment on 'crowding' or a moral comment on the nastiness of 'some people'? Cut it?" To which Black replies: "I did." As though they had any right to pronounce judgment on the content of a novel, rather than spelling and typos! Very well—this, too, is taken exactly from life, and I remain angry about it. In the original episode, I called the police, and told them, politely, that if they could not protect my children from getting beaten up, I would do it my way. No, I wasn't bluffing. After that, things settled down somewhat. But let's address the issue raised by Pencil: is this sequence irrelevant to the story? That depends on the level you're reading it. If you assume that the only relevant material is what happens directly to the protagonist, then the byplay of children seems incidental. But if you are looking at the society in the larger sense, and at fundamental motives, the context should become clear. Why would a man desert Earth for a perhaps-hazardous life on another planet? Why would a whole family do it? Is it

from high moral principles—"Man deserves to
conquer the Galaxy, and I must do my part!"—or
is it more likely to be from the frustrations of a
lifestyle that is deteriorating on every level, from
job security to the safety of children, so that a
complete new start becomes attractive? I assumed
that some few would do it from principle, but that
the greater number would do it from an accumula-
tion of mundane reasons such as these shown here.
Certainly *we* fought through the situation, and in
due course—a couple of years later, when we could
manage it economically—moved out of that neighborhood without regret. Up here we have concentrated much of our effort on preventing
development around us, preferring *no* neighbors to
the kind we had. (Actually, we also had some of the
world's best neighbors; had we been able to dictate
which neighbors to keep and which to get rid of,
there are some we would gladly have kept. But the
good neighbors don't intrude on one's awareness
the way the bad ones do.) We did not step to
another planet, but the contrast between city life
and deep forest is about as substantial as this globe
presently offers. This is the way Tully and his wife
now feel—and their decision intimately affects
Scot. I feel these examples are relevant to the theme
I am developing here. It may be that I misjudged
the case—but I believe, for both legal and social
reasons, that I should have been allowed to present
it my way. In short, even if I was wrong to adapt this
sequence—and I do not concede that—these
copyeds had no business second-guessing my decision. This was, after all, my novel, not theirs. What
the hell did they think they were doing, hacking out
entire scenes?! Oh, yes—there is worse to come!

32. Pencil marked this paragraph up, and Red cut it. Naturally they didn't understand the point I was making here: that no one could any longer be certain of surviving, economically, on Earth. That the pressure was greatest on those with family responsibilities, with children to protect. Adding insult to injury, Red says that Janice's decision to emigrate is too sudden. Perhaps it is—after my detailed documentation of their situation, patterned after the one that caused *my* family to emigrate to the forest, is deleted.

33. Black says: "Scot phones Fanny to come!" to which Red responds "So?"

34. Pencil writes: "Usage of 'Earth' bothers me—makes it unnatural, far away." But Red responds: "Modern usage—copy editor is old fogy." What have we here—backstabbing among copyeds? It strikes me as akin to a falling-out of thieves. No, I'm not making this up; this particular exchange occurs on page 32 of my original manuscript. They really are starting to sink their teeth into each other, in the absence of any semblance of discipline exerted by Editor.

35. Black says: "Fanny comes—is this the same day? (If so, Tully has bicycled 40 miles, 20 with a person behind)." Red retorts: "Elapsed time has been implied—I suppose I have to spell it out." Well, I did show it, by using a break with a centered asterisk, which is the standard way to signify the passage of time between scenes. But Pencil had deleted my asterisk in response to Black's creation of a "Part II" here. Maybe writers should open a school for copyeds, to teach them at least the fundamental literary conventions before they practice their ignorance on an author's manuscript.

36.   The copyeds left this paragraph untouched, except for routinely doubling the "l" in "pedaling," and adding an "a" at the beginning of "esthetically," but Writer deleted the whole thing. Writers of the second rank do not necessarily appreciate the nuances of description or characterization—which is of course why they *are* second-rank.

37.   Black says: "For no apparent reason Fanny is now ready to go to the planet Conquest (look at her on p. 5)!" She is referring to the manuscript page; the scene occurs on page 23 of this version. It is in the opening, where Fanny expresses no interest in leaving Earth. Red agrees: "God knows that has to change!" So Writer included an explanation: she had read the literature and talked with Janice, and concluded Conquest should be better than Earth. Well, now—did I goof? Why *did* I set her up as a woman subject to changes of mind without apparent reason? Well, first, this *is* the way women sometimes appear to men; they have inner seasons that men simply don't understand. They don't necessarily give their reasons. Second, Fanny *does* have reason—and here I have to do what a writer does not like to do, and give away future plans. You see, I had a sequel novel in mind, titled *And What of Conquest?* in which the story of the colonization of that planet was to be traced. Tully and family went there—and, as we shall see later, so did Fanny, alone. Why? Because she perceived in Tully a man worth having. Fanny, as I am showing here, is a very poised, reserved, self-interested woman with very little conscience. She goes to Conquest because she means to take Tully for herself. You are appalled? Well, people like this do exist, and this *is* her motive. Naturally she doesn't give Scot her

reason! At this stage she expects to go with him, and then see about Tully when they are on Conquest. First things first, for she is very practical. First get off Earth, then make the conquest on Conquest. As you might imagine, there is quite a story to tell on Conquest. But Editor bounced it as "juvenile." It hardly seems so to me! But as it turned out, that rejection was fortunate. I did not then know that people very like Fanny were doing to *Earth?* what Fanny is doing to Scot. I trust this suffices to show that I did have reason for the manner I presented Fanny's change of mind. I *wanted* the reader to be slightly perplexed at this point, so he would remember and understand, later. This is another example of the difference between a writer and a copyed: the former plans ahead, while the latter sees only the moment. It's another reason why no copyed should mess with the author's text. I would be satisfied simply to have my text rendered into print with *no* copy-editing, and face the music for any trifling errors of punctuation anyone thinks I made. I was once an English teacher; this hardly makes me an expert, but I have encountered no copyed—or, for that matter, editor—who knows more about the language than I do. I would prefer to see the copyeds dispensed with, and the money saved thereby added to the advance paid the author. That would eliminate a headache and serve as an inducement for better writing. But publishers are wedded to their arcane and money-losing ways.

38. Black says derisively: "She's ready to marry Scot immediately." Yes she is—but she is merely using him. If Scot had more sense he'd realize that this really is too good to be true, and that this

marriage would be a disaster for him. Miss Pencil and Miss Black are perhaps unsympathetic to characterization of this nature. They don't care to concede that *any* woman would marry a man for cynical practical reasons, though they have to know it is true. Fortunately, most women are not like that, as we shall see later in this novel.

39. Red marked this paragraph: "Improve that." Writer simply eliminated it. Sigh; none so blind . . .

40. Black says querulously: "Scot is feeling better—can he now pick up the child? This is the same day? If so, Tully has now bicycled— Must be days later!" Yes it is, Miss Black; remember that asterisk?

41. Black says: "3 days later—Scot can't go to Conquest because of the implied morals charge stemming from the accident—beyond belief!! (Does P. Anthony *hate* women?)" To which Red responds: "It would seem obvious that any clod could tell Scot isn't colony material, morals charge or not. However, spell it out again." So Writer inserted a reference to failure of a psychological examination. Very well—the termites are evidently having some trouble digesting this matter, so I'll clarify my intent: I am making a covert protest to the ponderosity and irrelevance of the processes of bureaucracy. Beyond belief? Hardly! Ask any person who has been denied a job because of anonymous misinformation in a secret FBI file, or had his credit-rating downgraded because of a computer error. Scot assumes he is in trouble because of the accident report, and that may be—but it could also be a simple glitch in the system. What *I* find almost beyond belief is the attitude of Miss Black. No, I

don't hate women—but in her case I'm considering an exception.

42. Red cut these two sentences, since the rationale for Scot's rejection has been changed. This is an example of how one change, like one lie, necessarily begets another. My motto is: He edits best who edits least.

43. Black cut out the paragraph, and the following line. Evidently Miss Black has some trouble with the notion that a man can be either romantic or idealistic, or that a woman could be to blame for his loss. She is entitled to her sexist opinions—*but not at the expense of my novel.*

44. This is one of several three-dot ellipses I used. Today I might use four dots to indicate the end of the sentence following the omitted words "disturbed him deeply"—but I am rendering this text unchanged, deliberately, faults and all.

45. Red says: "Get rid of this garbage and add something longer and more believable." Writer simply cut it.

46. The copyeds really took off on this one! Pencil says: "No explanation is given for Fanny's behavior. She was reluctant to emigrate. Why did she change her mind, let alone go off alone? Again, 'the nastiness of some people' seems the only answer. Cheap solution." And Black says: "Scot finally thinks to telephone Fanny—only to discover she's gone to Conquest—her parents think he's with her—they took her to the station, but didn't even look for him—they assumed he was on the train! Yet she was leaving home for good—their only daughter—they'd never see her again!" Right, Miss Black. When Fanny told them that Scot was already on the train, were they going to say "We

don't believe you—go locate him and bring him
back so we know you aren't lying, you disreputable
creature"? No—they trusted her to know what she
was doing, and they were blinded by love and tears;
it never occurred to them that Scot might *not* be
aboard. They are ordinary, caring people who believe in their daughter, odd as that may seem to ye
copyeds. The parents, like Scot (and Tully), were
completely deceived. Fanny is a manipulator; she
ran one extremely neat, cynical operation here—
and surely she is going to bring similar misery to
Tully on Conquest. Our Miss Black concludes:
"Why did Fanny go? —Yes, why hadn't she told
him? Why didn't P. Anthony tell us?" Well, Fanny
went, as I explained in a prior note, in order to nab
Tully, whom she had come to perceive as a winner
in the course of twenty miles on a tandem bike. He
had all the qualities she liked in his brother Scot,
plus some significant strengths where Scot had
weaknesses. She didn't tell Scot because he would
only have made an unpleasant fuss, and she doesn't
like fusses. I didn't tell the reader for the same
reason the author of a mystery doesn't announce
who-done-it on page five. I think, in any event, that
my explanation would have been wasted on these
rampaging females. They were more interested in
arguing than in answers; they never bothered to ask
me directly. I never saw these notes or even knew of
their existence until months after the novel was
published. If they had really wanted to clarify the
novel, why did they keep their questions a secret
from me? Because I might have refuted their
objections—exactly as I am doing now? And they
profess not to know Fanny's motive, these conniv-
ing bitches! What hypocrisy!

47.   Pencil crossed out the reference to the little girl, and Black says: "Scot waters the garden—if he misses a spot the plants *wilted.*" Apparently Black is uninformed about farming, too; young, tender plants are quick to wilt in the sun, if not properly watered. I have gardened, on and off, for years, and of course I was raised on a farm. Whatever possessed Black to challenge *this*? The arrogance of ignorance amazes me! But Writer, who may have had more exposure to rural life, compounds the error in his version by having the tomato plants promptly wilt *when watered.* The only rationale I can see for such a phenomenon is the drooping of plants in a downpour; they let their leaves down to avoid getting bashed by the force of the storm. Plants are smarter than we think; as a vegetarian I appreciate their qualities. But a gentle watering on a sunny day never made *my* tomatoes wilt!

48.   Red says: "Check energy book for a better system." The system described is the one we had at the time; it was operative and satisfactory, and cut our water-heating cost substantially. We finally got an electric timer that turned on the pump automatically in the morning, and off in the evening, but Tully hadn't yet gotten around to that. I could say a great deal about solar water-heating systems, but for now will merely point out that the "best" systems can be quite expensive, so most people settle for second-best. A highly-efficient solar water-heating system is no bargain if it saves you $500 a year in electricity but costs $15,000 to set up; it will spring a leak before it earns out.

49.   Black observes: "Scot was alone on his block—is this a farm? Scot talks to a neighbor in the next block." Very well, once more over this:

here in the Florida country the forest is platted in blocks one mile on a side. These are subdivided as convenient. Thus we have one immediate neighbor across the street, and three more (in three directions) a quarter-mile distant. We are on speaking terms with all of them, and exchange favors, such as feeding each other's animals when someone has to be away. We are the only residence on our block of 30 acres, but other blocks have several farms. I assume that similar setups exist elsewhere on the continent. Actually I visualized Tully's farm as closer in to town than ours, so he is near "the fringe of suburbia"—that is, not that far out of the more densely settled region, but definitely in the country. Got it straight now, city-girl?

50.   These lamps, again, are taken from my own experience. Faced with that short deadline for completing the novel, I found it easier to use the things I already knew, rather than inventing new ones as I might otherwise have preferred to do. The farm that I was raised on, in the Green Mountains of New England, had no electricity, so we used wood-burning stoves and kerosene lamps that operate exactly as described. But Writer thought he knew better, so he added this sentence: "After being pressurized with a little gadget attached to one side of the base, it burned with a pure white light." He's thinking of another kind of lamp. He should have let well enough alone.

51.   Red says: "Dumb. Worry about vandals, maybe, or mention trees and bushes shading unit part time." Well, of course the trees and house do shade the ground, which is why less sunlight reaches it; I thought that was obvious. But Writer took another route, having Scot install a hand pump for

water circulation. Now *that's* dumb! Let me explain a little more about solar water-heating, as we have used both the pump and the pumpless kind, and I do know whereof I speak. If you use a pump, you must run it pretty much continuously, because only a small amount of water heats at a time. You have to keep it circulating, the warm water being brought down to the tank and the cold water being forced up to the hot copper pipes of the collector. An electric pump is continuous, but a hand pump is not; you'd have to stand there all day pumping, slowly. So the practical answer is to put your collector below the holding-tank; then the warm water circulates automatically up and the cold down. That is the best of all systems, completely automatic; if a cloud hides the sun, the heating stops and the water stops moving, preserving the warm water in the tank. Once again, the arrogance of ignorance has struck, rendering my sense into nonsense. Why do people who haven't done something assume they know better than one who has?

52.   Now here is one I wince at: it makes it seem that he is in the city. He isn't; the civilized amenities, such as electricity and phone, emanate from the city, so he feels their impact out here. Bad phrasing.

53.   Black says: "Beauty knocks on door—she doesn't want to spend the night outside—what about the empty houses in that block?" Well, Miss Black, if you were a lone woman, would you trust yourself to a deserted house that could be hiding any man or beast and would have no civilized amenities? Or would you seek company you could trust, so that at least you could sleep without fear?

54.   Red circled this, with a question mark, and

Writer excised it. In case it is confusing to present
readers, I'll clarify the reference: When Fanny
suddenly agreed to go to Conquest, Scot could
hardly believe it, as he had expected her demurral.
Now he sees this woman, who evidently expected to
be turned down, reacting similarly, and he under-
stands. Experience is a great teacher.

55.   Red exclaims: "Gak! Do something about
that." So Writer fudged it some. Now Wanda is a
special person, honest with herself and others; I
portray her as I see her, in her hour of desperation.
She'd rather make a gift than suffer a theft, of
whatever nature. Specifically, she'd rather give a
man sex than get raped. I respect that. Another
woman might react differently; perhaps *most* wom-
en would. But this is not most women, this is
Wanda, an individual. What is there about this
portrayal that warrants this illiterate "Gak"?

56.   Red remarks wryly "He didn't even give her
a blanket, the cheap S.O.B." Well, Scot is simply
not smart about things like that—phones, blankets,
women or whatever. He just didn't think of it. He is
in fact a pretty unlikely hero. Fortunately, heroism
is not defined by things like that, as we shall see.

57.   Black says: "He checked around the farm
outside—with a stalled car *down the street*! Is it a
farm or a town?" Very well, ma'am, let's go to the
big dictionary: my 1913 Funk & Wagnalls, bought
second-hand for me as a gift for my tenth birthday,
over forty years ago and still my favorite reference.
This has several definitions of "street," one of
which is: "A public road or highway extending
through a considerable tract of country." As a
synonym it lists "Road." Now where the hell is the
problem, Miss Black? If that word "street" both-

ered you, why didn't you simply change it to "road"? I wouldn't have objected; upon reconsideration, I think "road" is the more appropriate term. But no, you had to Make an Issue—again. Don't you have better uses for your time than this? Or were you just trying to impress Editor by making mountains of molehills? As I understand it, you were hired right after this novel was accepted *as it stood*—whereupon you sought to prove yourself by quibbling it to death. Miss B, your kind should be abolished.

58. "This is springtime," Black remarks. Indeed it is; what of it? Do you have a point to make, or are you hinting at something?

59. This passage about stealing—Pencil, Blue, Red and Purple took off on this, and deleted it entire. They concluded that it didn't make sense. Doesn't it? Or is this a nuance that no one at this establishment was equipped to comprehend? Where was Black, on this one? When something ridiculous is going on, she's usually right in the thick of it. Ah, well—maybe she was in the Lady's Room at the moment.

60. Red circled this 150-word dialogue about decency, remarking that *he* was uncomfortable with it, and cut it all out. I'm not surprised. As far as I can tell, none of the folk associated with this outfit have much to do with decency.

61. Red crossed out the last two words, labeling them "crap." Need I comment?

62. Ah—Miss Black is back from the Lady's Room. Here she crosses out three lines. No, wait— that's *Blue* doing that.

63. *Now* Black is back! "He received a *letter* from Tully—63 light-years away! (And did he men-

tion Fanny, by chance?)" Sigh—I see I'll have to
clarify the obvious again. Because Conquest *is* 63
light-years away, there is no way to transmit a
message by radio or beam; it would take 63 years to
arrive. But the MT shuttles are going back and forth
regularly, carrying colonists there, returning empty.
Empty MT's, per the pun. So Tully sends a physical
letter back; there's plenty of room for it, and the
shuttle is going to Earth anyway. This is the only
feasible type of communication. No, Tully didn't
mention Fanny; he's a decent man who doesn't
want to rub salt in the wound.

64.   Here is one they should have challenged,
and didn't. When we built our new house in the
forest, we discovered that there are no sewers out
here. Most country houses are on septic tanks;
Tully's house should have been too. But composting
refuse is a good alternative.

65.   Writer killed them off instead. I regard this
as gratuitous violence.

66.   Blue cut most of three paragraphs.

67.   Red exclaims: "Wash it, you nincompoop!"
Um, Red, I'm tempted not to break this news to
you, but my conscience compels me: the problem
with many of these poisons is that they are ab-
sorbed by the leaves of the plants, and therefore
cannot be washed off. But you go ahead and wash
and eat it if you want to.

68.   Red marked this entire scene for deletion,
but Purple said "STET or whatever." Yes, Purple,
that was the correct term; Writer left the passage in,
except for the song. That could be a correct decision; I assumed the song was in the public domain,
but if it's not, then it shouldn't be quoted. Black,
meanwhile, has a sour note: "Bugs eating lettuce—

Wanda says let's stomp on them—Scot is chagrined that he doesn't think of this brilliant solution?" That's right, Miss B; wouldn't *you* be?

69.   Black again: "Only when Scot stays outside at night does he realize that when they're in the house at night someone could sneak up on them!" Right on, Black! The obvious can be the hardest thing to recognize—which is why women disrobe in lighted apartments with uncurtained windows, providing the men of the neighborhood with nightly entertainment. Ever do that yourself?

70.   "Prowler comes and goes—does nothing," Black remarks. "Scot checks area where prowler had been. Sure enough, there were footprints in the dirt—SURE 'NUFF!!" To which Red adds: "He expects maybe tire tracks?" All right, enjoy your feeble sarcasm, folks. In starlight innocent things may appear menacing, and the mind's eye can generate a human shape where only a moving branch exists. Would you have Scot *not* check the region? Then what is the basis for your ridicule? Forgive me if I'm getting paranoid, but somehow I perceive something other than helpful literary criticism operating here. In fact, I see something other than proper publishing practice operating throughout.

71.   "Do *something* about that," Red says, so Writer cuts it. I remind my readers that these notes are only samples; spot cuts are so common that it would be tedious to document them all. I have not found *one single page* of my manuscript unmolested. What, incidentally, was so bad about this passage?

72.   "Wanda suggests digging holes and covering them up—to protect the house. Scot thinks this is

INGENIOUS!" Black sneers. Red responds: "So
he's still stupid. So?" No, folks, Scot isn't stupid;
he's just an ordinary guy, learning as he goes. What
he does makes more sense to me than what this
clutch of would-be critics is doing here; I'd certainly
rather have him for a neighbor than *them*. But Red
does add one valid note: what Wanda describes is
not a deadfall.

73.   This entire 1,000-word scene, from the time
they go upstairs to this point, was eliminated by
Writer. Pencil says: "This whole discussion of sleeping vs. screwing seems *very* dated, but worse, very
drag-g-ed out. Boredom sets in on the 3rd paragraph." Black says: "I agree! Three pages of shall
we, shan't we—terrible." And Red says: "Yes." It is
evident that none of these folk have any patience
with the struggle of two people to come to terms
with themselves and their relationship. Well, I
prefer to let the reader judge; did boredom really set
in on the third paragraph? Is the scene terrible? I'm
sure I'll be hearing if this material is really that bad.
Meanwhile, I'm inclined to trust my own judgment,
which says that sexual engagement is no light
matter, and that characterization of this nature is
vital. We have to see how Scot handles his personal
commitments, in order to understand the basis for
his later actions, which affect the whole country.

74.   Black says: "'That's what I like about you,
Scot, you're a normal male.' HE IS!" To which Red
replies: "A normal prick, yes."

75.   Black continues: "Scot's digging, Wanda's
gathering wood. She pitches a shovelful of dirt at
him! (Impossible.)" To which Red responds: "No,
he isn't digging—you missed a sentence." Yep—
she doesn't have time to read carefully, but she

certainly has time to carp. How typical. But Red
carps too: "Cutesy-poo. Do something." And *I* say:
Yes, it is cutesy—but real-life dialogue gets that
way. Ordinary folk aren't as clever as copyeds.

76.   Black says: "They didn't talk 'cause they
didn't want to make any noise—they ate potato
salad. The rest of the neighborhood is making
noise." Red responds: "Well, potato salad isn't very
noisy."

77.   "THE NEIGHBORHOOD AGAIN" Black
exclaims indignantly, tossing her ebony tresses, but
Red responds soothingly, "The term does not refer
only to city blocks, you know." Purple is less
charitable: "Dumb copy-editor."

78.   Despite my objections to Miss Black's objections about the locale, I do feel that some of this
is imprecise. Obviously I was thinking partly of the
neighborhood I left, as well as of the one I was
coming to. You can hear voices and cars and dogs at
a distance of half a mile, but they have to be pretty
loud and you have to listen carefully. Obviously
Scot and Wanda *are* listening carefully now; still, I
am not quite at ease with this. If I were reworking
this, instead of showing it exactly as it was, I would
delete the "voices talking."

79.   "Scot has her in a bear hug—she's unconscious," Black says. "HE DIDN'T KNOW SHE'D
STOPPED STRUGGLING." So?

80.   Both Black and Purple had trouble with this
entire interrogation. Black says, "The triteness of
the interrogation of the girl intruder—this is all
padding. SCOT ADMIRES IT!" Purple says: "Get
some decent and less male-chauvinistic questions."
That's an interesting remark, since Wanda is doing
the questioning here. Maybe I'm dense; I just don't

see what's so male-chauvinistic about questions
like "Can you sit up?"; "Who are you?"; "Are you
hungry?"; and "Why were you wandering around
our yard?" Those were the ones asked on the page
where this comment was penned. Maybe Purple
considered the tone of the complete interrogation
to be male-chauvinistic, though it was conducted
by a woman. As for it being trite, the reader will
have to judge; how *do* you question someone in this
situation? Certainly it was not written as padding; I
was trying desperately to keep this novel short,
without sacrificing necessary elements.

81. Ouch! Downtown is ten miles away. I was
raised in the country, and we walked one and a half
miles to reach our mailbox, and four miles to town,
but ten miles is not a reasonable distance for Wanda
to walk alone to pick up an old newspaper. As Miss
Black would say—well, let's just let the subject
drop.

82. Ouch again! I had definitely slipped in my
thinking back to the metropolitan setting. Miss
Black does after all have a point, much as it galls me
to admit it.

83. I perceive a reader challenge developing
here: if two months have passed, hasn't the lettuce
matured yet? The answer is that they are staggering
their plantings, spacing them out so as always to
have new plants developing as the old ones mature.
In Florida, a garden can be maintained the year
around; the farther north you go, the more limited
the season becomes. I see this as a southern region,
not necessarily Florida—you don't see much snow
in Florida—but with a fairly extensive lettuce
season.

84. Now, mysteriously, the marks and com-

ments are thinning out; I don't know whether the copyeds in their wisdom decided that my text was improving, or whether they simply ran out of carps. (Maybe my confession that Miss Black did have half a point about the city-country confusion mollified her?) But here Blue changed "Negro" to "black." But reference to his race was deleted from the published version. Like sharks, these people seem to pounce on whatever gobbet has already been touched, each one adding his chomp. Now Brother Paul, here about to be introduced, is perhaps the most important single character I have generated; he is the main figure in my quartermillion word novel *Tarot* (published in three volumes, to my dismay; it was written as one) and appears in the *Cluster* series, which shares the framework that spreads across nine diverse volumes, with others contemplated. I don't like major figures getting messed-over.

85. Blue deleted this 100-word exchange. No reason given.

86. Here I used the subjunctive mood where it does not belong. Make that "was preaching" etc.

87. Blue deleted these 50 words.

88. Blue deleted these 50 words too. I don't think Bluebeard likes Brother Paul.

89. Purple exclaims "Do *something* about that!" and Red says "Gak!" so out came the whole paragraph. Now it happens that I have done composting, too; the compost pile assimilates the least-appetizing refuse and converts it to the soil on which most landbound life ultimately depends. It is a marvel, physically and philosophically. This is my favorite concept of this novel. What does it rate from these copyeds? An exclamation of disgust, and

excision from the text. Know what I think? I think
these folk have souls that reek of manure and
garbage, and they desperately need composting so
that they can learn to perceive the significance of a
compost pile. Meanwhile, annoyed that this concept was cut, I put it in *Tarot*, where it survives to
this day—and not one reader has cried "Gak!" to
me.

90.   Ye copyeds had another field day with this
sequence. Pencil says of this paragraph: "You believe this—you'll find the premise of this book
believable." Red says: "Right on!" Black says: "The
'thugs'' behavior is not believable. Scot's thinking
of p. 96 [the manuscript page—page 109 of this
book] is silly." To which Purple (maybe Red—
sometimes they're hard to distinguish) says "No
more unbelievable than the rest of the plot, but try
to liven it up a bit." It seems that not one of them
was willing to let the reader be the judge, or to let
the author handle his novel his own way, right or
wrong.

91.   The published version had Brother Paul
hurting the men somewhat—which misses the
point. The truly proficient martial artist can subdue
others efficiently *without* hurting them, and Brother
Paul is no hypocrite. Writer evidently didn't catch
on that it is a deliberately crude, TV-violence type
scene that is nevertheless concluded by pacifistic
means. You don't see that as often. The point made
here is not the merit of gratuitous violence, but that
of competent pacifism. I was raised as a Quaker
(The Religious Society of Friends), and a guiding
principle of Quakerism is to seek the nonviolent
solution. I did not join that faith, but I remain
impressed by its tenets, and they do guide my life in
subtle ways. As an agnostic I am not against
religion, just apart from it.

92. Most of this paragraph was deleted by Blue. Any hint of philosophy is anathema, it seems.

93. Writer changed this to a .25 automatic pistol with a magazine of six cartridges. I don't remember why I set up the gun as I did, but I normally draw from reality unless I have reason for fantasy. I believe I had reference to a derringer of this description—the kind of tiny gun that can kill. People tend to assume that all handguns are standard; they are not.

94. Writer deleted this prayer, apparently objecting to any religious expression. I am, as I said, agnostic, professing no belief in any religion or any supernatural phenomenon, but I respect those who *do* believe. Brother Paul is a deeply religious man, and so I portray him as he is. I do not feel it is the place of the writer to impose his private religious, political or moral code on the reader; thus you would not know from the text of the novel that I do not believe in God. I *do* feel it is the place of the writer to characterize people realistically, and I did my best with Brother Paul. This *is* the attitude Brother Paul has, and I daresay he's a better man than I am. He does pray openly when he feels it is appropriate—but *only* then. Nobody else had any business castrating him like this, cutting off his prayer. It is a matter of artistic integrity—a concept evidently foreign to these revisionists.

95. Black can't handle this. "Beethoven's 9th on a piccolo! (where did he get the piccolo?)—No—he's whistling, but it sounds like a piccolo—perfect pitch—while he's stacking wood (150 pound logs?)" Here we go again! Miss Black evidently was so eager to pan this scene that she started her note before completely reading the passage, then had to correct herself as she went

along. I've commented before on her evident motive: the sheer need to make her mark, regardless of the good of the novel. Here her ignorance about country life betrays her again. Brand is not at this point hoisting a 150-pound log, he's stacking split wood. To trace the process of reduction, that I did not feel was necessary in the novel (never underestimate the ignorance of the copied!): the 150-pound log was four feet long, a handy size for hauling in from the forest. It was then sawed into three sixteen-inch-long billets, each weighing about 50 pounds. These were split into quarters, each quarter weighing about twelve and a half pounds. It is these quarters Brand is stacking as he whistles. He's a powerful man; he can pick up such a piece of wood with one hand without bursting out in sweat or gasping from the strain. *I* do it all the time, preparing wood for our stove, and I'm not as strong as Brand is. This whole process, like so much of what I present in this novel, is taken directly from my own experience. I know whereof I speak, here. Yes, the whistling too: certainly it is possible to play the theme from Beethoven's Ninth on a piccolo; I can do it on the recorder, which is a flutelike instrument, or on the harmonica, or I can whistle it. I'm no musician, so I don't do it well, but anyone would recognize it. Brand is better at this than I am, so he does it well. You don't *have* to render Beethoven with a full orchestra; it's excellent music however you do it, and a haunting theme. I believe the song for the United Nations uses that tune: "Walk beside me, O my brother, . . ." Not only is it *possible* on such instruments, it's *easy*—one of the readiest classical themes to adapt. As Miss Black would have known, had she bothered to try it herself. Meanwhile, Writer checked with his wife—yes, his note to that effect is right there on the manuscript!—and she evidently reassured him about this point, so he left this scene in. This whole challenge was much ado about nothing. In fact, this whole blundering editing job—but I'm starting to froth at the mouth!

96. But our dear Miss Black simply can't let it alone. "Given the state of the world," she asks plaintively, "where did he learn these melodies—he's illiterate." To which Purple responds, with appropriately purple prose: "He isn't deaf, you jackass." Which misses the point of Black's objection; with the power out, there will be few radios playing for Brand to listen to, to pick up tunes. However, this is no problem: Brand wasn't born yesterday, and he has had most of his life to listen when there *was* plenty to listen to, before MT changed things. Melodies learned in childhood remain in adulthood.

97. Blue and Pencil marked this whole 500-word discussion of women for deletion, but Writer digested it down and kept part of it. Let me take this opportunity to clarify part of what I was doing here: the business about letting a small woman struggle with a tough chore like grinding grain. Naturally I've had considerable experience on exactly the type of hand-grinder described. Not only does it produce flour, it develops the arm and chest muscles. Well, Lucy craves a larger bosom, having correctly ascertained that this is the way to a certain man's eye. Childbirth and nursing will increase the mass of the mammary tissue—but what's a girl to do before that? Lucy realizes that the grinder represents her opportunity to develop the muscle-sheath

underneath the breast, hence a more prominent outline. This is a recognized technique; the muscle boosts the breast outward, and the effect is similar to additional mammary in appearance, though not in function. So she grinds. It's hard work, but she's determined; she's playing for high stakes here. Brand, perceiving this, agrees. He sees what Scot does not: that Lucy, not Wanda, is the proper woman for Scot. But it is necessary for time to pass before the grinding and the situation do their work. Scot really *is* rather foolish about women, as men tend to be. Naturally the female copyeds don't want this sort of thing publicized; trade secrets are precious.

98. Red challenged this figure, not for the first time: he feels that not enough people are being shipped to account for the observed impact on Earth. Well, this is an accelerating thing—ten million in the first year, more thereafter—from this country alone. Within a decade, at this progression, the nation will be entirely depopulated. That seems fast enough to me. But what of the initial stage, when fewer than a million were gone, yet things seemed to be falling apart? That I perceive as more an effect of the huge energy strain on the nation, to support the MT effort. The society contracted rapidly, leaving the fringes to wither. To save power, electricity was cut off first from the less-economic farm regions, and that caused the residents there to vacate rapidly. Had Scot resided in a big city, he would have noted relatively little change. Since it is my purpose as a novelist to dramatize the situation, I have him out in the country where the cutback and depopulation are most apparent.

99. Actually, in *Tarot* I go into Brother Paul's

background more deeply, and it turns out that Paul actually *was* his prior name. Sometimes it works that way. But the symbolism and significance remain; he did assume a new meaning for the name, as we are about to see.

100. More recent theory has it that Paul was epileptic—but the principle is the same.

101. This 1,000-word scene of religious discussion is condemned by Red as "Elementary Sunday School" material and eliminated by Blue.

102. Red marked this "Balls" and adds: "Remarkable cures—throw in some garbage on that."

103. More recent research suggests that the lemmings have been unfairly characterized; they *don't* blindly charge into the sea. But it remains an evocative analogy.

104. "What does it all mean?" Red asks plaintively, and Writer reworked and digested this section down so that the thesis on which the novel is based hardly shows. I suspect that what it all means is that copyeds should not tackle a manuscript they do not comprehend. Would a surgeon operate without understanding what he is doing?

105. Red expresses objection to these two paragraphs. "Does he have to be quite so obviously a teat man?" Beauty is in the eye of the beholder; these paragraphs discuss breasts, face, skin, health, hair, legs, arms and torso—yet all Red perceives is "teats." Well, not quite all; Red adds "And an MCP to boot." I believe the initials stand for "Male Chauvinist Pig." Thus the mere act of noticing the attractive qualities of a woman makes a man an "MCP." And what of a woman who notices the attractive qualities of a man? Is she automatically a Female Chauvinist Pig? Must we be limited to

noticing only the *un*attractive qualities of the opposite sex, to avoid being branded chauvinist pigs?
Why do I have this nagging feeling that this so-
called "editing" is mainly an exercise in name-
calling by closet bigots?

106.   Well, they had done a little of it before
Brother Paul arrived, but he had made it more
scientific.

107.   Red circled this clause, saying in his ex-
pressive way: "Gak! Yeast gone bad and unable to
get more." Not so, Red; this, again, is from my own
experience. The yeast culture bubbles along as long
as you take care of it, as with any living thing. You
simply have to keep it reasonably cool (to avoid
overactivity) and keep diluting it with new flour
and water every few days; when you want to bake,
you take some of this mixture and put it in the mix
in lieu of new yeast. It's the same stuff, in a different
form. The practice of cultivating yeast, like that of
baking itself, has been largely forgotten in recent
times, but it's the kind of thing that makes perfect
sense in the context of this novel. As a boy, I kept
my own yeast-culture, and every so often I would
eat some of it directly. I called it "fizzly pudding,"
for it fizzled on the tongue.

108.   Naturally they couldn't let this revelation
pass! Having missed the point about the grinding
and Scot's best choice of women, the copyeds are
enraged to have it revealed here. Pencil says "This
is all truly ridiculous. Must we?" Red says: "Both
MCP's—on Brand it's logical" and, on Scot's comment about there being more to a woman than a
bust, "Nice that he finally discovered the fact." But
as I have noted, Scot always was aware of that; it's
Red who is evidently hyper about "teats." So I agree

with Pencil: this is all truly ridiculous—only I'm not talking about the narrative. But Red isn't quite finished; Black (naturally you couldn't keep *her* out of this!) is looking for a better word than "bastard," so Red obligingly suggests: "asshole? prick?" Writer simply eliminated the whole sequence. Actually, "bastard" is not the ideal word; technically it means a person who was born when his parents weren't married, and if this signals a fault, it can hardly be in the person, who had no control over his generation. But it *is* a commonly used term for denigration or, in this case, admiration, and so I elected in this instance to go for realism rather than proper use.

109. Yes, you guessed it: all of the text following my last note was deleted by Writer.

110. Black remarks smugly: "Lucy reveals she stole Scot's car (that's what I thought when she fell into the pit and Scot thought he recognized her)" to which Red retorts: "So? We've already established that Scot is stupid." Very well: when I first drafted this novel, Lucy *wasn't* the one who stole his car. Then it occurred to me that there would be a certain poetic justice in this, so I pondered making her the car-thief. My wife, as I recall, was doubtful: misuse of coincidence, etc. But art prevailed over coincidence, and I made the change. Then, to be fair to the reader (a thing ye copyeds wouldn't understand) I put in the early references about her familiarity. That way, the perceptive readers could make the connection immediately, while others could wait for the revelation. This is not a mystery novel, but in ordinary fiction there can be elements of that. I feel this change worked out well, and I have no trouble myself, believing that Lucy is the

car-thief; had it not worked out, I would have changed it back. So Miss Black caught on early (she claims); that's no sign that the author of the novel is stupid. Some readers will be surprised at the revelation, learning Lucy's identity for the first time; that's no sign that those readers are stupid either. I like to write my novels so that they can be appreciated on more than one level, and this is an example of that. There are also different philosophic levels, that have been giving the copyeds even more trouble.

111.   Red circles these two paragraphs and says: "More psychology and less fucking." It's pretty plain what level *he's* reading on. So these paragraphs were eliminated.

112.   Pencil, Blue and Red ganged up on this scene and eliminated it, and Writer had them get married instead—just like that. This evidently is their notion of realism. Scot has in effect been jilted twice, and is on a double rebound, but suddenly he's sure? My portrayal is not intended to make of him an MCP, but a genuinely hurt and uncertain man who is not about to make the same mistake a third time. This may be ungallant, but it is realistic —and it's about time he got realistic. So he does *not* suddenly marry the car-thief; he takes time to be sure this is the proper course. Taking that extra measure of time to make an important decision has saved me an enormous amount of grief over the course of my life, and I'm sure it will do the same for Scot. But of course these copyeds have not been noted for thinking before shooting off their multi-colored pens.

113.   Blue marked this entire technical discussion for deletion, but Pencil said, "STET"—that is,

keep it in. In fact, Editor called me to ask for a
repetition of this explanation later in the novel, as
they didn't understand it. This shows how the first
instinct of these people is simply to cut what they
don't understand, regardless of its importance to
the novel. This is idiocy, of course—but it *does*
seem to be the operative principle. Meanwhile, Red
circled the reference to ease of sabotage and said:
"Really? Bullshit." Evidently Red thinks he knows
something I don't, again.

114. Red says, "*Show* the action, don't put it
offstage," so Writer amplified the scene. Now I had
reason for doing it the way I did—but let's let that
wait for now. Have no fear, I will discuss this at
length before the end of the novel.

115. Red says "Try to get this mildly plausible."
So Writer has Scot fight through, but fail to rescue
Donald. I have instead saved this material for a
flashback that occurs late in the novel. Why did I, a
writer who abhors unnecessary obfuscation, do
something as artificial as this? Why did I skimp on
detail here, where it seems most relevant? Well, my
reason obviously bypassed the massed wisdom of
ye copyeds—except, oddly, Pencil, who seemed to
perceive it, but disagreed. I'll clarify everything—
when I get to that flashback.

116. Red circled most of the fourth sentence of
this paragraph, saying: "Bullshit! They came in
from the outside. Rewrite this to comply with
history." Now this is an interesting view. History
happens to be a hobby of mine, and the largest
section of my private library is devoted to it—
several hundred books. Put very simply, in the fifth
century A.D., when the Huns overran Slavic and
Germanic Europe and contributed to the disinte-

gration of the Western Roman Empire, England
was left unprotected. The Teutonic Angles, Saxons
and Jutes raided and then colonized the island,
finally becoming dominant; hence the "Angle-
Land" became "England," as Brother Paul clarified
earlier in this novel. Actually, the invaders merged
with the prior population and, with an overlay of
Norman stock, became the modern-day civilized
kingdom. America was colonized by this British
amalgam, and by peoples from other regions, and
now there is further merging. Here in *Earth?* I am
showing cultural as well as technological reversion,
with modern stock assuming the attributes of ancient tribes, though of course this is only a semblance, not the actual original tribes. Details differ,
naturally. Red's comment, in the present context, is
nonsense. I suspect that he simply misunderstood
my thesis, and thought that I was saying that the
real Saxons formed from the remnants of some
prior civilization. He read carelessly, and in the
arrogance of his ignorance assumed that *I* was the
one talking nonsense.

117. "Why not Mongols? Or Zulus?" Red demands. Red has been harping on this, in prior
marginal notes. Now the Mongols are one of my
favorite historical subjects; my novel *Steppe* is
based on them. But the Mongols never invaded
America. Neither did the Zulus. The Saxons did, in
the manner I have described. Our contemporary
American heritage is thus more Saxon than Mongol
or Zulu, so that is the identification made here.
However, I do later have reference to the Huns.

118. "Saxons aren't nomads. (And nomads
don't, anyway.)," Red objects. Some things it seems
I must clarify again for you, Red. These aren't

exactly Saxons; they are a regressed, reconstituted tribe that our folk have chosen for convenience to call Saxons. Whatever the historical Teutons may have been at whatever stage of their evolution, these contemporary people are of necessity somewhat nomadic. They do take care of their horses—as did the true nomads of history, such as the Mongols.

119. Black says: "Man's arthritis abates because he is more satisfied with his life?" To which Purple replies: "Read up on medicine—it happens." True—which is why I mentioned it in the novel.

120. Of this statement of faith, Red says: "Totally unbelievable, but can it be improved?" And Purple says: "[Editor] or no, I won't have that gullible a priest. He was a city slicker just a couple of years ago." Now I could get into an extended discussion of what can be believed in the name of religion, such as crackers and wine converting into literal flesh and blood of a man almost two thousand years dead, but let's just say that I find this Priest of Lugus perfectly credible. He may also be insane, but he is credible. People have an enormous capacity to believe in what benefits them materially or stokes their self-esteem. Red himself, for example, believes that he is a good editor and an informed person.

121. "A crop of farmers led by Attilla of the soil," Purple chortles, evidently unaware (like some contemporary celebrities) that the name is properly accented on the first syllable and is spelled with a single "l."

122. Which is a deliberate reversal of the original maxim.

123. Black protests about this whole situation:

"Technology still transmitting people—with all the apparatus that implies—AT THE SAME TIME— Barbarian tribes building camps and fighting with bows and arrows. THIS REALLY IS NOT BE-LIEVABLE." Purple responds: "Ask one of your Eskimos about that sometime." Precisely—we have barbarian tribes in remote jungles today. I marvel at the sheltered life Miss Black has evidently led. She finds reality unbelievable. Perhaps she prefers it that way. But why, O Lord, did she have to be inflicted on my manuscript?

124.   Black is aghast: "The Druid priest is a former lawyer—the King, his superior, is 'God knows what' who believes in magic—a cloud passes in front of the sun—the King thinks its magic and lets the Druid priest have his way. [THIS IS DE-SCRIBED AS AN IMPRESSIVE MANEUVER.]" (Those are her brackets, not mine.) Exactly, Miss Black. What is your point?

125.   Black again, outraged: "The whole joust with its false conclusion is silly. This followed by a no sleeping no eating contest!" Purple responds "But takes up space." Now it is interesting that these folk who seek so constantly to advise me on realism and history do not recognize the point: This tribe has adopted its mode of Celtic culture, and is true to that mode. This includes acceptance of some magic, single-combat, and an appeals proce-dure of exactly the nature described here. Contem-porary folk may feel it is "silly," but this *is* the way the Celts did it. Let's face it, copyeds: you can't condemn me for being untrue to history (rightly or wrongly) and also condemn those scenes that *are* true to history. And I remind you again that regardless of the merit of a particular scene, or your

private opinion of it, this is *my* novel, not yours, and you should not be interfering with it. If you believe you can write better novels yourselves, by all means do so—on your own contracts. The attempt might have a salutary effect on your attitude.

126. Red protests: "You've already said that about 6 times." Really? That the emigration of Earth's best and brightest might have caused the reversion? Seems to me that when I mentioned this before, it was to present the notion that the diminishing population caused the regression, without comment on the quality of the exodus. I could be wrong. I'd like to see page-and-line references to those prior six times, Red.

127. "But chest muscles aren't used in carrying—back muscles are. Put something less banal in there," Red says. Well, now; it depends how you carry. Having kinked my back more than once by lifting a heavy load improperly, I have learned caution, and I now try to lift with a vertical torso. For that, and for carrying, I believe I use my arm and chest muscles, which are better developed than those of most other writers. I did 30 chins in the morning on my study rafter, and 75 Japanese pushups three times a week until tendinitis wiped them out. I don't do any back-muscle exercises. So I believe Lucy could carry things the same way I do—and would have trouble if she lacked those chest muscles. But that's not really the point. The point is, how do these men see it? They are making polite conversation, seeking some way out of their dilemma. Scot could be in error on this matter—but he still could say it, and the Saxon could agree. I don't believe it's banal. Here we are seeing the

gradual mellowing of their contact, as the two men come to respect each other. But this is of course an aspect of characterization that Red is not equipped to perceive.

128.   Black corrects my "we" to "us." Yes, I'll buy that; I can still foul up on we/us and who/whom even though I once taught such usage. Were it any character *except* this educated Druid speaking, I would not accept the correction, however, because most people do not use the language perfectly.

129.   But nobody corrected this to "vassalage." Well, consider it corrected now; I, too, have a more critical perception when editing than when writing, and my base of information is broader than that of these meddlers.

130.   "Scot's wife is pregnant?" Black demands. "Is Scot married to Lucy?" Red retorts: "Never heard of common-law marriage?" I suppose I'll have to comment. Yes, Scot and Lucy are married now, and she really is pregnant. But it is my preference to have the reader wonder at this reference, exactly as Miss Black does. (Women do prefer to be married before being pregnant, for some reason.) If Scot is married, when did it happen? Or is he just *saying* it? What's going on here? Well, a minor mystery is what's going on here, for now.

131.   "The Saxon's sister is matching up with Brand—" Miss Black protests, evidently sneaking a peek ahead. "This is getting just too silly!" "Agreed," Purple agrees. "Banal dialogue," Red puts in banally. But Writer keeps that matchup. The fact is, Brand has expressed his interest in finding a suitable woman several times, and here for the first time we encounter an available one of the required type. The matchup is not unreasonable; it has been

a long time coming. One might protest that the encounter is coincidental—but the fact is, almost *any* initial encounter between people is coincidental, and the majority of contacts are transitory, such as folk passing each other on the street. But when this random sampling produces a promising prospect, the average person follows it up, and thereafter it is not coincidental. The factors that brought me to attend college, when I had not planned on a college education, were to a considerable extent coincidental, and largely random events put me on a dishwashing crew with a coed whose attendance was perhaps similarly unlikely. Such an encounter probably would not happen again, if our lives were rerun with any modification at all. But as I retyped this novel for this republication, we celebrated our 28th wedding anniversary, and had our 33rd by the time of publication. Miss Black would surely find this silly. Miss Black is surely unmarried.

132. And here is the crucial revelation of this novel, on which the title is based: man is colonizing the planets of distant stars—*but what of Earth?* Earth needs his attention more than any of those other worlds do. This realization changes Scot's life. But—Writer eliminated this entire Celtic-appeals-endurance contest, and this vital revelation with it, rendering the novel relatively pointless. He substituted what seems to me an ineffective decision to have Brand and the Saxon fight again; to head that off, and free himself from harassment, Scot agrees to swear fealty to the King. I feel that this endurance-contest is the most effective part of the novel, mirroring as it does the struggle of the whole Earth, which is being depleted much the way Scot is being depleted. Not least is the matter of

honor—both Scot and the Saxon have it, and it
shows here, and it is a major part of the key to
settlement. But of course such artistry and symbolism are wasted on this bunch; these folk perceive
only silliness and banality here.

133.   If there is a feeling of *déjà vu* here, it is
because of the oblique references to Brother Paul's
presentation of the conversion of the Apostle Paul
—which material was deleted by the copyeds. Indeed, Scot is experiencing a similar, if muted,
conversion; from this point on he has a mission as
important as Paul's was.

134.   "Too goddam formal for a previously uneducated man," Red complains. Strange—I don't
perceive the Saxon as uneducated. Live and learn.

135.   "Dumb," Red grumps. "He can't just get
handed a wife—have to show some previous interest." Red, you forget you're among Celtics now.

136.   The changes in the text become so substantial in the later stages of the novel that it's
difficult even to define them, so I'll continue with
spot notes on the markings on the manuscript. This
paragraph was emphatically ripped out by Blue; I
don't know why, as it seems innocuous. I suppose
copyeds don't have to have reason for what they do.

137.   Again I misused the term. We all have our
smudges of ignorance.

138.   If you are wondering why I should develop
Brother Paul so carefully, then write him all the way
out of the novel—it is in part because he is no
longer on Earth. You must go to *Tarot* to find him.
No, on reconsideration, years have passed; he has
been back long since, and is now married and
raising his own family. But it can be tricky to
coordinate the characters of different novels; if I

had Brother Paul appear again in *Earth*? it would limit him for his own novel, and I needed him free. An author dares not wield his godlike power over his characters carelessly.

139. This is overly optimistic. As we see in the *Cluster* series, which takes history a couple thousand years forward, man does not change his nature. Man merely discovers better ways to exploit the galaxy. But it's a nice dream Lucy has.

140. Black inquires querulously: "They sleep in a parked car?" Yes; what's wrong with that? But Writer obligingly has them sleep in an alley instead. I trust Miss Black approved. She seems to be suspicious about what goes on in parked cars.

141. This sentence was excised by Pencil. How these copyeds resent any effort by a writer to state his theme! This whole novel draws a parallel between the individual situation and the planetary one. Without that allegory, this becomes just another entertainment—which is evidently what this publisher wanted. No wonder this line of books was noted chiefly for its mediocrity; in the end it possessed neither literary nor commercial appeal, and collapsed. Don't misunderstand me: I find nothing wrong in entertainment fiction. The wrong is in requiring that entertainment be the *only* value of fiction. To me, the ideal novel is one that both entertains and stretches awareness, so that it is an experience that embraces the reader. *Earth?* attempted to be such a novel; I fear it failed, and in the process may be insufficiently entertaining and stretching—but by this time it should be evident that the effort was made. Far better to try, and fail, than not even to try.

142. "DID LUCY ENTER A COMPLAINT

THAT SHE HAD BEEN ATTACKED?" Miss Black demands imperiously. She's sort of pretty in her fashion when she gets her dander up. "There was only a suspicion of a *morals charge,* remember?" Good point. But Lucy was not the one who made the charge; that was done by witnesses who saw Scot seemingly attacking a young woman in a car. Such charges, in a bureaucratic file, assume the force of facts, even if they are nonsense. This whole morals-charge business is outrageous—but such things do happen in life. I speak as one who was surcharged and ridered for *all* mental disease on his insurance—because of my complaint of slight fatigue stemming from then-undiagnosed diabetes. It took ten years to get that straightened out. (And to forestall objection by the insurance industry: yes, I *know* that policies are either surcharged or ridered for a specific liability, not both; I was after all once an insurance salesman myself. But it was done to me. I bounced the policy and demanded a refund. They granted it, probably by then being certain I was crazy. I would have some rather unkind things to say about the medical and psychiatric professions' perception of sanity, if I got going on that subject. But it can indeed be difficult to tell sane from insane, as I learned when I worked at a mental hospital.) Now my insurance surcharges me for the diabetes, though I am in fact one of the healthiest men of my age-range; my diabetes is a marginal condition requiring no medication. That's why it took so long to diagnose: no sugar in the urine. Meanwhile, that same insurance ignores the fact that my wife smokes. I am not a doctor (though I was at one time engaged in a collaborative nonfiction book on kidney disease—and *there's* a type of illness to avoid, if you have any choice!), but I could get rather disparaging about the bases on which insurance companies rider and fail to rider. All of which would no doubt serve as the final proof for both the medical and the insurance industries that I *am* insane. Such industries have a very convenient shelter from common sense. Anyway, I stand by my assertion that people can be severely penalized for ludicrous reasons, as I think anyone who has lived in the real world for any length of time will agree.

143. Naturally Pencil snatched this exchange out. Note the reference, just above this, where Lucy voided her charge of attack. She had never *made* the charge—she didn't even know his identity at the time—but now she formally withdraws it. This is the way you have to deal with the bureaucracy. It reminds me of the man who was unremittingly billed by a computer for $0.00. Nothing could get him off that dunning list—until at last he got smart and wrote a check for $0.00. That satisfied the computer.

144. Black objects: "Lucy asks if they mightn't consider emigration after all—WITHOUT THEIR CHILDREN." Miss B, Lucy isn't serious. It's like a person with acrophobia, wondering how it would be to jump from a high building. We are ironically tempted by absolute folly, sometimes. As the following lines show, she is near hysteria, from the tension—just as you seem to be, Miss B.

145. Black notes: "BRAND arrested?—man comes in. 'Anyone here know BRAND?'" So?

146. Yes, of course Pencil took this out. Ye copyeds were intent on destroying my theme. I proffer these insights for consideration: You can learn a lot about an editor by noting what he edits

out of a manuscript. And the person who believes
that the end justifies the means is apt to have an end
that is unjustified.

147.   Naturally Miss Black objects: "The offi-
cials couldn't find the manual but Scot and Lucy
can—in the bathroom!" Yes, because Brand had
mentioned going to the bathroom; I thought it was
a reasonably obvious connection for Scot to make.
They probably discussed such exigencies before
they embarked on this mission: "If we get separated, and I have the manual and am about to get
caught, I'll hide it under a red chair, or maybe the
bathroom . . ." Do we need to spell out every single
detail?

148.   I'm not satisfied with this; I wish they had
a better place to be. But the day is getting on, and I
suppose they can't be choosy.

149.   All hell broke loose here, of course. Pencil
didn't like his poking around inside her shirt to
help get the snow out. Black had objections to their
making love and to their being unwilling to wait a
month lest they be arrested. A month? I believe it
was a 24-hour extension. Red said: "Oh, come on!
Have to put something plausible in there." And this
was the place that I had to add in a redundant
technical explanation, because Editor didn't remember the one I had had before. I am giving my
original version here, as I'm sure that you, the
reader, don't need such repetition. Red had so
much trouble with it anyway that he finally
growled, "Rewrite the whole damn ending," and
Writer did. But if I had it to do over, I would make
some changes, because if Scot and Lucy are wearing
clothing heavy enough to keep them comfortable
when sitting in snow, it would have been tricky to
get much snow down her front, and trickier to make

effective love. Can be done, I'm sure; I just would have made it easier on them. I live in Florida now, so haven't had much recent experience making love in snow. Sigh.

150. Ah—there's the one month Miss Black notes. Still, that's no alternative, because they *would* be arrested, and have no chance to complete their mission. Maybe Miss B favors MT, and wants them to be arrested. And to be confined in separate cells, so they can't engage in any more nasty s-x.

151. Need you ask? Naturally that exchange was deleted by Pencil.

152. Red had trouble with that, but then blacked out his own comment, so I don't know what he said. You know, years later a reviewer criticized my awkward dialogue, so I wrote to him to ask for examples. He sent some, among which was "I love you." Now dialogue is another subject I could expound on at length, as many writers have distorted notions of its nature, but the essence is that it is often necessary for me to use a kind of shorthand in rendering it so that it doesn't become tedious. "I love you" can be such a shorthand—but I would not call it awkward. It is my suspicion that the person who objects to this sort of expression on the grounds of awkwardness or lack of realism actually has some other reason for his or her opposition—such as, perhaps, being turned off by the honest expression of emotion. There is a lot of alienation in our society, and true love and understanding can be hard to find—but very precious when it *is* found. Scot and Lucy, after their difficult beginning, have found it.

153. "It's 5 A.M." Miss Black protests. "THIS HAS ALL TAKEN PLACE IN THE MIDDLE OF THE NIGHT." Yes—they spent the night in the

snow outside, talking, clearing snow out of clothing, making love, perhaps sleeping, talking again, poring over the obscure manual, puzzling it out, working out the details. Not comfortable at all, but this is a desperate business. Miss Black, you will remember, was the one who objected to them sleeping in a parked car, before. Something about a man and a woman spending time together that sets her off, apparently.

154. Black says: "They get into the bldg—what about guards and dogs—they were there yesterday!" Yes they were—but that was afternoon; this is early morning. Somebody is being slack about guard duty. I know how it is, having served on guard duty in the U.S. Army.

155. Red demands: "If he's blowing up the whole place, why does he care?" I'm referring to the workmen in the area *before* the blowup, Red, who might spot something amiss.

156. "WHY?" Red demands. Well, a lot of people are being processed, at enormous expense; the government just can't fool around with those who change their minds. So an arbitrary limit was set: one chance only. That encourages people to be decisive, and prevents any quibbling about which world they prefer to go to. Take it or leave it— forever. It's not a compassionate policy, but it's effective, and easier for the bureaucracy to handle than a policy of free choice would be.

157. Pencil objects: "Dialogue/situation too elementary. Shall we re-write?" These copyeds, having misunderstood or deleted anything in the novel that threatens to become *other* than elementary, are now objecting to what remains. As Red would say, Gak!

158.   Black says: "They're within 2 miles of the center of a blast like that of an old-fashioned H-Bomb! The scene strikes Scot as *déjà-vu!* (his house burning)." Actually, the *blast* was not like that of a hydrogen bomb, but the *cloud* reminded Scot of the films he had seen. Try reading the passage more carefully, Miss Black. As you may not know, the mushroom-shaped or globe-shaped cloud can derive from other types of explosion—and in this case it does. But there is not the same type of damage, and no lethal radiation; it's relatively sanitary. (There has not been an explosion of this nature on Earth before, so I'm free to define it as seems reasonable to me. At such time as such an explosion does occur, I'll update my description.) But the effect does indeed send Scot into a searing memory he had pretty much suppressed before. Now at last we discover what happened when he plunged into his burning house.

159.   Note the imperfect syntax: a comma instead of "and" in the first sentence of this paragraph. I have on occasion been challenged for such usage, the challenger assuming that I did not know how to do it properly. No, I know the grammatical rules; I merely set them aside when they interfere with my effect. Here Scot is in a desperate strait, and my style is intended to reflect this. If the sentence seems forced, so is his situation. I have had trouble from the outset of my career with copyeds who laboriously "correct" my usage, thereby damaging my prose. Yes, of course Pencil did that to this; could you have doubted that?

160.   Here is where Pencil shows a modicum of perception: "OK—this is a flash-back to the fire at the farm. It's a good idea, but I'm not sure it *quite*

works yet. What do you think?" Very well—think
about it for a while, and I'll have another note at the
end of it.

161.   Note the Biblical reference, again, signaling a significant change of outlook, as in the Apostle
Paul's conversion to Christianity. Naturally this
was excised from my text; I suspect that in this case
the copyeds understood the symbolism and perse-
cuted it.

162.   Pencil says here: "Let's move this description up to p. 137: the details of the house, building
and change in mode of life." Red agrees: "*Right!*"
So Writer moved it to that place in my narrative, so
that the story carried through with no break and no
flashback. Meanwhile, the riddle continues: why
did I set it up this way? Tune in to Footnote #164,
coming up soon.

163.   Pencil amputated that with an indignant
exclamation point. Remember my comment about
judging an editor by what he (she) excises?

164.   All right. Flashback ends, and it's time for
explanations, as this flashback was perhaps the
most controversial aspect of this novel. Why did I
do it? Well, I found I had a problem with this novel:
it built up, peaked, and then lost force toward the
end. A novel's climax—its height of tension, its
point of critical decision—normally comes near
the end, not in the middle. This one had the wrong
dramatic configuration; once it was evident that
Scot had found and married the right girl, and had
the will and the means to destroy the MT program,
all else seemed anticlimactic. What to do? So,
though I much prefer to tell a story straight through
from beginning to end unless I am trying for
something special, I decided in this case to revise
the structure—not the story, but the *presentation*

—so as to place that climax where it belonged, near the end. This had the advantage of making clear the parallel between the carelessness of an MT technician at great cost to his hosts—and the MT program itself, which was heedlessly depleting the planet, at the cost of civilization. This was a deliberately artistic juxtaposition of events: the heat and violence and destruction of the fire, versus that of *MT*'s blowup. The loss of Scot's house that actually leads to a more stable family life, vs. the destruction of the MT program that actually will lead to a better Earth. I did not place this scene here to confuse my readers; I did it to clarify the real message of the novel, and finish with the double impact of physical *and* philosophical climax. The personal and the global, culminating together. And Scot's marriage to Lucy, superimposed on the moment. And the obvious justice of Donald's disastrous visit providing them with the tool they needed to bring similar destruction on the effort Donald represented, MT. This sort of thing seldom happens in life, but it can happen in art—and I deemed it my responsibility, as the artist here, to make it happen.

Obviously the significance of this effort of mine bypassed the massed copyeds, whose perception of literature seems inextricably limited to the pedestrian. It also bypassed the Writer, who did their ignorant bidding. It even bypassed a reviewer, of whom there will be more in the terminal essay. (Unless you are reading these Notes last, in which case you have already encountered Reviewer.) If it also bypassed you, my Readers, then I am truly sorry; I was attempting to enhance your pleasure and contemplation of significance in this novel. There are writers who confine themselves to the pedestrian level, but I like to think that I cater to a

readership that desires, appreciates, and indeed
expects more than that.

165. "Scot and Lucy walk away hand in hand,"
Black sneers. May God preserve the man who tries
to hold *your* hand, Miss Black!

166. "Get them farther away," Red says, evidently concerned about their proximity to what the
copyeds assumed was a hydrogen-bomb blast. So
Writer reworked the ending to provide them two
hours' lead time before the detonation. But it seems
that the copyeds weren't satisfied even with that;
Writer advised me later that they had reworked *his*
ending. Indeed, Editor phoned me to inform me
how brilliant that ending was; obviously he was
proud of it. He mentioned the phenomenal exodus
from the MT site. Well, let's sample that ending. In
it, Scot and Lucy tell the folk of the city what is
about to happen, so that people have a chance to
escape.

By now the flood of people was outside the
town moving down the main road toward the
open countryside. A few children whimpered,
but for the most part, an unearthly silence
enveloped the people. Were they relieved now
that it was finally over, Scot wondered. He
grasped Lucy's hand and turned to look at the
trail of refugees.

Thousands formed the exodus—men, wom-
en, and children hurrying away from the center
of the impending holocaust, their faces mirroring the pathos and grim strength that has
sustained every group of refugees. Scot wondered if the two hours they had were enough to
insure that all would make it in time. What

about the stragglers? Especially the old, the lame?

That sort of thing; there's more. I'm not sure I should be too civilized here, as I'm not a disinterested observer, but just let me pose one question: if everybody knew, two hours before the event, that MT was going to blow—why didn't the MT technicians use the time to undo Scot's sabotage? All they had to do was remove the faulty calibrator. Of course, Writer reworked that aspect too—but if the damage was too great for the technicians to fix in two hours, why didn't they simply shut down operations until they got it fixed? Certainly they didn't have to wait for the detonation! Where was Miss Black's acerbic critique on that one? My logical conclusion was deleted in favor of nonsense!

And at the end of the published version, Scot hugs Brand and Lucy to him, laughs, and says "Let's go back to the farm." So it seems that holding hands is only worthy of a sneer, but hugging is all right.

167. Remember, I said Editor asked me to add a prologue and an epilogue, so I did, though I felt that neither was necessary. They ran the prologue, as noted above, but deleted the epilogue. Accordingly, I give it here:

Epilogue:

There could hardly have been a less likely savior of Earth than Scot Krebs; yet he had performed as his nature and the circumstances dictated. He returned to his Saxon King, who conferred with the Druid, who in turn consulted with his counterpart in the Holy Order of Vision. Now the way to stop MT had been shown, and the need to act—or fail to act—was upon them.

The Saxons sent emissaries to the Huns and to other tribes, bearing this key information. Swift horses raced to all the centers of culture across the continent, and Viking boats crossed the oceans, spreading the word. And in very short order, all of the MT units of the world were shut down. Not all were destroyed, but those spared were curbed. The Age of Emigration—some called it the Dark Age—was over.

Almost half Earth's human population remained on the planet. This was more than enough to restore civilization. There was a period of reorganization and uncertainty. But out of this, in time, emerged a much more disciplined program of colonization that considered the welfare of Earth as well as that of its colonies.[168]

Eventually an organized interstellar empire developed, using the much more economical physical space travel rather than energy-wasteful matter transmission. This was Sol Sphere, expanding to a radius of a hundred light-years. Contact was made with non-human spacefaring species, ushering in an entirely new era. Man, having surmounted his planetary shortcomings, was now a Galactic species. His real history was only beginning.

And what of the man who had made it all possible? Like many of the world's true benefactors, Scot Krebs disappeared into anonymity. His personal fate is unknown—but it is presumed that he was satisfied, and that he lived in simple health and achievement with his family, friends and neighbors: loving and loved. That was, after all, his dream.

168. Pencil remarks: "Well—it's hard to find believable a barbarian mode of life can combine with the technology and sophistication necessary to become a Galactic power."

CONCLUSION

So the deed was done, and my solo novel had been illicitly rendered into this abomination. What happened thereafter?

Well, I wrote a six-page missive to my agent, dated October 14, 1976. In it I summarized the history of the novel and described what had been done to it, pointing out the clear violation of the contract. This was an "open" letter, intended for wider circulation, as my agent understood. In fact, he made copies of it and distributed them to Editor, Writer, Editor's boss whom I shall call Publisher, and I'm not sure who else. Naturally the feces hit the fan. It turned out that Publisher had not known what was going on either. He sent my agent an apology and reversion of the novel. That meant I could have it republished elsewhere without penalty—which is what I am doing here. The entire line of science fiction books was shut down and

Editor was fired. This means, I suspect, that the various copyeds lost their jobs, and Writer lost his major market. I have little sympathy.

Now I can't honestly claim that this was all because of my letter; this line of books had developed into such a disaster in terms of quality and sales that it could not continue much longer. Condemnation of the merit of the line was widespread, and sales of individual novels, instead of being in the projected quarter-million class, were in the 10,000 class. The final statement on *But What of Earth?* showed total sales of 8,489. Only $664.47 had been earned toward the advance of $2,500 to me and $500 to Writer. In my letter I had said that Writer should be paid all the royalties accruing beyond the advance until his share of the money matched mine, and that they should be split evenly thereafter, because I believed that even an unauthorized promise to an innocent person should be honored. Honor is perhaps the guiding principle of my life—a fact that the great majority of people I have interacted with have failed signally to understand. My word *is* my bond, in letter and spirit, even when, as in this case, my word has been given without my consent. Thus I now had a commitment to share the money evenly with Writer—and a similar commitment to destroy Editor.

I did not know, at that stage, that my offer had been rendered meaningless by reality. Sales of 250,000 copies would have earned out the advance many times over; sales of under 10,000 left us in the hole. We did not have to return any money, but we never got any more on that novel from that publisher.

So probably I did not single-handedly close down this operation—but I believe I could have, had that been required. I could have sued for the contract-violation and the detriment to my literary reputation done by this outfit. But Publisher was not really at fault, not having known what was going on; in fact Publisher took a phenomenal bath on this line of books. Certainly, after my letter, Editor had no further prospects in the science fiction genre; he faded quickly from the scene. If I were to mention his name here, the vast majority of my readers would draw a blank.

Meanwhile, I wanted to establish the relative merits of the two versions of the novel, so I arranged with the editor of an amateur genre magazine (fanzine) to have both texts reviewed by an independent reviewer, who would publish his conclusion: which version was better, my original or the published one? Naturally my commentary here is one-sided; I am after all the aggrieved party. It was only fair to have a competent third party decide the issue of merit. The reviewer was selected—one whose prior comment on my work had been generally unfavorable. In fact, the one who later quoted "I love you" as an example of my awkward dialogue. (See Note 152.) Sigh. But I kept my mouth shut and waited with a certain dread for the verdict. I *knew* my version was superior, but was hardly assured that *he* would see it that way. I have had much to say about the inadequacies of copy-editors here; I could go into a similar discussion of reviewers. Any writer could!

But when the day of reckoning came, this reviewer concluded, as I remember, that though the published edition had substantially benefited the novel by eliminating my flashback (see Note 164 for my rationale on that), and by having Scot marry Lucy (somehow he got the notion that I had never

bothered to get them married), the characterization
of my version was better. He found both versions
mediocre, but the published one slightly worse than
my original. Now this was hardly any striking
recommendation, but it did validate my point:
After all the struggles of up to five copyeds and a
reWriter, what had been accomplished? A worse
novel than the one they had started with! What
better argument can there be than that for keeping
other fingers *out* of an author's novel?

When it comes to that, why should *any* changes
be made other than correction of spelling, obvious
grammatical flaws, and deletion of anything obviously libelous or obscene or inaccurate? I, for one,
am ready to face the music with my fiction *exactly
as I write it,* spelling and all. I feel that copyeds
generally do more harm than good to my text, often
introducing errors of spelling, syntax or fact, and
eliminating important and necessary material, such
as the rationale for destroying the matter transmit-
ter. This is not the only publisher with whom I have
had a copyed problem; this is just the most egre-
gious example. Copyeds strike me as resembling
termites, tunneling through the supporting frames
of the structure. They may think they are improving
it, but their unchecked attention can cause it to
collapse. I suspect that publishers could publish
better material, and save money, by simply eliminating the copy-editing stage. Somehow they seem
to assume that the author is illiterate, and that any
young woman hired off the street can do a better
job. It just isn't so! I hold a B.A. degree in Creative
Writing, and I have been a proofreader and an
English teacher, and I have an excellent literary and
commercial track record, and, not least, I *do* know
how to write. I will concede that writers may exist

who are less literate than the typical copyed, but I am not one of them. When, oh when, will I be suffered to present my work in peace?

Actually, I may now have an answer to that rhetorical question: When more publishers computerize their typesetting. Then material can go directly from the author's word-processor to the publisher's typesetting system, untouched by any human hand. I am, I understand, the next-to-last well-established writer to convert to the computer, as of this book. I held out because the computer companies claimed they couldn't provide my Dvorak keyboard, and in part because I knew my manual office Olympia typewriter was more reliable than any computer, considering things like accidental wipeouts and power failures. The first situation has changed, and I bought a unit to protect my power supply, so this reworked novel was the first I did on my Digital Rainbow system. I did write this concluding essay in pencil, and this particular paragraph during a four-hour power failure; nothing's perfect. But they no longer make good manual typewriters, and my present machine has ten years and ten million words on it and was beginning to tire; my hand had been forced, and if I *had* to go electric, I concluded I might as well go whole-hog. Especially if it offered future leverage to cut out the copy-editing middleman. Publishers will battle to the very end to avoid taking such a reasonable step, so we won't see it soon, but some starlight glimmers at the end of the tunnel.

I don't claim that *everything* done to my novel was evil. Writer changed the system of measurements from mile, acre and such to metric: kilometer, hectare and such. Certainly metric is more sensible than our chaotic present system. A hectare is a square 100 meters on a side, or almost two and a half acres, which happens to be the size (but not the shape) of the local lots. But logically, it doesn't wash; Americans are simply not going to change over, now or in the near future, so it is more realistic to show the society as it is, flaws and all.

Some questions remain. Whatever possessed Editor to suppose that he could do something like this to an ornery writer like me? I can only conjecture that he simply deceived himself about the likely consequence, just as contemporary politicians do about an ongoing budgetary deficit. He had allowed his copyeds to run wild, then had to cover up their mischief by hiding it from me. I cannot believe it was an accident that prevented the galley-proofs from reaching me; had I seen them, I would have acted instantly to prevent publication of the novel in that form, and I would have required them to revert it to its original form. Perhaps he deluded himself that the collaborative version of *Earth?* actually represented an improvement, and that I really would be pleased. But mostly, I suspect that he had dug himself into such a hole that he could do nothing but carry on with blinders, praying to God for deliverance. Well, God delivered him into minor religious publishing, where he remained the last I heard of him. Mainly, Editor lacked plain common sense—but because he was a persuasive promoter, he built himself quite an edifice on sand before the tide swept it away.

How could something like this have happened in our fair genre? Well, it happened because most people, like me, prefer to believe in the good faith and common sense of others. We are not paranoid; we accept assurances as given, and we assume that contracts and standard practices will be honored. A great deal of business is instigated on faith. Publishers extend faith all the time—and money too!—that an author's promise to deliver an original and satisfactory manuscript will be honored. Most writers do indeed honor such pledges; the few who don't quickly achieve a bad name, and have increasing difficulty getting contracts. Most editors, too, are honorable by their peculiar code. I have dealt with a number, and seldom have been met with outright dishonor. If a writer deals with an established publisher, I believe the chances are 20 to 1 in favor of the given commitments being honored in the major, if not the minor compass. This does not mean that such publishers can't be rapacious; they can exploit unagented authors unmercifully, they can misrepresent their sales figures to the authors' disfavor (so as to avoid paying royalties), they can give novels shoddy treatment, and they can blacklist authors who protest. I have been the route! That's why I am considered ornery: because I do stand up for my rights, and will take action against those who violate them. But many publishers don't regard such behavior as dishonorable; they think of it as good business practice. They will correct such errors if jogged in the right manner. It's a bit like a runner in baseball taking a lead off first base: if challenged by a throw to first, he will return to it quickly enough. The writer simply has to keep his eyes open and assert himself politely when necessary (an agent is useful for this, and sometimes a lawyer), and he will get along. Note that the Publisher of *Earth?* quickly accommodated my complaints, when I made them formally. Perhaps I should say that God helps those who help themselves; publishers are as honorable as the writer requires them to be. Unfortunately, many writers rather resemble sheep in this respect, and so they do get shorn, but it doesn't *have* to be that way. Publishers can on occasion be generous, too; at times I have been treated with greater kindness than the contract required, and not just because of my increasing leverage. So Parnassus may be a mixed bag, but honor and even generosity are sometimes to be found. This general trust and good feeling does leave open avenues for abuse, but on the whole we're better off with it than without it.

How can we prevent any recurrence of such mischief? Only by continued vigilance. It is my regret that so-called writers' organizations are not very consistent in policing the trade; sometimes they do excellent service, but sometimes their involvement only exacerbates a situation. The individual writer has to watch his own jacket and wallet. But he *can* do this; a little backbone helps. If it were not possible for a writer to stand his ground and ultimately prosper, though scarred by just such abuses as this one, I would not be presenting this present commentary.